SUDDENLY, THE HEADLESS HORSEMAN!

As Ichabod approached the stream his heart began to thump; he summoned up, however, all his resolution, gave his horse half a score of kicks in the ribs, and attempted to dash briskly across the bridge; but instead, the perverse old animal made a lateral movement and ran broadside against the fence!

The schoolmaster now bestowed both whip and heel upon old Gunpowder, who dashed forward, snuffling and snorting, but again came to a stand . . . Just at this moment, Ichabod heard a plashy tramp. In the dark shadows on the margin of the brook, he beheld something huge, misshapen, black and towering.

It gathered up in the gloom, like a monster ready to spring!

THE LEGEND OF SLEEPY HOLLOW & OTHER STORIES

WASHINGTON IRVING

MAGNUM EASY EYE BOOKS
MAGNUM BOOKS • NEW YORK

THE LEGEND OF SLEEPY HOLLOW
& OTHER STORIES

Magnum Easy Eye Books are published by

LANCER BOOKS INC. • 18 EAST 41ST STREET
NEW YORK, N.Y. 10017

CONTENTS

CONTENTS

THE AUTHOR'S
ACCOUNT OF HIMSELF

"I am of this mind with Homer, that as the snaile that crept out of her shel was turned eftsoons into a toad, and thereby was forced to make a stoole to sit on; so the traveller that straggleth from his owne country is in a short time transformed into so monstrous a shape, that he is faine to alter his mansion with his manners, and to live where he can, not where he would."—

LYLY'S *Euphues*

I was always fond of visiting new scenes, and observing strange characters and manners. Even when a mere child I began my travels, and made many tours of discovery into foreign parts and unknown regions of my native city, to the frequent alarm of my parents, and the emolument of the town-crier. As I grew, into boyhood, I extended the range of my observations. My holiday afternoons were spent in rambles about the surrounding country. I made myself familiar with all its places famous in history or fable. I knew every spot where a murder or robbery had been committed, or a ghost seen. I visited the neighboring villages, and added greatly to my stock of knowledge by noting their habits and customs, and conversing with their sages and great men. I even journeyed one long summer's day to the summit of the most distant hill, whence I stretched my eye over many a mile of *terra incognita,* and was astonished to find how vast a globe I inhabited.

This rambling propensity strengthened with my years. Books of voyages and travels became my passion, and in devouring their contents, I neglected the regular exercises of the school. How wistfully would I wander about the pierheads in fine weather, and watch the parting ships, bound to distant climes; with what longing eyes would I gaze after their lessening sails, and waft myself in imagination to the ends of the earth!

Further reading and thinking, though they brought this vague inclination into more reasonable bounds, only served to make it more decided. I visited various parts of my own country; and had I been merely a lover of fine scenery, I should have felt little desire to seek elsewhere its gratification, for on no country have the charms of nature been more prodigally lavished. Her mighty lakes, like oceans of liquid silver; her mountains, with their bright aerial tints; her valleys, teeming with wild fertility; her tremendous cataracts, thundering in their solitudes; her boundless plains, waving with spontaneous verdure; her broad deep rivers, rolling in solemn silence to the ocean; her trackless forests, where vegetation puts forth all its magnificence; her skies, kindling with the magic of summer clouds and glorious sunshine;—no, never need an American look beyond his own country for the sublime and beautiful of natural scenery.

But Europe held forth the charms of storied and poetical association. There were to be seen the masterpieces of art, the refinements of highly cultivated society, the quaint peculiarities of ancient and local custom. My native country was full of youthful promise: Europe was rich in the accumulated treasures of age. Her very ruins told the history of times gone by, and every mouldering stone was a chronicle. I longed to wander over the scenes of renowned achievement— to tread, as it were, in the footsteps of antiquity—to loiter about the ruined castle—to meditate on the falling tower—to escape, in short, from the commonplace realities of the present, and lose myself among the shadowy grandeurs of the past.

I had, beside all this, an earnest desire to see the great men of the earth. We have, it is true, our great men in America: not a city but has an ample share of them. I have mingled among them in my time, and been almost withered by the shade into which they cast me; for there is nothing so baleful to a small man as the shade of a great one, particularly the great man of a city. But I was anxious to see the great men of Europe; for I had read in the works of various philosophers, that all animals degenerated in America, and man among the number. A great man of Europe, thought I, must therefore be as superior to a great man of America, as a peak of the Alps to a highland of the Hudson; and in this idea I was confirmed, by observing the comparative importance and swelling magnitude of many English travellers among us, who, I was assured, were very little people in their own country. I will visit this land of wonder, though I, and see the gigantic race from which I am degenerated.

It has been either my good or evil lot to have my roving passion gratified. I have wandered through different countries, and witnessed many of the shifting scenes of life. I cannot say that I have studied them with the eye of a philosopher, but rather with the sauntering gaze with which humble lovers of the picturesque stroll from the window of one print-shop to another, caught sometimes by the delineations of beauty, sometimes by the distortions of caricature, and sometimes by the loveliness of landscape. As it is the fashion for modern tourists to travel pencil in hand, and bring home their portfolios filled with sketches, I am disposed to get up a few for the entertainment of my friends. When, however, I look over the hints and memorandums I have taken down for the purpose, my heart almost fails me at finding how my idle humor has led me aside from the great objects studied by every regular traveller who would make a book. I fear I shall give equal disappointment with an unlucky landscape-painter, who had travelled on the continent, but, following the bent of his vagrant inclination, had sketched in nooks, and corners, and by-places. His sketch-book was accordingly crowded with cottages, and landscapes, and obscure ruins; but he had neglected to paint St. Peter's, or the Coliseum; the cascade of Terni, or the bay of Naples; and had not a single glacier or volcano in his whole collection.

THE LEGEND OF SLEEPY HOLLOW

Found Among the Papers of the Late Diedrich
Knickerbocker

A pleasing land of drowsy head it was,
 Of dreams that wave before the half-shut eye;
And of gay castles in the clouds that pass,
 For ever flushing round a summer sky.
                              CASTLE OF INDOLENCE

In the bosom of one of those spacious coves which in-
dent the eastern shore of the Hudson, at that broad
expansion of the river denominated by the ancient
Dutch navigators the Tappan Zee, and where they always prudently shortened sail, and implored the protection of St. Nicholas when they crossed, there lies a
small market town or rural port, which by some is
called Greensburgh, but which is more generally and
properly known by the name of Tarry Town. This
name was given, we are told, in former days, by the

good housewives of the adjacent country, from the inveterate propensity of their husbands to linger about the village tavern on market days. Be that as it may, I do not vouch for the fact, but merely advert to it, for the sake of being precise and authentic. Not far from this village, perhaps about two miles, there is a little valley, or rather lap of land, among high hills, which is one of the quietest places in the whole world. A small brook glides through it, with just murmur enough to lull one to repose; and the occasional whistle of a quail or tapping of a woodpecker is almost the only sound that ever breaks in upon the uniform tranquillity.

I recollect that, when a stripling, my first exploit in squirrel shooting was in a grove of tall walnut trees that shades one side of the valley. I had wandered into it at noontime, when all nature is peculiarly quiet, and was startled by the roar of my own gun, as it broke the Sabbath stillness around, and was prolonged and reverberated by the angry echoes. If ever I should wish for a retreat, whither I might steal from the world and its distractions and dream quietly away the remnant of a troubled life, I know of none more promising than this little valley.

From the listless repose of the place, and the peculiar character of its inhabitants, who are descendants from the original Dutch settlers, this sequestered glen has long been known by the name of SLEEPY HOLLOW, and its rustic lads are called the Sleepy Hollow Boys throughout all the neighboring country. A drowsy, dreamy influence seems to hang over the land, and to pervade the very atmosphere. Some say that the place was bewitched by a high German doctor during the early days of the settlement; others, that an old Indian chief, the prophet or wizard of his tribe, held his pow-wows there before the country was discovered by Master Hendrick Hudson. Certain it is, the place still continues under the sway of some witching power that holds a spell over the minds of the good people, causing them to walk in a continual reverie. They are given to all kinds of marvelous beliefs, are subject to trances and visions, and frequently see strange sights, and hear music and voices in the air. The whole neighborhood abounds with local tales, haunted spots, and twilight superstitions; stars shoot and meteors glare oftener across the valley than in any other part of the country, and the nightmare, with her whole ninefold, seems to make it the favorite scene of her gambols.

The dominant spirit, however, that haunts this enchanted region and seems to be commander-in-chief of all the powers of the air is the apparition of a figure on horseback without a head. It is said by some to be the ghost of a Hessian trooper, whose head had been carried away by a cannon ball, in some nameless battle during the Revolutionary War, and who is ever and anon seen by the country folk, hurrying along in the gloom of night, as if on the wings of the wind. His haunts are not confined to the valley, but extend at times to the adjacent roads, and especially to the vicinity of a church at no great distance. Indeed, certain of the most authentic historians of those parts, who have been careful in collecting and collating the floating facts concerning this specter, allege that the body of the trooper, having been buried in the churchyard, the ghost rides forth to the scene of battle in nightly quest of his head; and that the rushing speed with which he sometimes passes along the Hollow, like a midnight blast, is owing to his being belated, and in a hurry to get back to the churchyard before daybreak.

Such is the general purport of this legendary superstition, which has furnished materials for many a wild story in that region of shadows; and the specter is known, at all the country firesides, by the name of the Headless Horseman of Sleepy Hollow.

It is remarkable that the visionary propensity I have mentioned is not confined to the native inhabitants of the valley, but is unconsciously imbibed by everyone who resides there for a time. However wide awake they may have been before they entered that sleepy region, they are sure, in a little time, to inhale the witching influence of the air, and begin to grow imaginative— to dream dreams and see apparitions.

I mention this peaceful spot with all possible laud; for it is in such little retired Dutch valleys, found here and there embosomed in the great State of New York, that population, manners, and customs remain fixed; while the great torrent of migration and improvement, which is making such incessant changes in other parts of this restless country, sweeps by them unobserved. They are like those little nooks of still water which border a rapid stream, where we may see the straw and bubble riding quietly at anchor, or slowly revolving in their mimic harbor, undisturbed by the rush of the passing current. Though many years have elapsed since I trod the drowsy shades of Sleepy Hollow, yet I question whether I should not still find the same trees and the same families vegetating in its sheltered bosom.

In this by-place of nature there abode, in a remote period of American history, that is to say, some thirty years since, a worthy wight of the name of Ichabod Crane, who sojourned, or, as he expressed it, "tarried," in Sleepy Hollow, for the purpose of instructing the children of the vicinity. He was a native of Connecticut, a State which supplies the Union with pioneers for the mind as well as for the forest, and sends forth yearly its legions of frontier woodsmen and country schoolmasters. The cognomen of Crane was not inapplicable to his person. He was tall, but exceedingly lank, with narrow shoulders, long arms and legs, hands that dangled a mile out of his sleeves, feet that might have served for shovels, and his whole frame most loosely hung together. His head was small, and flat at top, with huge ears, large green glassy eyes, and a long snipe nose, so that it looked like a weathercock, perched upon his spindle neck, to tell which way the wind blew. To see him striding along the profile of a hill on a windy day, with his clothes bagging and fluttering about him, one might have mistaken him for the genius of famine descending upon the earth, or some scarecrow eloped from a cornfield.

His schoolhouse was a low building of one large

room, rudely constructed of logs, the windows partly glazed, and partly patched with leaves of old copybooks. It was most ingeniously secured at vacant hours by a withe twisted in the handle of the door and stakes set against the window shutters, so that, though a thief might get in with perfect ease, he would find some embarrassment in getting out; an idea most probably borrowed by the architect, Yost Van Houten, from the mystery of an eel pot. The schoolhouse stood in a rather lonely but pleasant situation, just at the foot of a woody hill, with a brook running close by, and a formidable birch tree growing at one end of it. From hence the low murmur of his pupils' voices, conning over their lessons, might be heard in a drowsy summer's day, like the hum of a beehive, interrupted now and then by the authoritative voice of the master, in the tone of menace or command, or, peradventure, by the appalling sound of the birch, as he urged some tardy loiterer along the flowery path of knowledge. Truth to say, he was a conscientious man, and ever bore in mind the golden maxim, "Spare the rod and spoil the child." Ichabod Crane's scholars certainly were not spoiled.

I would not have it imagined, however, that he was one of those cruel potentates of the school who joy in the smart of their subjects; on the contrary, he administered justice with discrimination rather than severity, taking the burthen off the backs of the weak, and laying it on those of the strong. Your mere puny stripling that winced at the least flourish of the rod was passed by with indulgence; but the claims of justice were satisfied by inflicting a double portion on some little, tough, wrong-headed, broad-skirted Dutch urchin, who sulked and swelled and grew dogged and sullen beneath the birch. All this he called "doing his duty by their parents"; and he never inflicted a chastisement without following it by the assurance, so consolatory to the smarting urchin, that "he would remember it, and thank him for it the longest day he had to live."

When school hours were over, he was even the companion and playmate of the larger boys; and on holiday afternoons would convoy some of the smaller ones home, who happened to have pretty sisters, or good housewives for mothers, noted for the comforts of the cupboard. Indeed it behooved him to keep on good terms with his pupils. The revenue arising from his school was small, and would have been scarcely sufficient to furnish him with daily bread, for he was a huge feeder, and though lank, had the dilating powers of an anaconda; but to help out his maintenance, he was, according to country custom in those parts, boarded and lodged at the houses of the farmers whose children he instructed. With these he lived successively a week at a time; thus going the rounds of the neighborhood, with all his worldly effects tied up in a cotton handkerchief.

That all this might not be too onerous on the purses of his rustic patrons, who are apt to consider the costs of schooling a grievous burden and schoolmasters as mere drones, he had various ways of rendering himself both useful and agreeable. He assisted the farmers occasionally in the lighter labors of their farms, helped to make hay, mended the fences, took the horses to water, drove the cows from pasture, and cut wood for the winter fire. He laid aside, too, all the dominant dignity and absolute sway with which he lorded it in his little empire, the school, and became wonderfully gentle and ingratiating. He found favor in the eyes of the mothers by petting the children, particularly the youngest; and like the lion bold, which whilom so magnanimously the lamb did hold, he would sit with a child on one knee, and rock a cradle with his foot for whole hours together.

In addition to his other vocations, he was the singing master of the neighborhood, and picked up many bright shillings by instructing the young folks in psalmody. It was a matter of no little vanity to him, on Sundays, to take his station in front of the church gallery, with a band of chosen singers; where, in his own mind, he completely carried away the palm from the parson. Certain it is, his voice resounded far above all the rest of the congregation; and there are peculiar quavers still to be heard in that church, and which may even be heard half a mile off, quite to the opposite side of the millpond, on a still Sunday morning, which are said to be legitimately descended from the nose of Ichabod Crane. Thus, by diverse little makeshifts in that ingenious way which is commonly denominated "by hook and by crook," the worthy pedagogue got on tolerably enough, and was thought, by all who understood nothing of the labor of headwork, to have a wonderfully easy life of it.

The schoolmaster is generally a man of some importance in the female circle of a rural neighborhood, being considered a kind of idle gentlemanlike personage, of vastly superior taste and accomplishments to the rough country swains, and, indeed, inferior in learning only to the parson. His appearance, therefore, is apt to occasion some little stir at the tea table of a farmhouse, and the addition of a supernumerary dish of cakes or sweetmeats, or, peradventure, the parade of a silver teapot. Our man of letters, therefore, was peculiarly happy in the smiles of all the country damsels. How he would figure among them in the churchyard, between services on Sundays! gathering grapes for them from the wild vines that overrun the surrounding trees, reciting for their amusement all the epitaphs on the tombstones, or sauntering, with a whole bevy of them, along the banks of the adjacent millpond, while the more bashful country bumpkins hung sheepishly back, envying his superior elegance and address.

From his half-itinerant life, also, he was a kind of traveling gazette, carrying the whole budget of local gossip from house to house, so that his appearance was always greeted with satisfaction. He was, moreover, esteemed by the women as a man of great erudition, for he had read several books quite through, and was a perfect master of Cotton Mather's *History of New England Witchcraft,* in which, by the way, he most firmly and potently believed.

He was, in fact, an odd mixture of small shrewdness and simple credulity. His appetite for the marvelous, and his powers of digesting it, were equally extraordinary; and both had been increased by his residence in this spellbound region. No tale was too gross or monstrous for his capacious swallow. It was often his delight, after his school was dismissed in the afternoon, to stretch himself on the rich bed of clover, bordering the little brook that whimpered by his schoolhouse, and there con over old Mather's direful tales, until the gathering dusk of the evening made the printed page a mere mist before his eyes. Then, as he wended his way, by swamp and stream and awful woodland, to the farmhouse where he happened to be quartered, every sound of nature, at that witching hour, fluttered his excited imagination: the moan of the whippoorwill* from the hillside; the boding cry of the tree toad, that harbinger of storm; the dreary hooting of the screech owl, or the sudden rustling in the thicket of birds frightened from their roost. The fireflies, too, which sparkled most vividly in the darkest places, now and then startled him, as one of uncommon brightness would stream across his path; and if, by chance, a huge blockhead of a beetle came winging his blundering flight against him, the poor varlet was ready to give up the ghost, with the idea that he was struck with a witch's token. His only resource on such occasions, either to drown thought or drive away evil spirits, was to sing psalm tunes, and the good people of Sleepy Hollow, as they sat by their

* The whippoorwill is a bird which is only heard at night. It receives its name from its note, which is thought to resemble those words.

doors of an evening, were often filled with awe, at hearing his nasal melody, "in linked sweetness long drawn out," floating from the distant hill or along the dusky road.

Another of his sources of fearful pleasure was to pass long winter evenings with the old Dutch wives as they sat spinning by the fire, with a row of apples roasting and spluttering along the hearth, and listen to their marvelous tales of ghosts and goblins, and haunted fields, and haunted brooks, and haunted bridges, and haunted houses, and particularly of the headless horseman, or galloping Hessian of the Hollow, as they sometimes called him. He would delight them equally by his anecdotes of witchcraft, and of the direful omens and portentous sights and sounds in the air, which prevailed in the earlier times of Connecticut; and would frighten them woefully with speculations upon comets and shooting stars, and with the alarming fact that the world did absolutely turn around, and that they were half the time topsy-turvy!

But if there was a pleasure in all this, while snugly cuddling in the chimney corner of a chamber that was all of a ruddy glow from the crackling wood fire, and where, of course, no specter dared to show his face, it was dearly purchased by the terrors of his subsequent walk homewards. What fearful shapes and shadows beset his path amidst the dim and ghastly glare of a snowy night! With what wistful look did he eye every trembling ray of light streaming across the waste fields from some distant window! How often was he appalled by some shrub covered with snow, which, like a sheeted specter, beset his very path! How often did he shrink with curdling awe at the sound of his own steps on the frosty crust beneath his feet; and dread to look over his shoulder, lest he should behold some uncouth being tramping close behind him! And how often was he thrown into complete dismay by some rushing blast, howling among the trees, in the idea that it was the Galloping Hessian on one of his nightly scourings!

All these, however, were mere terrors of the night, phantoms of the mind that walk in darkness; and though he had seen many specters in his time, and been more than once beset by Satan in diverse shapes, in his lonely perambulations, yet day-light put an end to all these evils; and he would have passed a pleasant life of it, in despite of the devil and all his works, if his path had not been crossed by a being that causes more perplexity to mortal man than ghosts, goblins, and the whole race of witches put together, and that was—a woman.

Among the musical disciples who assembled, one evening in each week, to receive his instructions in psalmody, was Katrina Van Tassel, the daughter and only child of a substantial Dutch farmer. She was a blooming lass of fresh eighteen, plump as a partridge, ripe and melting and rosy-cheeked as one of her father's peaches, and universally famed, not merely for her beauty, but her vast expectations. She was withal a little of a coquette, as might be perceived even in her dress, which was a mixture of ancient and modern fashions, as most suited to set off her charms. She wore the ornaments of pure yellow gold, which her great-great-grandmother had brought over from Saardam; the tempting stomacher of the olden time; and withal a provokingly short petticoat, to display the prettiest foot and ankle in the country around.

Ichabod Crane had a soft and foolish heart toward the sex; and it is not to be wondered at that so tempting a morsel soon found favor in his eyes, more especially after he had visited her in her paternal mansion. Old Baltus Van Tassel was a perfect picture of a thriving, contented, liberal-hearted farmer. He seldom, it is true, sent either his eyes or his thoughts beyond the boundaries of his own farm; but within those everything was snug, happy, and well-conditioned. He was satisfied with his wealth, but not proud of it; and piqued himself upon the hearty abundance, rather than the style in which he lived. His stronghold was situated on the banks of the Hudson, in one of those green, sheltered, fertile nooks, in which the Dutch farmers are so fond of nestling. A great elm tree spread its broad branches over it, at the foot of which bubbled up a spring of the softest and sweetest water, in a little well, formed of a barrel, and then stole sparkling away through the grass, to a neighboring brook that bubbled along among alders and dwarf willows. Hard by the farmhouse was a vast barn that might have served for a church; every window and crevice of which seemed bursting forth with the treasures of the farm; the flail was busily resounding within it from morning to night; swallows and martins skimmed twittering about the eaves; and rows of pigeons, some with one eye turned up, as if watching the weather, some with their heads under their wings, or buried in their bosoms, and others swelling, and cooing, and bowing about their dames, were enjoying the sunshine on the roof. Sleek unwieldy porkers were grunting in the repose and abundance of their pens; whence sallied forth, now and then, troops of sucking pigs, as if to snuff the air. A stately squadron of snowy geese were riding in an adjoining pond, convoying whole fleets of ducks; regiments of turkeys were gobbling through the farmyard, and guinea fowls freeting about it, like ill-tempered housewives, with their peevish discontented cry. Before the barn door strutted the gallant cock, that pattern of a husband, a warrior, and a fine gentleman, clapping his burnished wings and crowing in the pride and gladness of his heart—sometimes tearing up the earth with his feet, and then generously calling his ever-hungry family of wives and children to enjoy the rich morsel which he had discovered.

The pedagogue's mouth watered as he looked upon this sumptuous promise of luxurious winter fare. In his devouring mind's eye he pictured to himself every roasting pig running about with a pudding in his belly and an apple in his mouth; the pigeons were snugly put to bed in a comfortable pie, and tucked in with a coverlet of crust; the geese were swimming in their own gravy; and the ducks pairing cozily in dishes, like snug married couples, with a decent competency of onion sauce. In the porkers he saw carved out the future sleek side of bacon, and juicy relishing ham;

not a turkey but he beheld daintily trussed up, with its gizzard under its wing, and, peradventure, a necklace of savory sausages; and even bright chanticleer himself lay sprawling on his back, in a sidedish, with uplifted claws, as if craving that quarter which his chivalrous spirit disdained to ask while living.

As the enraptured Ichabod fancied all this, and as he rolled his great green eyes over the fat meadow lands, the rich fields of wheat, of rye, of buckwheat, and Indian corn, and the orchards burthened with ruddy fruit, which surrounded the warm tenement of Van Tassel, his heart yearned after the damsel who was to inherit these domains, and his imagination expanded with the idea how they might be readily turned into cash, and the money invested in immense tracts of wild land, and shingle palaces in the wilderness. Nay, his busy fancy already realized his hopes, and presented to him the blooming Katrina, with a whole family of children, mounted on the top of a wagon loaded with household trumpery, with pots and kettles dangling beneath; and he beheld himself bestriding a pacing mare, with a colt at her heels, setting out for Kentucky, Tennessee, or the Lord knows where.

When he entered the house the conquest of his heart was complete. It was one of those spacious farmhouses, with high-ridged, but lowly sloping roofs, built in the style handed down from the first Dutch settlers, the low projecting eaves forming a piazza along the front, capable of being closed up in bad weather. Under this were hung flails, harness, various utensils of husbandry, and nets for fishing in the neighboring river. Benches were built along the sides for summer use; and a great spinning wheel at one end, and a churn at the other, showed the various uses to which this important porch might be devoted. From this piazza the wondering Ichabod entered the hall, which formed the center of the mansion and the place of usual residence. Here, rows of resplendent pewter, ranged on a long dresser, dazzled his eyes. In one corner stood a huge bag of wool ready to be spun; in another a quantity of linsey-woolsey just from the loom; ears of Indian corn and strings of dried apples and peaches hung in gay festoons along the walls, mingled with the gaud of red peppers; and a door left ajar gave him a peep into the best parlor, where the claw-footed chairs and dark mahogany tables shone like mirrors; and irons, with their accompanying shovel and tongs, glistened from their covert of asparagus tops; mock oranges and conch shells decorated the mantelpiece; strings of various colored birds' eggs were suspended above it; a great ostrich egg was hung from the center of the room, and a corner cupboard, knowingly left open, displayed immense treasures of old silver and well-mended china.

From the moment Ichabod laid his eyes upon these regions of delight, the peace of his mind was at an end, and his only study was how to gain the affections of the peerless daughter of Van Tassel. In this enterprise, however, he had more real difficulties than generally fell to the lot of a knight-errant of yore, who seldom had anything but giants, enchanters, fiery

dragons, and such like easily conquered adversaries
to contend with; and had to make his way merely
through gates of iron and brass, and walls of adamant,
to the castle keep, where the lady of his heart was
confined; all which he achieved as easily as a man
would carve his way to the center of a Christmas pie;
and then the lady gave him her hand as a matter of
course. Ichabod, on the contrary, had to win his
way to the heart of a country coquette, beset with a
labyrinth of whims and caprices, which were forever
presenting new difficulties and impediments; and he
had to encounter a host of fearful adversaries of real
flesh and blood, the numerous rustic admirers, who
beset every portal to her heart, keeping a watchful
and angry eye upon each other, but ready to fly out
in the common cause against any new competitor.

Among these the most formidable was a burly,
roaring, roystering blade, of the name of Abraham,
or, according to the Dutch abbreviation, Brom Van
Brunt, the hero of the country round, which rang
with his feats of strength and hardihood. He was
broad-shouldered and double-jointed, with short curly
black hair, and a bluff but not unpleasant countenance,
having a mingled air of fun and arrogance. From his
Herculean frame and great powers of limb, he had received the nickname of BOOM BONES, by which he
was universally known. He was famed for great knowledge and skill in horsemanship, being as dexterous on
horseback as a Tartar. He was foremost at all races
and cockfights; and, with the ascendency which bod-
ily strength acquires in rustic life, was the umpire in

all disputes, setting his hat on one side and giving his decisions with an air and tone admitting of no gainsay or appeal. He was always ready for either a fight or a frolic; but had more mischief than ill will in his composition, and, with all his overbearing roughness, there was a strong dash of waggish good humor at bottom. He had three or four boon companions, who regarded him as their model and at the head of whom he scoured the country, attending every scene of feud or merriment for miles around. In cold weather he was distinguishd by a fur cap, surmounted with a flaunting fox's tail; and when the folks at a country gathering descried this well-known crest at a distance, whisking about among a squad of hard riders, they always stood by for a squall. Sometimes his crew would be heard dashing along past the farmhouses at midnight, with whoop and halloo, like a troop of Don Cossacks; and the old dames, startled out of their sleep, would listen for a moment till the hurry-scurry had clattered by, and then exclaim, "Ay, there goes Brom Bones and his gang!" The neighbors looked upon him with a mixture of awe, admiration, and good will; and when any madcap prank or rustic brawl occurred in the vicinity, always shook their heads and warranted Brom Bones was at the bottom of it.

This rantipole hero had for some time singled out the blooming Katrina for the object of his uncouth gallantries, and though his amorous toyings were something like the gentle caresses and endearments of a bear, yet it was whispered that she did not altogether discourage his hopes. Certain it is, his advances were signals for rival candidates to retire, who felt no inclination to cross a lion in his amours; insomuch, that when his horse was seen tied to Van Tassel's paling, on a Sunday night, a sure sign that his master was courting, or, as it is termed, "sparking," within, all other suitors passed by in despair, and carried the war into other quarters.

Such was the formidable rival with whom Ichabod Crane had to contend, and, considering all things, a stouter man than he would have shrunk from the competition, and a wiser man would have despaired. He had, however, a happy mixture of pliability and perseverance in his nature; he was in form and spirit like a supple jack—yielding, but tough; though he bent, he never broke; and though he bowed beneath the slightest pressure, yet, the moment it was away—jerk! he was as erect, and carried his head as high as ever.

To have taken the field openly against his rival would have been madness, for he was not a man to be thwarted in his amours, any more than that stormy lover Achilles. Ichabod, therefore, made his advances in a quiet and gently insinuating manner. Under cover of his character of singing master, he made frequent visits to the farmhouse; not that he had anything to apprehend from the meddlesome interference of parents, which is so often a stumbling block in the path of lovers. Balt Van Tassel was an easy indulgent soul; he loved his daughter better even than his pipe, and, like a reasonable man and an excellent father, let her have her way in everything. His notable little wife, too, had enough to do to attend to her housekeeping and manage her poultry; for, as she sagely observed, ducks and geese are foolish things, and must be looked after, but girls can take care of themselves. Thus while the busy dame bustled about the house, or plied her spinning wheel at one end of the piazza, honest Balt would sit smoking his evening pipe at the other, watching the achievements of a little wooden warrior, who, armed with a sword in each hand, was most valiantly fighting the wind on the pinnacle of the barn. In the meantime, Ichabod would carry on his suit with the daughter by the side of the spring under the great elm, or sauntering along in the twilight, that hour so favorable to the lover's eloquence.

I profess not to know how women's hearts are wooed and won. To me they have always been matters of riddle and admiration. Some seem to have but one vulnerable point, or door of access, while others have a thousand avenues, and may be captured in a thousand different ways. It is a great triumph of skill to gain the former, but a still greater proof of generalship to maintain possession of the latter, for the man must battle for his fortress at every door and window. He who wins a thousand common hearts is therefore entitled to some renown; but he who keeps undisputed sway over the heart of a coquette is indeed a hero. Certain it is, this was not the case with the redoubtable Brom Bones; and from the moment Ichabod Crane made his advances, the interests of the former evidently declined; his horse was no longer seen tied at the palings on Sunday nights, and a deadly feud gradually arose between him and the preceptor of Sleepy Hollow.

Brom, who had a degree of rough chivalry in his nature, would fain have carried matters to open war-fare, and have settled their pretensions to the lady ac-cording to the mode of those most concise and simple reasoners, the knights-errant of yore—by single com-bat; but Ichabod was too conscious of the superior might of his adversary to enter the lists against him. He had overheard a boast of Bones that he would "double the schoolmaster up, and lay him on a shelf of his own schoolhouse," and he was too wary to give him an opportunity. There was something extremely provoking in this obstinately pacific system; it left Brom no alternative but to draw upon the funds of rustic waggery in his disposition, and to play off boor-ish practical jokes upon his rival. Ichabod became the object of whimsical persecution to Bones and his gang of rough riders. They harried his hitherto peaceful domains; smoked out his singing school by stopping up the chimney; broke into the schoolhouse at night, in spite of its formidable fastenings of withe and win-dow stakes, and turned everything topsy-turvy, so that the poor schoolmaster began to think all the witches in the country held their meetings there. But what was still more annoying, Brom took all opportunities of turning him into ridicule in presence of his mistress, and had a scoundrel dog whom he taught to whine in the most ludicrous manner, and introduced as a rival of Ichabod's to instruct her in psalmody.

In this way matters went on for sometime, without producing any material effect on the relative situation of the contending powers. On a fine autumnal afternoon, Ichabod, in pensive mood, sat enthroned on the lofty stool whence he usually watched all the concerns of his little literary realm. In his hand he swayed a ferule, that scepter of despotic power; the birch of justice reposed on three nails, behind the throne, a constant terror to evil-doers; while on the desk before him might be seen sundry contraband articles and prohibited weapons, detected upon the persons of idle urchins, such as half-munched apples, popguns, whirligigs, fly cages, and whole legions of rampant little paper gamecocks. Apparently there had been some appalling act of justice recently inflicted, for his scholars were all busily intent upon their books, or slyly whispering behind them with one eye kept upon the master; and a kind of buzzing stillness reigned throughout the schoolroom. It was suddenly interrupted by the appearance of a Negro, in towcloth jacket and trousers, a round-crowned fragment of a hat, like the cap of Mercury, and mounted on the back of a ragged, wild, half-broken colt, which he managed with a rope by way of halter. He came clattering up to the school door with an invitation to Ichabod to attend a merrymaking or "quilting frolic" to be held that evening at Mynheer Van Tassel's; and having delivered his message with that air of importance and effort at fine language which a Negro is apt to display on petty embassies of the kind, he dashed over the brook and was seen scampering away up the hollow, full of the importance and hurry of his mission.

All was now bustle and hubbub in the late quiet schoolroom. The scholars were hurried through their lessons, without stopping at trifles; those who were nimble skipped over half with impunity, and those who were tardy had a smart application now and then in the rear to quicken their speed or help them over a tall word. Books were flung aside without being put away on the shelves, ink-stands were overturned, benches thrown down, and the whole school was turned loose an hour before the usual time, bursting forth like a legion of young imps, yelping and racketing about the green, in joy at their early emancipation.

The gallant Ichabod now spent at least an extra half hour at his toilet, brushing and furbishing up his best and indeed only suit of rusty black, and arranging his looks by a bit of broken looking glass that hung up in the schoolhouse. That he might make his appearance before his mistress in the true style of a cavalier he borrowed a horse from the farmer with whom he was domiciliated, a choleric old Dutchman of the name of Hans Van Ripper, and, thus gallantly mounted, issued forth, like a knight-errant in quest of adventures. But it is meet I should, in the true spirit of romantic story, give some account of the looks and equipments of my hero and his steed. The animal he bestrode was a broken-down plow horse that had outlived almost everything but his viciousness. He was gaunt and shagged, with a ewe neck and a head like a hammer; his rusty mane and tail were tangled and knotted with burrs; one eye had lost its pupil and was glaring and spectral, but the other had the gleam of a genuine devil in it. Still he must have had fire and mettle in his day, if we may judge from the name he bore of Gunpowder. He had, in fact, been a favorite steed of his master's, the choleric Van Ripper, who was a furious rider, and had infused, very probably, some of his own spirit into the animal, for, old and broken-down as he looked, there was more of the lurking devil in him than in any young filly in the country.

Ichabod was a suitable figure for such a steed. He rode with short stirrups, which brought his knees nearly up to the pommel of the saddle; his sharp elbows stuck out like grasshoppers'; he carried his ship perpendicularly in his hand, like a scepter, and, as his horse jogged on, the motion of his arms was not unlike the flapping of a pair of wings. A small wool hat rested on the top of his nose, for so his scanty strip of forehead might be called; and the skirts of his black coat fluttered out almost to the horse's tail. Such was the appearance of Ichabod and his steed, as they shambled out of the gate of Hans Van Ripper, and it was altogether such an apparition as is seldom to be met with in broad daylight.

It was, as I have said, a fine autumnal day, the sky was clear and serene, and nature wore that rich and golden livery which we always associate with the idea of abundance. The forests had put on their sober brown and yellow, while some trees of the tenderer kind had been nipped by the frosts into brilliant dyes of orange, purple, and scarlet. Streaming files of wild ducks began to make their appearance high in the air; the bark of the squirrel might be heard from the groves of beech and hickory nuts, and the pensive whistle of the quail at intervals from the neighboring stubble field.

The small birds were taking their farewell banquets. In the fullness of their revelry, they fluttered, chirping and frolicking, from bush to bush, and tree to tree, capricious from the very profusion and variety around them. There was the honest cock robin, the favorite game of stripling sportsmen, with its loud querulous note; and the twittering blackbirds flying in sable clouds; and the golden-winged woodpecker, with his crimson crest, his broad black gorget, and splendid plumage; and the cedar bird, with its red-tipped wings and yellow-tipped tail, and its little monteiro cap of feathers; and the blue jay, that noisy coxcomb, in his gay light-blue coat and white underclothes; screaming and chattering, nodding and bobbing and bowing, and pretending to be on good terms with every songster of the grove.

As Ichabod jogged slowly on his way, his eye, ever open to every symptom of culinary abundance, ranged with delight over the treasures of jolly autumn. On all sides he beheld vast store of apples, some hanging in oppressive opulence on the trees, some gathered into baskets and barrels for the market, others heaped up in rich piles for the cider press. Farther on he beheld great fields of Indian corn, with its golden ears peeping from their leafy coverts and holding out the promise of cakes and hasty pudding; and the yellow pumpkins lying beneath them, turning up their fair round bellies to the sun, and giving ample prospects of the most luxurious of pies; and anon he passed the fragrant buckwheat fields, breathing the odor of the beehive, and as he beheld them, soft anticipations stole over his mind of dainty slapjacks, well buttered and garnished with honey or treacle, by the delicate little dimpled hand of Katrina Van Tassel.

Thus feeding his mind with many sweet thoughts and "sugared suppositions," he journeyed along the sides of a range of hills which look out upon some of the goodliest scenes of the mighty Hudson. The sun gradually wheeled his broad disk down into the west. The wide bosom of the Tappan Zee lay motionless and glassy, excepting that here and there a gentle undulation waved and prolonged the blue shadow of the distant mountain. A few amber clouds floated in the sky, without a breath of air to move them. The horizon was of a fine golden tint, changing gradually into a pure apple green, and from that into the deep blue of the mid-heaven. A slanting ray lingered on the woody crests of the precipices that overhung some parts of the river, giving greater depth to the dark-gray and purple of their rocky sides. A sloop was loitering in the distance, dropping slowly down with the tide, her sail hanging uselessly against the mast; and as the reflection of the sky gleamed along the still water, it seemed as if the vessel was suspended in the air.

It was toward evening that Ichabod arrived at the castle of the Heer Van Tassel, which he found thronged with the pride and flower of the adjacent country. Old farmers, a spare leathern-faced race, in homespun coats and breeches, blue stockings, huge shoes, and magnificent pewter buckles. Their brisk withered little dames, in close-crimped caps, long-waisted short gowns, homespun petticoats, with scissors and pincushions and gay calico pockets hanging on the outside. Buxom lasses, almost as antiquated as their mothers, excepting where a straw hat, a fine ribbon, or perhaps a white frock gave symptoms of city innovation. The sons, in short square-skirted coats with rows of stupendous brass buttons, and their hair generally queued in the fashion of the times, especially if they could procure an eel skin for the purpose, it being esteemed throughout the country as a potent nourisher and strengthener of the hair.

Brom Bones, however, was the hero of the scene, having come to the gathering on his favorite steed Dare-devil, a creature, like himself, full of mettle and mischief, and which no one but himself could manage. He was, in fact, noted for preferring vicious animals, given to all kinds of tricks, which kept the rider in constant risk of his neck, for he held a tractable well-broken horse as unworthy of a lad of spirit.

Fain would I pause to dwell upon the world of charms that burst upon the enraptured gaze of my hero as he entered the state parlor of Van Tassel's mansion. Not those of the bevy of buxom lasses, with their luxurious display of red and white, but the ample charms of a genuine Dutch country tea table, in the sumptuous time of autumn. Such heaped-up platters of cakes of various and almost indescribable kinds, known only to experienced Dutch housewives! There was the doughty doughnut, the tenderer oly koek, and the crisp and crumbling cruller; sweet cakes and shortcakes, ginger cakes and honey cakes, and the whole family of cakes. And then there were apple pies and peach pies and pumpkins pies; besides slices of ham and smoked beef; and moreover delectable dishes of preserved plums, and peaches, and pears, and quinces; not to mention broiled shad and roasted chickens; together with bowls of milk and cream, all mingled higgledy-piggledy, pretty much as I have enumerated them, with the motherly teapot sending up its clouds of vapor from the midst—Heaven bless the mark! I want breath and time to discuss this banquet as it deserves, and am too eager to get on with my story. Happily, Ichabod Crane was not in so great a hurry as his historian, but did ample justcie to every dainty.

He was a kind and thankful creature whose heart dilated in proportion as his skin was filled with good cheer, and whose spirits rose with eating as some men's do with drink. He could not help, too, rolling his large eyes around him as he ate, and chuckling with the possibility that he might one day be lord of all this scene of almost unimaginable luxury and splendor. Then, he thought, how soon he'd turn his back upon the old schoolhouse; snap his fingers in the face of Hans Van Ripper, and every other niggardly patron, and kick any itinerant pedagogue out of doors that should dare to call him comrade!

Old Baltus Van Tassel moved about among his guests with a face dilated with content and good humor, round and jolly as the harvest moon. His hospitable attentions were brief, but expressive, being confined to a shake of the hand, a slap on the shoulder, a loud laugh, and a pressing invitation to "fall to, and help themselves."

And now the sound of the music from the common room, or hall, summoned to the dance. The musician was an old gray-headed Negro, who had been the itinerant orchestra of the neighborhood for more than half a century. His instrument was as old and battered as himself. The greater part of the time he scraped on two or three strings, accompanying every movement of the bow with a motion of the head; bowing almost to the ground and stamping with his foot whenever a fresh couple were to start.

Ichabod prided himself upon his dancing as much as upon his vocal powers. Not a limb, not a fiber about him was idle; and to have seen his loosely hung frame in full motion, and clattering about the room, you would have thought Saint Vitus himself, that blessed patron of the dance, was figuring before you in person. He was the admiration of all the Negroes, who, having gathered, of all ages and sizes, from the farm and the neighborhood, stood forming a pyramid of shining black faces at every door and window, gaz-

ing with delight at the scene, rolling their white eye-
balls, and showing grinning rows of ivory from ear
to ear. How could the flogger of urchins be otherwise
than animated and joyous? The lady of his heart was
his partner in the dance, and smiling graciously in
reply to all his amorous oglings, while Brom Bones,
sorely smitten with love and jealousy, sat brooding by
himself in one corner.

When the dance was at an end, Ichabod was attracted to a knot of the sager folks, who, with old
Van Tassel, sat smoking at one end of the piazza,
gossiping over former times, and drawing out long
stories about the war.

This neighborhood, at the time of which I am
speaking, was one of those highly favored places which
abound with chronicle and great men. The British
and American line had run near it during the war; it
had, therefore, been the scene of marauding, and infested with refugees, cowboys, and all kinds of border
chivalry. Just sufficient time had elapsed to enable
each storyteller to dress up his tale with a little becoming fiction, and, in the indistinctness of his recollection, to make himself the hero of every exploit.

There was the story of Doffue Martling, a large
blue-bearded Dutchman, who had nearly taken a
British frigate with an old iron nine-pounder from a
mud breastwork, only that his gun burst at the sixth
discharge. And there was an old gentleman who shall
be nameless, being too rich a mynheer to be lightly
mentioned, who, in the Battle of White Plains, being
an excellent master of defense, parried a musket ball

with a small sword, insomuch that he absolutely felt
it whiz around the blade and glance off at the hilt, in
proof of which he was ready at any time to show the
sword, with the hilt a little bent. There were several
more that had been equally great in the field, not one
of whom but was persuaded that he had a considerable hand in bringing the war to a happy termination.

But all these were nothing to the tales of ghosts and
apparitions that succeeded. The neighborhood is rich
in legendary treasures of the kind. Local tales and
superstitions thrive best in these sheltered long-settled
retreats, but are trampled under foot by the shifting
throng that forms the population of most of our country places. Besides, there is no encouragement for
ghosts in most of our villages, for they have scarcely
had time to finish their first nap and turn themselves
in their graves before their surviving friends have trav-
eled away from the neighborhood; so that when they
turn out at night to walk their rounds they have no
acquaintance left to call upon. This is perhaps the
reason why we so seldom hear of ghosts except in our
long-established Dutch communities.

The immediate cause, however, of the prevalence
of supernatural stories in these parts was doubtless
owing to the vicinity of Sleepy Hollow. There was a
contagion in the very air that blew from that haunted
region; it breathed forth an atmosphere of dreams and
fancies infecting all the land. Several of the Sleepy
Hollow people were present at Van Tassel's, and, as
usual, were doling out their wild and wonderful legends. Many dismal tales were told about funeral trains,

and mourning cries and wailings heard and seen about the great tree where the unfortunate Major André was taken, and which stood in the neighborhood. Some mention was made also of the woman in white that haunted the dark glen at Raven Rock, and was often heard to shriek on winter nights before a storm, having perished there in the snow. The chief part of the stories, however, turned upon the favorite specter of Sleepy Hollow, the headless horseman, who had been heard several times of late, patrolling the country, and, it was said, tethered his horse nightly among the graves in the churchyard.

The sequestered situation of this church seems always to have made it a favorite haunt of troubled spirits. It stands on a knoll, surrounded by locust trees and lofty elms, from among which its decent whitewashed walls shine modestly forth, like Christian purity baeming through the shades of retirement. A gentle slope descends from it to a silver sheet of water, bordered by high trees, between which peeps may be caught at the blue hills of the Hudson. To look upon its grass-grown yard, where the sunbeams seem to sleep so quietly, one would think that there at least the dead might rest in peace. On one side of the church extends a wide woody dell, along which raves a large brook among broken rocks and trunks of fallen trees. Over a deep black part of the stream, not far from the church, was formerly thrown a wooden bridge; the road that led to it, and the bridge itself, were thickly shaded by overhanging trees, which cast a gloom about it, even in the daytime, but occasioned a fearful

darkness at night. This was one of the favorite haunts
of the headless horseman, and the place where he was
most frequently encountered. The tale was told of old
Brouwer, a most heretical disbeliever in ghosts, how
he met the horseman returning from his foray into
Sleepy Hollow, and was obliged to get up behind him;
how they galloped over bush and brake, over hill and
swamp, until they reached the bridge, when the horseman suddenly turned into a skeleton, threw old
Brouwer into the brook, and sprang away over the
treetops with a clap of thunder.

This story was immediately matched by a thrice
marvelous adventure of Brom Bones, who made light
of the galloping Hessian as an arrant jockey. He affirmed that, on returning one night from the neighboring village of Sing Sing, he had been overtaken
by this midnight trooper; that he had offered to race
with him for a bowl of punch, and should have won it
too, for Daredevil beat the goblin horse all hollow,
but, just as they came to the church bridge, the Hessian bolted and vanished in a flash of fire.

All these tales, told in that drowsy undertone with
which men talk in the dark, the countenance of the
listeners only now and then receiving a casual gleam
from the glare of a pipe, sank deep in the mind of
Ichabod. He repaid them in kind with large extracts
from his invaluable author, Cotton Mather, and added
many marvelous events that had taken place in his
native State of Connecticut, and fearful sights which
he had seen in his nightly walks about Sleepy Hollow.

The revel now gradually broke up. The old farmers

gathered together their families in their wagons, and were heard for some time rattling along the hollow roads and over the distant hills. Some of the damsels mounted on pillions behind their favorite swains, and their lighthearted laughter, mingling with the clatter of hoofs, echoed along the silent woodlands, sounding fainter and fainter until they gradually died away—and the late scene of noise and frolic was all silent and deserted. Ichabod only lingered behind, according to the custom of country lovers, to have a tête-à-tête with the heiress, fully convinced that he was now on the high road to success. What passed at this interview I will not pretend to say, for in fact I do not know. Something, however, I fear me, must have gone wrong, for he certainly sallied forth, after no very great interval, with an air quite desolate and chopfallen. Oh these women! these women! Could that girl have been playing off any of her coquettish tricks? Was her encouragement of the poor pedagogue all a mere sham to secure her conquest of his rival? Heaven only knows, not I! Let it suffice to say, Ichabod stole forth with the air of one who had been sacking a hen roost rather than a fair lady's heart. Without looking to the right or left to notice the scene of rural wealth, on which he had so often gloated, he went straight to the stable, and with several hearty cuffs and kicks roused his steed most uncourteously from the comfortable quarters in which he was soundly sleeping, dreaming of mountains of corn and oats, and whole valleys of timothy and clover.

It was the very witching time of night that Ichabod,

heavy-hearted and crestfallen, pursued his travel homeward, along the sides of the lofty hills which rise above Tarry Town, and which he had traversed so cheerily in the afternoon. The hour was as dismal as himself. Far below him, the Tappan Zee spread its dusky and indistinct waste of waters, with here and there the tall mast of a sloop, riding quietly at anchor under the land. In the dead hush of midnight he could even hear the barking of the watchdog from the opposite shore of the Hudson, but it was so vague and faint as only to give an idea of his distance from this faithful companion of man. Now and then, too, the long-drawn crowing of a cock, accidentally awakened, would sound far, far off, from some farmhouse away among the hills—but it was like a dreaming sound in his ear. No signs of life occurred near him, but occasionally the melancholy chirp of a cricket, or perhaps the guttural twang of a bullfrog, from a neighboring marsh, as if sleeping uncomfortably and turning suddenly in his bed.

All the stories of ghosts and goblins that he had heard in the afternoon now came crowding upon his recollection. The night grew darker and darker; the stars seemed to sink deeper in the sky, and driving clouds occasionally hid them from his sight. He had never felt so lonely and dismal. He was, moreover, approaching the very place where many of the scenes of the ghosts stories had been laid. In the center of the road stood an enormous tulip tree, which towered like a giant above all the other trees of the neighborhood and formed a kind of landmark. Its limbs were gnarled and fantastic, large enough to form trunks for ordinary trees, twisting down almost to the earth and rising again into the air. It was connected with the tragical story of the unfortunate André, who had been taken prisoner hard by; and was universally known by the name of Major André's tree. The common people regarded it with a mixture of respect and superstition, partly out of sympathy for the fate of its ill-starred namesake, and partly from the tales of strange sights and doleful lamentations told concerning it.

As Ichabod approached this fearful tree, he began to whistle; he thought his whistle was answered—it was but a blast sweeping sharply through the dry branches. As he approached a little nearer, he thought he saw something white hanging in the midst of the tree—he paused and ceased whistling; but on looking more narrowly, perceived that it was a place where the tree had been scathed by lightning and the white wood laid bare. Suddenly he heard a groan—his teeth chattered and his knees smote against the saddle; it was but the rubbing of one huge bough upon another as they were swayed about by the breeze. He passed the trees in safety, but new perils lay before him.

About two hundred yards from the tree a small brook crossed the road and ran into a marshy and thickly wooded glen, known by the name of Wiley's swamp. A few rough logs, laid side by side, served for a bridge over this stream. On that side of the road where the brook entered the wood, a group of oaks and chestnuts, matted thick with wild grapevines, threw a cavernous gloom over it. To pass this bridge was the severest trial. It was at this identical spot that the unfortunate André was captured, and under the covert of those chestnuts and vines were the sturdy yeomen concealed who surprised him. This has ever since been considered a haunted stream, and fearful are the feelings of the schoolboy who has to pass it alone after dark.

As he approached the stream his heart began to thump; he summoned up, however, all his resolution, gave his horse half a score of kicks in the ribs, and attempted to dash briskly across the bridge; but instead of starting forward, the perverse old animal made a lateral movement and ran broadside against the fence. Ichabod, whose fears increased with the delay, jerked the reins on the other side, and kicked lustily with the contrary foot; it was all in vain; his steed started, it is true, but it was only to plunge to the opposite side of the road into a thicket of brambles and alder bushes. The schoolmaster now bestowed both whip and heel upon the starveling ribs of old Gunpowder, who dashed forward, snuffling and snorting, but came to a stand just by the bridge with a suddenness that had nearly sent his rider sprawling over his head. Just at this moment a plashy tramp by the side of the bridge caught the sensitive ear of Ichabod. In the dark shadow of the grove, on the margin of the brook, he beheld something huge, misshapen, black and towering. It stirred not, but seemed gathered up in the gloom, like some gigantic monster ready to spring upon the traveler.

The hair of the affrighted pedagogue rose upon his head with terror. What was to be done? To turn and fly was now too late; and besides, what chance was there of escaping ghost or goblins, if such it was, which could ride upon the wings of the wind? Summoning up, therefore, a show of courage, he demanded in stammering accents—"Who are you?" He received no reply. He repeated his demand in a still more agitated voice. Still there was no answer. Once more he cudgeled the sides of the inflexible Gunpowder, and, shutting his eyes, broke forth with involuntary fervor into a psalm tune. Just then the shadowy object of alarm put itself in motion, and, with a scramble and a bound, stood at once in the middle of the road. Though the night was dark and dismal, yet the form of the unknown might now in some degree be ascertained. He appeared to be a horseman of large dimensions, and mounted on a black horse of powerful frame. He made no offer of molestation or sociability, but kept aloof on one side of the road, jogging along on the blind side of old Gunpowder, who had now got over his fright and waywardness.

Ichabod, who had no relish for this strange midnight companion, and bethought himself of the adventure of Brom Bones with the Galloping Hessian, now quickened his steed, in hopes of leaving him behind. The stranger, however, quickened his horse to an equal pace. Ichabod pulled up, and fell into a walk, thinking to lag behind—the other did the same. His heart began to sink within him; he endeavored to resume his psalm tune, but his parched tongue clove to the

roof of his mouth, and he could not utter a stave.
There was something in the moody and dogged silence
of this pertinacious companion that was mysterious
and appalling. It was soon fearfully accounted for.
On mounting a rising ground, which brought the figure of his fellow-traveler in relief against the sky,
gigantic in height, and muffled in a cloak, Ichabod
was horror-struck on perceiving that he was headless!
But his horror was still more increased on observing
that the head, which should have rested on his shoulders, was carried before him on the pommel of the
saddle. His terror rose to desperation; he rained a
shower of kicks and blows upon Gunpowder, hoping,
by a sudden movement, to give his companion the
slip—but the specter started full jump with him. Away
then they dashed, through thick and thin, stones flying and sparks flashing at every bound. Ichabod's
flimsy garments fluttered in the air as he stretched his
long lank body away over his horse's head, in the
eagerness of his flight.

They had now reached the road which turns off to
Sleepy Hollow; but Gunpowder, who seemed possessed
with a demon, instead of keeping up it, made an opposite turn, and plunged headlong downhill to the left.
This road leads through a sandy hollow, shaded by
trees for about a quarter of a mile, where it crosses
the bridge famous in goblin story, and just beyond
swells the green knoll on which stands the whitewashed church.

As yet the panic of the steed had given his unskillful rider an apparent advantage in the chase; but just

as he had got halfway through the hollow, the girths of the saddle gave way, and he felt it slipping from under him. He seized it by the pommel and endeavored to hold it firm, but in vain; and had just time to save himself by clasping old Gunpowder around the neck when the saddle fell to the earth, and he heard it trampled under foot by his pursuer. For a moment the terror of Hans Van Ripper's wrath passed across his mind—for it was his Sunday saddle; but this was no time for petty fears; the goblin was hard on his haunches, and (unskillful rider that he was!) he had much ado to maintain his seat, sometimes slipping on one side, sometimes on the other, and sometimes jolted on the high ridge of his horse's backbone with a violence that he verily feared would cleave him asunder.

An opening in the trees now cheered him with the hopes that the church bridge was at hand. The wavering reflection of a silver star in the bosom of the brook told him that he was not mistaken. He saw the walls of the church dimly glaring under the trees beyond. He recollected the place where Brom Bones's ghostly competitor had disappeared. "If I can but reach that bridge," thought Ichabod, "I am safe." Just then he heard the black steed panting and blowing close behind him; he even fancied that he felt his hot breath. Another convulsive kick in the ribs and old Gunpowder sprang upon the bridge; he thundered over the resounding planks; he gained the opposite side; and now Ichabod cast a look behind to see if his pursuer should vanish, according to rule, in a flash of fire and brimstone. Just then he saw the goblin rising in his stirrups, and in the very act of hurling his head at him. Ichabod endeavored to dodge the horrible missile, but too late. It encountered his cranium with a tremendous crash—he was tumbled headlong into the dust, and Gunpowder, the black steed, and the goblin rider, passed by like a whirlwind.

The next morning the old horse was found without his saddle, and with the bridle under his feet, soberly cropping the grass at his master's gate. Ichabod did ont make his appearance at breakfast—dinner hour came, but no Ichabod. The boys assembled at the schoolhouse, and strolled idly about the banks of the brook; but no schoolmaster. Hans Van Ripper now began to feel some uneasiness about the fate of poor Ichabod, and his saddle. An inquiry was set on foot, and after diligent investigation they came upon his traces. In one part of the road leading to the church was found the saddle trampled in the dirt; the tracks of horses' hoofs deeply dented in the road, and evidently at furious speed, were traced to the bridge, beyond which, on the bank of a broad part of the brook, where the water ran deep and black, was found the hat of the unfortunate Ichabod, and close beside it a shattered pumpkin.

The brook was searched, but the body of the schoolmaster was not to be discovered. Hans Van Ripper, as executor of his estate, examined the bundle which contained all his worldly effects. They consisted of two shirts and a half, two stocks for the neck, a pair or two of worsted stockings, an old pair of corduroy small clothes, a rusty razor, a book of psalm tunes full of dogs' ears, and a broken pitch-pipe. As to the books and furniture of the school-house, they belonged to the community, excepting Cotton Mather's *History of Witchcraft, a New England Almanac,* and a book of dreams and fortune-telling; in which last was a sheet of foolscap much scribbled and blotted in several fruitless attempts to make a copy of verses in honor of the heiress of Van Tassel. These magic books and the poetic scrawl were forthwith consigned to the flames by Hans Van Ripper, who from that time forward determined to send his children no more to school, observing that he never knew any good come of this same reading and writing. Whatever money the schoolmaster possessed, and he had received his quarter's pay but a day or two before, he must have had about his person at the time of his disappearance.

The mysterious event caused much speculation at the church on the following Sunday. Knots of gazers and gossips were collected in the churchyard, at the bridge, and at the spot where the hat and pumpkin had been found. The stories of Brouwer, of Bones, and a whole budget of others were called to mind; and when they had deligently considered them all and compared them with the symptoms of the present case, they shook their heads and came to the conclusion that Ichabod had been carried off by the galloping Hessian. As he was a bachelor and in nobody's debt, nobody troubled his head any more about him. The school was removed to a different quarter of the hollow, and another pedagogue reigned in his stead.

It is true an old farmer, who had been down to New York on a visit several years after, and from whom this account of the ghostly adventure was received, brought home the intelligence that Ichabod Crane was still alive; that he had left the neighborhood, partly through fear of the goblin and Hans Van Ripper, and partly in mortification at having been suddenly dismissed by the heiress; that he had changed his quarters to a distant part of the country, had kept school and studied law at the same time, had been admitted to the bar, turned politician, electioneered, written for the newspapers, and finally had been made a justice of the Ten Pound Court. Brom Bones too, who shortly after his rival's disappearance conducted the blooming Katrina in triumph to the altar, was observed to look exceedingly knowing whenever the story of Ichabod was related, and always burst into a hearty laugh at the mention of the pumpkin, which led some to suspect that he knew more about the matter than he chose to tell.

The old country wives, however, who are the best judges of these matters, maintain to this day that Ichabod was spirited away by supernatural means; and it is a favorite story often told about the neighborhood around the winter evening fire. The bridge became more than ever an object of superstitious awe, and that may be the reason why the road has been altered of late years, so as to approach the church by the border of the millpond. The schoolhouse, being deserted, soon fell to decay, and was reported to be haunted by the ghost of the unfortunate pedagogue; and the plowboy, loitering homeward of a still summer evening, has often fancied his voice at a distance, chanting a melancholy psalm tune among the tranquil solitudes of Sleepy Hollow.

POSTSCRIPT

FOUND IN THE HANDWRITING OF MR. KNICKERBOCKER

The preceding Tale is given, almost in the precise words in which I heard it related at a Corporation meeting of the ancient city of Manhattoes, at which were present many of its sagest and most illustrious burghers. The narrator was a pleasant, shabby, gentlemanly old fellow, in pepper-and-salt clothes, with a sadly humorous face, and one whom I strongly suspected of being poor—he made such efforts to be entertaining. When his story was concluded, there was much laughter and approbation, particularly from two or three deputy aldermen, who had been asleep a greater part of the time. There was, however, one tall, dry-looking old gentleman with beetling eyebrows, who maintained a grave and rather severe face throughout, now and then folding his arms, inclining his head, and looking down upon the floor, as if turning a doubt over in his mind. He was one of your wary men, who never laugh but upon good grounds—when they have reason and the law on their side. When the mirth of the rest of the company had subsided and silence was restored, he leaned once arm on the elbow of his chair, and, sticking the other akimbo, demanded, with a sight but exceedingly sage motion of the head, and contraction of the brow, what was the moral of the story, and what it went to prove?

The storyteller, who was just putting a glass of wine to his lips as a refreshment after his toils, paused for a moment, looked at his inquirer with an air of infinite deference, and, lowering the glass slowly to the table, observed that the story was intended most logically to prove:

"That there is no situation in life but has its advantages and pleasures—provided we will but take a joke as we find it.

"That, therefore, he that runs races with goblin troopers is likely to have rough riding of it.

"Ergo, for a country schoolmaster to be refused the hand of a Dutch heiress is a certain step to high preferment in the state."

The cautious old gentleman knit his brows tenfold closer after this explanation, being sorely puzzled by the ratiocination of the syllogism; while, methought, the one in pepper-and-salt eyed him with something of a triumphant leer. At length, he observed, that all this was very well, but still he thought the story a little on the extravagant—there were one or two points on which he had his doubts.

"Faith, sir," replied the storyteller, "as to that matter, I don't believe one-half of it myself."

D. K.

RIP VAN WINKLE

A Posthumous Writing of Diedrich Knickerbocker

By Woden, God of Saxons,
From whence comes Wensday, that is Wodensday,
Truth is a thing that ever I will keep
Unto thylke day in which I creep into
My sepulchre————

CARTWRIGHT

[The following Tale was found among the papers of the late Diedrich Knickerbocker, an old gentleman of New York, who was very curious in the Dutch history of the province and the manners of the descendants from its primitive settlers. His historical researchers, however, did not lie so much among books as among men, for the former are lamentably scantly on his favorite topics, whereas he found the old burghers, and still more their wives, rich in that legendary lore so invaluable to true history.

Whenenever, therefore, he happened upon a genuine Dutch family, snugly shut up in its low-roofed farmhouse, under a spreading sycamore, he looked upon it as a little clasped volume of black letter and studied it with the zeal of a bookworm.

The result of all these researchers was a history of the province during the reign of the Dutch governors, which he published some years since. There have been various opinions as to the literary character of his work, and, to tell the truth, it is not a whit better than it should be. Its chief merit is its scrupulous accuracy, which indeed was a little questioned on its first appearance, but has since been completely established, and it is now admitted into all historical collections as a book of unquestionable authority.

The old gentleman died shortly after the publication of his work, and now that he is dead and gone, it cannot do much harm to his memory to say that his time might have been much better employed in weightier labors. He, however, was apt to ride his hobby his own way; and though it did now and then kick up the dust a little in the eyes of his neighbors and grieve the spirit of some friends, for whom he felt the truest deference and affection, yet his errors and follies are remembered "more in sorrow than in anger," and it begins to be suspected that he never intended to injure or offend. But however his memory may be appreciated by critics, it is held dear by many folks, whose good opinion is well worth having; particularly by certain biscuit bakers, who have gone so far as to imprint his likeness on their new-year cakes, and have thus given him a chance for immortality, almost equal to being stamped on a Waterloo Medal, or a Queen Anne's Farthing.]

Whoever has made a voyage up the Hudson must remember the Kaatskill Mountains. They are a dismembered branch of the great Appalachian family, and are seen away to the west of the river, swelling up to a noble height and lording it over the surrounding country. Every change of season, every change of weather, indeed, every hour of the day produces some change in the magical hues and shapes of these mountains, and they are regarded by all the good wives, far and near, as perfect barometers. When the weather is fair and settled, they are clothed in blue and purple, and print their bold outlines on the clear evening sky; but, sometimes, when the rest of the landscape is cloudless, they will gather a hood of gray vapors about their summits, which, in the last rays of the setting sun, will glow and light up like a crown of glory.

At the foot of these fairy mountains, the voyager may have described the light smoke curling up from a village, whose shingle roofs gleam among the trees, just where the blue tints of the upland melt away into the fresh green of the nearer landscape. It is a little village of great antiquity, having been founded by some of the Dutch colonists in the early times of the province, just about the beginning of the government of the good Peter Stuyvesant (may he rest in peace!), and there were some of the houses of the original settlers standing within a few years, built of small yellow bricks brought from Holland, having latticed windows and gable fronts, surmounted with weathercocks.

In that same village, and in one of these very houses (which, to tell the precise truth, was sadly time-worn and weather-beaten), there lived many years since, while the country was yet a province of Great Britain, a simple, good-natured fellow of the name of Rip Van Winkle. He was a descendant of the Van Winkles who figured so gallantly in the chivalrous days of Peter Stuyvesant, and accompanied him to the siege of Fort Christina. He inherited, however, but little of the martial character of his ancestors. I have observed that he was a simple, good-natured man; he was, moreover, a kind neighbor, and an obedient, henpecked husband. Indeed, to the latter circumstance might be owing that meekness of spirit which gained him such universal popularity, for those men are most apt to be obsequious and conciliating abroad who are under the discipline of shrews at home. Their tempers, doubtless, are rendered pliant and malleable in the fiery furnace of domestic tribulation, and a curtain lecture is worth all the sermons in the world for teaching the virtues of patience and long-suffering. A termagant wife may, therefore, in some respects, be considered a tolerable blessing; and if so, Rip Van Winkle was thrice blessed.

Certain it is that he was a great favorite among

all the good wives of the village, who, as usual with the amiable sex, took his part in all family squabbles and never failed, whenever they talked those matters over in their evening gossipings, to lay all the blame on Dame Van Winkle. The children of the village, too, would shout with joy whenever he approached. He assisted at their sports, made their playthings, taught them to fly kites and shoot marbles, and told them long stories of ghosts, witches, and Indians. Whenever he went dodging about the village, he was surrounded by a troop of them, hanging on his skirts, clambering on his back, and playing a thousand tricks on him with impunity; and not a dog would bark at him throughout the neighborhood.

The great error in Rip's composition was an insuperable aversion to all kinds of profitable labor. It could not be from the want of assiduity or perseverance, for he would sit on a wet rock, with a rod as long and heavy as a Tartar's lance, and fish all day without a murmur, even though he should not be encouraged by a single nibble. He would carry a fowling piece on his shoulder for hours together, trudging through woods and swamps and up hill and down dale to shoot a few squirrels or wild pigeons. He would never refuse to assist a neighbor even in the roughest toil, and was a foremost man at all country frolics for husking Indian corn or building stone fences; the women of the village, too, used to employ him to run their errands and to do such little odd jobs as their less obliging husbands would not do for them. In a word, Rip was ready to attend to anybody's business but his own; but as to doing family duty and keeping his farm in order, he found it impossible.

In fact, he declared it was of no use to work on his farm; it was the most pestilent little piece of ground in the whole country; everything about it went wrong, and would go wrong, in spite of him. His fences were continually falling to pieces; his cow would either go astray or get among the cabbages; weeds were sure to grow quicker in his fields than anywhere else; the rain always made a point of setting in just as he had some outdoor work to do; so that though his patrimonial estate had dwindled away under his management, acre by acre, until there was little more left than a mere patch of Indian corn and potatoes, yet it was the worst-conditioned farm in the neighborhood.

His children, too, were as ragged and wild as if they belonged to nobody. His son Rip, an urchin begotten in his own likeness, promised to inherit the habits, with the old clothes, of his father. He was generally seen trooping like a colt at his mother's heels, equipped in a pair of his father's cast-off galligaskins, which he had much ado to hold up with one hand as a fine lady does her train in bad weather.

Rip Van Winkle, however, was one of those happy mortals of foolish, well-oiled dispositions who take the world easy, eat white bread or brown, whichever can be got with least thought or trouble, and would rather starve on a penny than work for a pound. If left to himself, he would have whistled life away in perfect contentment; but his wife kept continually dinning in his ears about his idleness, his carelessness, and the ruin he was bringing on his family. Morning, noon, and night, her tongue was incessantly going, and everything he said or did was sure to produce a torrent of household eloquence. Rip had but one way of replying to all lectures of the kind, and that, by frequent use, had grown into a habit. He shrugged his shoulders, shook his head, cast up his eyes, but said nothing. This, however, always provoked a fresh volley from his wife, so that he was fain to draw off his forces and take to the outside of the house—the only side which, in truth, belongs to a henpecked husband.

Rip's sole domestic adherent was his dog, Wolf, who was as much henpecked as his master, for Dame Van Winkle regarded them as companions in idleness, and even looked upon Wolf with an evil eye as the cause of his master's going so often astray. True it is, in all points of spirit befitting an honorable dog, he was an courageous an animal as ever scoured the woods—but what courage can withstand the ever-during and all-besetting terrors of a woman's tongue? The moment Wolf entered the house his crest fell, his tail drooped to the ground, or curled between his legs, he sneaked about with a gallows air, casting many a sidelong glance at Dame Van Winkle, and at the least flourish of a broomstick or ladle he would fly to the door with yelping precipitation.

Times grew worse and worse with Rip Van Winkle as years of matrimony rolled on; a tart temper never mellows with age, and a sharp tongue is the only edged tool that grows keener with constant use. For a long while he used to console himself, when driven from home, by frequenting a kind of perpetual club of the sages, philosophers, and other idle personages of the village, which held its sessions on a bench before a small inn, designated by a rubicund portrait of His Majesty George the Third. Here they used to sit in the shade through a long, lazy summer's day, talking listlessly over village gossip or telling endless sleepy stories about nothing. But it would have been worth any statesman's money to have heard the profound discussions that sometimes took place when by chance an old newspaper fell into their hands from some passing traveler. How solemnly they would listen to the contents, as drawled out by Derrick Van Bummel, the schoolmaster, a dapper, learned little man who was not to be daunted by the most gigantic word in the dictionary; and how sagely they would deliberate upon public events some months after they had taken place.

The opinions of this junto were completely controlled by Nicholas Vedder, a patriarch of the village and landlord of the inn, at the door of which he took his seat from morning till night, just moving sufficiently to avoid the sun and keep in the shade of a large tree, so that the neighbors could tell the hour by his movements as accurately as by a sundial.

It is true he was rarely heard to speak, but smoked his pipe incessantly. His adherents, however (for every great man has his adherents), perfectly understood him, and knew how to gather his opinions. When anything that was read or related displeased him, he was observed to smoke his pipe vehemently and to send forth short, frequent, and angry puffs; but when pleased, he would inhale the smoke slowly and tranquilly and emit it in light and placid clouds, and sometimes, taking the pipe from his mouth and letting the fragrant vapor curl about his nose, would gravely nod his head in token of perfect approbation.

From even this stronghold the unlucky Rip was at length routed by his termagant wife, who would suddenly break in upon the tranquillity of the assemblage and call the members all to naught; nor was that august personage, Nicholas Vedder himself, sacred from the daring tongue of this terrible virago, who charged him outright with encouraging her husband in habits of idleness.

Poor Rip was at last reduced almost to despair, and his only alternative, to escape from the labor of the farm and clamor of his wife, was to take gun in hand and stroll away into the woods. Here he would sometimes seat himself at the foot of a tree and share the contents of his wallet with Wolf, with whom he sympathized as a fellow sufferer in persecution. "Poor Wolf," he would say, "thy mistress leads thee a dog's life of it; but never mind, my lad, whilst I live thou shalt never want a friend to stand by thee!" Wolf would wag his tail, look wistfully in his master's face, and if dogs can feel pity, I verily believe he reciprocated the sentiment with all his heart.

In a long ramble of the kind of a fine autumnal day, Rip had unconsciously scrambled to one of the highest parts of the Kaatskill Mountains. He was after his favorite sport of squirrel shooting, and the still solitudes had echoed and re-echoed with the reports of his gun. Panting and fatigued, he threw himself, late in the afternoon, on a green knoll, covered with mountain herbage, that crowned the brow of a precipice. From an opening between the trees he could overlook all the lower country for many a mile of rich woodland. He saw at a distance the lordly Hudson, far, far below him, moving on its silent but majestic course, with the reflection of a purple cloud or the sail of a lagging bark here and there sleeping on its glassy bosom, and at last losing itself in the blue highlands.

On the other side he looked down into a deep mountain glen, wild, lonely, and shagged, the bottom filled with fragments from the impending cliffs, and scarcely lighted by the reflected rays of the setting sun. For some time Rip lay musing on this scene. Evening was gradually advancing; the mountains began to throw their long blue shadows over the valleys. He saw that it would be dark long before he could reach the village, and he heaved a heavy sigh when he thought of encountering the terrors of Dame Van Winkle.

As he was about to descend, he heard a voice from a distance, hallooing, "Rip Van Winkle! Rip Van Winkle!" He looked around, but could see nothing but a crow winging its solitary flight across the mountain. He thought his fancy must have deceived him, and turned again to descend, when he heard the same cry ring through the still evening air, "Rip Van Winkle! Rip Van Winkle!" At the same time Wolf bristled up his back and, giving a low growl, skulked to his master's side, looking fearfully down into the glen. Rip now felt a vague apprehension stealing over him; he looked anxiously in the same direction and perceived a strange figure slowly toiling up the rocks, and bending under the weight of something he carried on his back. He was surprised to see any human being in this lonely and unfrequented place, but supposing it to be some one of the neighborhood in need of his assistance, he hastened down to yield it.

On nearer approach he was still more surprised at the singularity of the stranger's appearance. He was a short, square-built old fellow, with thick, bushy hair and a grizzled beard. His dress was of the antique Dutch fashion—a cloth jerkin strapped around the waist and several pairs of breeches, the outer one of ample volume, decorated with rows of buttons down the sides and bunches at the knees. He bore on his shoulder a stout keg that seemed full of liquor, and made signs for Rip to approach and assist him with the load. Though rather shy and distrustful of this new acquaintance, Rip complied with his usual alacrity, and mutually relieving one another, they clambered up a narrow gully, apparently the dry bed of a mountain torrent. As they ascended, Rip every now and then heard long rolling peals, like distant thunder, that seemed to issue out of a deep ravine, or rather cleft, between lofty rocks, toward which their rugged path conducted. He paused for an instant, but supposing it to be the muttering of one of those transient thunder showers which often take place in mountain heights, he proceeded. Passing through the ravine, they came to a hollow, like a small amphitheater, surrounded by perpendicular precipices, over the brinks of which impending trees shot their branches, so that you only caught glimpses of the azure sky and the bright evening cloud. During the whole time, Rip and his companion had labored on in silence, for though the former marveled greatly what could be the object of carrying a keg of liquor up this wild mountain, yet there was something strange and incomprehensible about the unknown that inspired awe and checked familiarity.

On entering the amphitheater, new objects of wonder were to be seen. On a level spot in the center was a company of odd-looking persons playing at ninepins. They were dressed in a quaint, outlandish fashion; some wore short doublets, others jerkins, with long knives in their belts, and most of them had enormous breeches, of similar style with that of the guide's. Their visages, too, were peculiar; one had a large beard, broad face, and small piggish eyes, the face of another seemed to consist entirely of nose and was surmounted by a white sugarloaf hat set off with a little red cock's tail. They all had beards, of various shapes and colors. There was one who seemed to be the commander. He was a stout old gentleman, with a weather-beaten countenance; he wore a laced doublet, broad belt and hanger, high-crowned hat and feather, red stockings, and high-heeled shoes, with roses in them. The whole group reminded Rip of the figures in an old Flemish painting, in the parlor of Dominie Van Shaick, the village parson, and which had been brought over from Holland at the time of the settlement.

What seemed particularly odd to Rip was that though these folks were evidently amusing themselves, yet they maintained the gravest faces, the most mysterious silence, and were, withal, the most melancholy party of pleasure he had ever witnessed. Nothing interrupted the sillness of the scene but the noise of the balls, which, whenever they were rolled, echoed along the mountains like rumbling peals of thunder.

As Rip and his companion approached them, they suddenly desisted from their play and stared at him with such fixed, statuelike gaze and such strange, uncouth, lackluster countenances that his heart turned within him and his knees smote together. His companion now emptied the contents of the keg into large flagons and made signs to him to wait upon the company. He obeyed with fear and trembling; they quaffed the liquor in profound silence and then returned to their game.

By degrees Rip's awe and apprehension subsided. He even ventured, when no eye was fixed upon him, to taste the beverage, which he found had much of the flavor of excellent Hollands. He was naturally a thirsty soul and was soon tempted to repeat the draft. One taste provoked another; and he reiterated his visits to the flagon so often that at length his senses were overpowered, his eyes swam in his head, his head gradually declined, and he fell into a deep sleep.

On waking, he found himself on the green knoll whence he had first seen the old man of the glen. He rubbed his eyes—it was a bright, sunny morning. The birds were hopping and twittering among the bushes, and the eagle was wheeling aloft and breasting the pure mountain breeze. "Surely," thought Rip, "I have not slept here all night." He recalled the occurrences before he fell asleep. The strange man with a keg of liquor—the mountain ravine—the wild retreat among the rocks—the woebegone party at ninepins—the flagon—"Oh! That flagon! That wicked flagon!" thought Rip. "What excuse shall I make to Dame Van Winkle"

He looked around for his gun, but in place of the clean, well-oiled fowling piece he found an old firelock lying by him, the barrel encrusted with rust, the lock falling off, and the stock worm-eaten. He now suspected that the grave roysters of the mountain had put a trick upon him, and, having dosed him with liquor, had robbed him of his gun. Wolf, too, had disappeared, but he might have strayed away after a squirrel or partridge. He whistled after him and shouted his name, but all in vain; the echoes repeated his whistle and shout, but no dog was to be seen.

He determined to revisit the scene of the last evening's gambol, and if he met with any of the party, to demand his dog and gun. As he rose to walk, he found himself stiff in the joints and wanting in his usual activity. "These mountain beds do not agree with me," thought Rip, "and if this frolic should lay me up with a fit of the rheumatism, I shall have a blessed time with Dame Van Winkle." With some difficulty he got down into the glen; he found the gully up which he and his companion had ascended the preceding evening, but to his astonishment a mountain stream was now foaming down it, leaping from rock to rock and filling the glen with babbling murmurs. He, however, made shift to scramble up its sides, working his toilsome way through thickets of birch, sassafras, and witch hazel, and sometimes tripped up or entangled by the wild grapevines that twisted their coils or tendrils from tree to tree and spread a kind of network in his path.

At length he reached to where the ravine had opened through the cliffs to the amphitheater, but no trades of such opening remained. The rocks presented a high, impenetrable wall over which the torrent came tumbling in a sheet of feathery foam and fell into a broad, deep basin, black from the shadows of the surrounding forest. Here, then, poor Rip was brought to a stand. He again called and whistled after his dog; he was only answered by the cawing of a flock of idle crows, sporting high in air about a dry tree that overhung a sunny precipice, and who, secure in their elevation, seemed to look down and scoff at the poor man's perplexities. What was to be done? The morning was passing away, and Rip felt famished for want of his breakfast. He grieved to give up his dog and gun; he dreaded to meet his wife, but it would not do to starve among the mountains. He shook his head, shouldered the rusty firelock, and, with a heart full of trouble and anxiety, turned his steps homeward.

As he approached the village he met a number of people, but none whom he knew, which somewhat surprised him, for he had thought himself acquainted with every one in the country around. Their dress, too, was of a different fashion from that to which he was accustomed. They all stared at him with equal marks of surprise, and whenever they cast their eyes upon him invariably stroked their chins. The constant recurrence of this gesture induced Rip, involuntarily, to do the same, when, to his astonishment, he found his beard had grown a foot long!

He had now entered the skirts of the village. A troop of strange children ran at his heels, hooting after him and pointing at his gray beard. The dogs, too, not one of which he recognized for an old acquaintance, barked at him as he passed. The very village was altered; it was larger and more populous. There were rows of houses which he had never seen before, and those which had been his familiar haunts had disappeared. Strange names were over the doors—strange faces at the windows—everything was strange. His mind now misgave him; he began to doubt whether both he and the world around him were not bewitched. Surely this was his native village, which he had left but the day before. There stood the Kaatskill Mountains—there ran the silver Hudson at a distance—there was every hill and dale precisely as it had always been. Rip was sorely perplexed. "That flagon last night," thought he, "has addled my poor head sadly!"

It was with some difficulty that he found the way to his own house, which he approached with silent awe, expecting every moment to hear the shrill voice of Dame Van Winkle. He found the house gone to decay—the roof fallen in, the windows shattered, and the doors off the hinges. A half-starved dog that looked like Wolf was skulking about it. Rip called him by name, but the cur snarled, showed his teeth, and passed on. This was an unkind cut indeed. "My very dog," sighed poor Rip, "has forgotten me!"

He entered the house, which, to tell the truth, Dame Van Winkle had always kept in neat order. It was empty, forlorn, and apparently abandoned. This desolateness overcame all his connubial fears—he called loudly for his wife and children; the lonely chambers rang for a moment with his voice, and then all again was silence.

He now hurried forth and hastened to his old resort, the village inn—but it too was gone. A large, rickety, wooden building stood in its place, with great gaping windows, some of them broken and mended with old hats and petticoats, and over the door was painted, "the Union Hotel, by Jonathan Doolittle." Instead of the great tree that used to shelter the quiet little Dutch inn of yore, there now was reared a tall, naked pole, with something on the top that looked like a red nightcap, and from it was fluttering a flag, on which was a singular assemblage of stars and stripes—all this was strange and incomprehensible. He recognized on the sing, however, the ruby face of King George, under which he had smoked so many a peaceful pipe; but even this was singularly metamorphosed. The red coat was changed for one of blue and buff, a sword was held in the hand instead of a scepter, the head was decorated with a cocked hat, and underneath was painted in large characters, GENERAL WASHINGTON.

There was, as usual, a crowd of folk about the door, but none that Rip recollected. The very character of the people seemed changed. There was a busy, bustling, disputatious tone about it, instead of the accustomed phlegm and drowsy tranquillity. He looked in vain for the sage Nicholas Vedder, with his broad face, double chin, and fair long pipe, uttering clouds of tobacco smoke instead of idle speeches; or Van Bummel, the schoolmaster, doling forth the contents of an ancient newspaper. In place of these, a lean, billious-looking fellow, with his pockets full of handbills, was haranguing vehemently about rights of citizens—elections—members of conress—liberty—Bunker's Hill—heroes of seventy-six —and other words, which were a perfect Babylonish jargon to the bewildered Van Winkle.

The appearance of Rip, with his long, grizzled beard, his rusty fowling piece, his uncouth dress, and an army of women and children at his heels, soon attracted the attention of the tavern politicians. They crowded around him, eying him from head to foot with great curiosity. The orator bustled up to him and, drawing him partly aside, inquired "on which side he voted?" Rip stared in vacant stupidity. Another short but busy little fellow pulled him by the arm, and, rising on tiptoe, inquired in his ear, "whether he was Federal or Democrat?" Rip was equally at a loss to comprehend the question; when a knowing, self-important old gentleman in a sharp cocked hat made his way through the crowd, putting them to the right and left with his elbows as he passed, and, planting himself before Van Winkle, with one arm akimbo, the other resting on his cane, his keen eyes and sharp hat penetrating, as it were, into his very soul, demanded in an austere tone, "what brought him to the election with a gun on his shoulder, and a mob at his heels, and whether he meant to breed a riot in the village?" "Alas! Gentlemen," cried Rip, somewhat dismayed, "I am a poor, quiet man, a native of the place, and a loyal subject of the king, God bless him!"

Here a general shout burst from the bystanders. "A tory! A tory! A spy! A refugee! Hustle him! Away with him!" It was with great difficulty that the self-important man in the cocked hat restored order; and, having assumed a tenfold austerity of brow, demanded again of the unknown culprit what he came there for and whom eh was seeking. The poor man humbly assured him that he meant no harm, but merely came there in search of some of his neighbors, who used to keep about the tavern.

"Well—who are they? Name them."

Rip bethought himself a moment, and inquired, "Where's Nicholas Vedder?"

There was a silence for a little while, when an old man replied, in a thin, piping voice, "Nicholas Vedder! Why, he is dead and gone these eighteen years! There was a wooden tombstone in the churchyard that used to tell all about him, but that's rotten and gone too."

"Where's Brom Dutcher?"

"Oh, he went off to the army in the beginning of the war; some say he was killed at the storming of Stony Point—others say he was drowned in a squall at the foot of Antony's Nose. I don't know—he never came back again."

"Where's Van Bummel, the schoolmaster?"

"He went off to the wars, too, was a great militia general, and is now in congress."

Rip's heart died away at hearing of these sad changes in his home and friends, and finding himself thus alone in the world. Every answer puzzled him, too, by treating of such enormous lapses of time and of matters which he could not understand: war—congress—Stony Point. He had no courage to ask after any more friends, but cried out in despair, "Does nobody here know Rip Van Winkle?"

"Oh, Rip Van Winkle!" exclaimed two or three. "Oh, to be sure! That's Rip Van Winkle yonder, leaning against the tree."

Rip looked, and beheld a precise counterpart of himself as he went up the mountain: apparently as lazy, and certainly as ragged. The poor fellow was now completely confounded. He doubted his own identity, and whether he was himself or another man. In the midst of his bewilderment, the man in the cocked hat demanded who he was, and what was his name?

"God knows," exclaimed he, at his wit's end. "I'm not myself—I'm somebody else—that's me yonder—no—that's somebody else got into my shoes—I was myself last night, but I fell asleep on the mountain, and they've changed my gun, and everything's changed, and I'm changed, and I can't tell what's my name, or who I am!"

The bystanders began now to look at each other,

nod, wink significantly, and tap their fingers against their foreheads. There was a whisper also about securing the gun and keeping the old fellow from doing mischief, at the very suggestion of which the self-important man in the cocked hat retired with some precipitation. At this critical moment a fresh, comely woman pressed through the throng to get a peep at the gray-bearded man. She had a chubby child in her arms, which, frightened at his looks, began to cry. "Hush, Rip," cried she, "hush, you little fool; the old man won't hurt you." The name of the child, the air of the mother, the tone of her voice, all awakened a train of recollections in his mind. "What is your name, my good woman?" asked he.

"Judith Gardenier."

"And your father's name?"

"Ah, poor man, Rip Van Winkle was his name, but it's twenty years since he went away from home with his gun, and never has been heard of since— his dog came home without him; but whether he shot himself, or was carried away by the Indians, nobody can tell. I was then but a little girl."

Rip had but one question more to ask; but he put it with a faltering voice:

"Where's your mother?"

"Oh, she too had died but a short time since; she broke a blood vessel in a fit of passion at a New England peddler."

There was a drop of comfort, at least, in this

intelligence. The honest man could contain himself no longer. He caught his daughter and her child in his arms. "I am your father!" cried he. "Young Rip Van Winkle once—old Rip Van Winkle now! Does nobody know poor Rip Van Winkle?"

All stood amazed, until an old woman, tottering out from among the crowd, put her hand to her brow and, peering under it in his face for a moment, exclaimed, "Sure enough! It is Rip Van Winkle—it is himself! Welcome home again, old neighbor. Why, where have you been these twenty long years?"

Rip's story was soon told, for the whole twenty years had been to him but as one night. The neighbors stared when they heard it; some were seen to wink at each other and put their tongues in their cheeks, and the self-important man in the cocked hat, who, when the alarm was over, had returned to the field, screwed down the corners of his mouth and shook his head—upon which there was a general shaking of the head throughout the assemblage.

It was determined, however, to take the opinion of old Peter Vanderdonk, who was seen slowly advancing up the road. He was a descendant of the historian of that name, who wrote one of the earliest accounts of the province. Peter was the most ancient inhabitant of the village, and well versed in all the wonderful events and traditions of the neighborhood. He recollected Rip at once and corroborated his story in the most satisfactory manner. He assured the company that it was a fact, handed down from his ancestor the historian, that the Kaatskill Mountains had always been haunted by strange beings. That it was affirmed that the great Hendrick Hudson, the first discoverer of the river and country, kept a kind of vigil there every twenty years, with his crew of the *Half Moon,* being permitted in this way to revisit the scenes of his enterprise and keep a guardian eye upon the river and the great city called by his name. That his father had once seen them in their old Dutch dresses playing at ninepins in a hollow of the mountain, and that he himself had heard, one summer afternoon, the sound of their balls, like distant peals of thunder.

To make a long story short, the company broke up and returned to the more important concerns of the election. Rip's daughter took him home to live with her; she had a snug, well-furnished house, and a stout, cheery farmer for a husband, whom Rip recollected for one of the urchins that used to climb upon his back. As to Rip's son and heir, who was the ditto of himself, seen leaning against the tree, he was employed to work on the farm, but evinced a hereditary disposition to attend to anything else but his business.

Rip now resumed his old walks and habits; he soon found many of his former cronies, though all rather the worse for the wear and tear of time, and preferred making friends among the rising generation, with whom he soon grew into great favor.

Having nothing to do at home, and being arrived

at that happy age when a man can be idle with impunity, he took his place once more on the bench at the inn door and was reverenced as one of the patriarchs of the village, and a chronicle of the old times "before the war." It was some time before he could get into the regular track of gossip, or could be made to comprehend the strange events that had taken place during his torpor. How that there had been a revolutionary war—that the country had thrown off the yoke of old England—and that, instead of being a subject of his Majesty George the Third, he was now a free citizen of the United States. Rip, in fact, was no politician—the changes of states and empires made but little impression on him; but there was one species of despotism under which he had long groaned, and that was —petticoat government. Happily that was at an end; he had got his neck out of the yoke of matrimony and could go in and out whenever he pleased, without dreading the tyranny of Dame Van Winkle. Whenever her name was mentioned, however, he shook his head, shrugged his shoulders, and cast up his eyes, which might pass either for an expression of resignation to his fate or joy at his deliverance.

He used to tell his story to every stranger that arrived at Mr. Doolittle's hotel. He was observed, at first, to vary on some points every time he told it, which was, doubtless, owing to his having so recently awaked. It at last settled down precisely to the tale I have related, and not a man, woman, or child in the neighborhood but knew it by heart. Some always pretended to doubt the reality of it, and insisted that Rip had been out of his head, and that this was one point on which he always remained flighty. The old Dutch inhabitants, however, almost universally gave it full credit. Even to this day they never hear a thunderstorm of a summer afternoon about the Kaatskill but they say Hendrink Hudson and his crew are at their game of ninepins; and it is a common wish of all henpecked husbands in the neighborhood, when life hangs heavy on their hands, that they might have a quieting draft out of Rip Van Winkle's flagon.

NOTE

The foregoing Tale, one would suspect, had been suggested to Mr. Knickerbocker by a little German superstition about the Emperor Frederick *der Rothbart* and the Kypphaüser mountain. The subjoined note, however, which he had appended to the tale, shows that it is an absolute fact, narrated with his usual fidelity:

"The story of Rip Van Winkle may seem incredible to many, but nevertheless I give it my full belief, for I know the vicinity of our old Dutch settlements to have been very subject to marvelous events and appearances. Indeed, I have heard many stranger stories than this, in the villages along the Hudson, all of which were too well authenticated to admit of a doubt. I have even talked with Rip Van Winkle myself, who, when last I saw him, was a very venerable old man and so perfectly rational and consistent on every other point that I think no conscientious person could refuse to take this into the bargain; nay, I have seen a certificate on the subject taken before a country justice and signed with a cross, in the justice's own handwriting. The story, therefore, is beyond the possibility of doubt.

D.K."

POSTSCRIPT

The following are traveling notes from a memorandum book of Mr. Knickerbocker:

The Kaatsberg, or Catskill Mountains, have always been a region full of fable. The Indians considered them the abode of spirits, who influenced the weather, spreading sunshine or clouds over the landscape, and sending good or bad hunting seasons. They were ruled by an old squaw spirit, said to be their mother. She dwelt on the highest peak of the Catskills and had charge of the doors of day and night, to open and shut them at the proper hour. She hung up the new moons in the skies and cut up the old ones into stars. In times of drought, if properly propitiated, she would spin light summer clouds out of cobwebs and morning dew and send them off from the crest of the mountain, flake after flake, like flakes of carded cotton, to float in the air; until, dissolved by the heat of the sun, they would fall in gentle showers, causing the grass to spring, the fruits to ripen, and the corn to grow an inch an hour. If displeased, however, she would brew up clouds black as ink, sitting in the midst of them like a bottle-bellied spider in the midst of its web; and when these clouds broke, woe betide the valleys!

In old times, say the Indian traditions, there was a kind of Manitou or Spirit, who kept about the wildest recesses of the Catskill Mountains, and took a mischievous pleasure in wreaking all kinds of evils and vexations upon the red men. Sometimes he would assume the form of a bear, a panther, or a deer, lead the bewildered hunter a weary chase through tangled forests and among ragged rocks, and then spring off with a loud ho! ho! leaving him aghast on the brink of a beetling precipice or raging torrent.

The favorite abode of this Manitou is still shown. It is a great rock or cliff on the loneliest part of the mountains, and, from the flowering vines which clamber about it and the wild flowers which abound in its neighborhood, is known by the name of the Garden Rock. Near the foot of it is a small lake, the haunt of the solitary bittern, with water snakes basking in the sun on the leaves of the pond lilies which lie on the surface. This place was held in great awe by the Indians, insomuch that the boldest hunter would not pursue his game within its precincts. Once upon a time, however, a hunter who had lost his way penetrated to the Garden Rock, where he beheld a number of gourds placed in the crotches of trees. One of these he seized and made off with, but in the hurry of his retreat he let it fall among the rocks, when a great stream gushed forth, which washed him away and swept him down precipices, where he was dashed to pieces, and the stream made its way to the Hudson and continues to flow to the present day; being the identical stream known by the name of the Kaaters-kill.

THE SPECTER BRIDEGROOM

A Traveler's Tale*

> *He that supper for is dight,*
> *He lyes full cold, I trow, this night!*
> *Yestreen to chamber I him led,*
> *This night Gray-Steel has made his bed.*
> SIR EGER, SIR GRAHAME, AND SIR GRAY-STEEL

On the summit of one of the heights of the Odenwald, a wild and romantic tract of Upper Germany that lies not far from the confluence of the Main and the Rhine, there stood, many, many years since, the Castle of the Baron Von Landshort. It is now quite fallen to decay and almost buried among beech trees and

* The erudite reader, well versed in good-for-nothing lore, will perceive that the above Tale must have been suggested to the old Swiss by a little French anecdote, a circumstance said to have taken place at Paris.

dark firs, above which, however, its old watchtower may still be seen, struggling, like the former possessor I have mentioned, to carry a high head and look down upon the neighboring country.

The baron was a dry branch of the great family of Katzenellenbogen,* and inherited the relics of the property and all the pride of his ancestors. Though the warlike disposition of his predecessors had much impaired the family possessions, yet the baron still endeavored to keep up some show of former state. The times were peacable, and the German nobles, in general, had abandoned their inconvenient old castles, perched like eagles' nests among the mountains, and had built more convenient residences in the valleys; still the baron remained proudly drawn up in his little fortress, cherishing, with hereditary inveteracy, all the old family feuds, so that he was on ill terms with some of his nearest neighbors on account of disputes that had happened between their great-great-grandfathers.

The baron had but one child, a daughter; but nature, when she grants but one child, always compensates by making it a prodigy, and so it was with the daughter of the baron. All the nurses, gossips, and country cousins assured her father that she had not her equal for beauty in all Germany; and who should

* *I.e.,* CAT'S-ELBOW. The name of a family of those parts very powerful in former times. The appellation, we are told, was given in compliment to a peerless dame of the family, celebrated for her fine arm.

know better than they? She had, moreover, been brought up with great care under the superintendence of two maiden aunts, who had spent some years of their early life at one of the little German courts and were skilled in all the branches of knowledge necessary to the education of a fine lady. Under their instructions she became a miracle of accomplishments. By the time she was eighteen she could embroider to admiration and had worked whole histories of the saints in tapestry with such strength of expression in their countenances that they looked like so many souls in purgatory. She could read without great difficulty, and had spelled her way through several church legends and almost all the chivalric wonders of the Heldenbuch. She had even made considerable proficiency in writing, could sign her own name without missing a letter, and so legibly that her aunts could read it without spectacles. She excelled in making little elegant good-for-nothing ladylike knick-knacks of all kinds; was versed in the most abstruse dancing of the day; played a number of airs on the harp and guitar; and knew all the tender ballads of the Minnelieders by heart.

Her aunts, too, having been great flirts and coquettes in their younger days, were admirably calculated to be vigilant guardians and strict censors of the conduct of their niece, for there is no duenna so rigidly prudent and inexorably decorous as a superannuated coquette. She was rarely suffered out of their sight; never went beyond the domains of the castle, unless well attended, or rather well watched; had continual lectures read to her about strict decorum and implicit obedience; and, as to the men—pah!—she was taught to hold them at such a distance, and in such absolute distrust, that, unless properly authorized, she would not have cast a glance upon the handsomest cavalier in the world—no, not if he were even dying at her feet.

The good effects of this system were wonderfully apparent. The young lady was a pattern of docility and correctness. While others were wasting their sweetness in the glare of the world and liable to be plucked and thrown aside by every hand, she was coyly blooming into fresh and lovely womanhood under the protection of those immaculate spinsters, like a rosebud blushing forth among guardian thorns. Her aunts looked upon her with pride and exultation, and vaunted that though all the other young ladies in the world might go astray, yet, thank Heaven, nothing of the kind could happen to the heiress of Katzenellenbogen.

But, however scantily the Baron Von Landshort might be provided with children, his household was by no means a small one, for Providence had enriched him with abundance of poor relations. They, one and all, possessed the affectionate disposition common to humble relatives, were wonderfully attached to the baron, and took every possible occasion to come in swarms and enliven the castle. All family festivals were commemorated by these good

people at the baron's expense; and, when they were
filled with good cheer they would declare that there
was nothing on earth so delightful as these family
meetings, these jubilees of the heart.

The baron, though a small man, had a large soul,
and it swelled with satisfaction at the consciousness
of being the greatest man in the little world about
him. He loved to tell long stories about the dark old
warriors whose portraits looked grimly down from
the walls around, and he found no listeners equal to
those that fed at his expense. He was much given
to the marvelous, and a firm believer in all those supernatural tales with which every mountain and
valley in Germany abounds. The faith of his guests
exceeded even his own; they listened to every tale
of wonder with open eyes and mouth, and never
failed to be astonished, even though repeated for
the hundredth time. Thus lived the Baron Von Landshort, the oracle of his table, the absolute monarch
of his little territory, and happy, above all things, in
the persuasion that he was the wisest man of the age.

At the time of which my story treats there was a
great family gathering at the castle, on an affair of
the utmost importance: it was to receive the destined
bridegroom of the baron's daughter. A negotiation
had been carried on between the father and an old
nobleman of Bavaria to unite the dignity of their
houses by the marriage of their children. The pre-
liminaries had been conducted with proper punctilio.
The young people were betrothed without seeing

each other, and the time was appointed for the marriage ceremony. The young Count Von Altenburg had been recalled from the army for the purpose, and was actually on his way to the baron's to receive his bride. Missives had even been received from him, from Würzburg, where he was accidentally detained, mentioning the day and hour when he might be expected to arrive.

The castle was in a tumult of preparation to give him a suitable welcome. The fair bride had been decked out with uncommon care. The two aunts had superintended her toilet and quarreled the whole morning about every article of her dress. The young lady had taken advantage of their contest to follow the bent of her own taste, and fortunately it was a good one. She looked as lovely as youthful bridegroom could desire, and the flutter of expectation heightened the luster of her charms.

The suffusions that mantled her face and neck, the gentle heaving of the bosom, the eye now and then lost in reverie, all betrayed the soft tumult that was going on in her little heart. The aunts were continually hovering around her, for maiden aunts are apt to take great interest in affairs of this nature. They were giving her a world of staid counsel how to deport herself, what to say, and in what manner to receive the expected lover.

The baron was no less busied in preparations. He had, in truth, nothing exactly to do, but he was naturally a fuming bustling little man, and could not

remain passive when all the world was in a hurry. He
worried from top to bottom of the castle with an air
of infinite anxiety; he continually called the servants
from their work to exhort them to be diligent; and
buzzed about every hall and chamber, as idly restless
and importunate as a bluebottle fly on a warm summer's day.

In the meantime the fatted calf had been killed; the
forests had rung with the clamor of the huntsmen; the
kitchen was crowded with good cheer; the cellars had
yielded up whole oceans of *Rhein-wein* and *Ferne-
wein;* and even the great Heidelberg tun had been laid
under contribution. Everything was ready to receive the distinguished guest with *Saus und Braus*
in the true spirit of German hospitality—but the guest
delayed to make his appearance. Hour rolled after
hour. The sun that had poured his downward rays
upon the rich forest of the Odenwald now just
gleamed along the summits of the mountains. The
baron mounted the highest tower, and strained his
eyes in hope of catching a distant sight of the count
and his attendants. Once he thought he beheld them;
the sound of horns came floating from the valley,
prolonged by the mountain echoes. A number of
horsemen were seen far below, slowly advancing
along the road; but when they had nearly reached
the foot of the mountain they suddenly struck off in
a different direction. The last ray of sunshine departed—the bats began to flit by in the twilight—
the road grew dimmer and dimmer to the view; and

nothing appeared stirring in it but now and then a peasant lagging homeward from his labor.

While the old castle of Landshort was in this state of perplexity a very interesting scene was transacting in a different part of the Odenwald.

The young Count Von Altenburg was tranquilly pursuing his route in that sober jog-trot way, in which a man travels toward matrimony when his friends have taken all the trouble and uncertainty of courtship off his hands, and a bride is waiting for him as certainly as a dinner at the end of his journey. He had encountered at Würzburg a youthful companion in arms with whom he had seen some service on the frontiers, Herman Von Starkenfaust, one of the stoutest hands and worthiest hearts of German chivalry, who was now returning from the army. His father's castle was not far distant from the old fortress of Landshort, although an hereditary feud rendered the families hostile and strangers to each other.

In the warmhearted moment of recognition the young friends related all their past adventures and fortunes, and the count gave the whole history of his intended nuptials with a young lady whom he had never seen but of whose charms he had received the most enrapturing descriptions.

As the route of the friends lay in the same direction, they agreed to perform the rest of their journey together; and, that they might do it the more leisurely, set off from Würzburg at an early hour, the count having given directions for his retinue to follow and overtake him.

They beguiled their wayfaring with recollections of their military scenes and adventures; but the count was apt to be a little tedious, now and then, about the reputed charms of his bride, and the felicity that awaited him.

In this way they had entered among the mountains of the Odenwald, and were traversing one of its most lonely and thickly wooded passes. It is well known that the forests of Germany have always been as much infested by robbers as its castles by specters; and at this time the former were particularly numerous, from the hordes of disbanded soldiers wandering about the country. It will not appear extraordinary, therefore, that the cavaliers were attacked by a gang of these stragglers in the midst of the forest. They defended themselves with bravery, but were nearly overpowered, when the count's retinue arrived to their assistance. At sight of them the robbers fled, but not until the count had received a mortal wound. He was slowly and carefully conveyed back to the city of Würzburg, and a friar summoned from a neighboring convent, who was famous for his skill in administering to both soul and body; but half of his skill was superfluous; the moments of the unfortunate count were numbered.

With his dying breath he entreated his friend to repair instantly to the castle of Landshort and explain the fatal cause of his not keeping his appointment with his bride. Though not the most ardent of lovers, he was one of the most punctilious of men, and appeared earnestly solicitous that his mission should be speedily and courteously executed. "Unless this is done," said he, "I shall not sleep quietly in my grave!" He repeated these last words with peculiar solemnity. A request, at a moment so impressive, admitted no hesitation. Starkenfaust endeavored to soothe him to calmness, promised faithfully to execute his wish, and gave him his hand in solemn pledge. The dying man pressed it in acknowledgment, but soon lapsed into delirium—raved about his bride —his engagements—his plighted word; ordered his horse that he might ride to the castle of Landshort; and expired in the fancied act of vaulting into the saddle.

Starkenfaust bestowed a sigh and a soldiers's tear on the untimely fate of his comrade, and then pondered on the awkward mission he had undertaken. His heart was heavy and his head perplexed, for he was to present himself an unbidden guest among hostile people, and to damp their festivity with tidings fatal to their hopes. Still there were certain whisperings of curiosity in his bosom to see this far-famed beauty of Katzenellenbogen, so cautiously shut up from the world, for he was a passionate admirer of the sex, and there was a dash of eccentricity and enterprise in his character that made him fond of all singular adventure.

Previous to his departure he made all due arrangements with the holy fraternity of the convent for the funeral solemnities of his friend, who was to be buried

in the cathedral of Würzburg, near some of his illustrious relatives; and the mourning retinue of the
count took charge of his remains.

It is now high time that we should return to the
ancient family of Katzenellenbogen, who were impatient for their guest, and still more for their dinner; and to the worthy little baron, whom we left
airing himself on the watchtower.

Night closed in, but still no guest arrived. The
baron descended from the tower in despair. The banquet, which had been delayed from hour to hour,
could no longer be postponed. The meats were already overdone; the cook in an agony; and the
whole household had the look of a garrison that had
been reduced by famine. The baron was obliged re-
luctantly to give orders for the feast without the
presence of the guest. All were seated at the table, and
just on the point of commencing when the sound of a
horn from without the gate gave notice of the approach of a stranger. Another long blast filled the old
courts of the castle with its echoes, and was answered by the warder from the walls. The baron
hastened to receive his future son-in-law.

The drawbridge had been let down, and the stranger
was before the gate. He was a tall, gallant cavalier,
mounted on a black steed. His countenance was pale,
but he had a beaming, romantic eye, and an air of
stately melancholy. The baron was a little mortified
that he should have come in this simple, solitary style.
His dignity for a moment was ruffled, and he felt dis-

posed to consider it a want of proper respect for the important occasion and the important family with which he was to be connected. He pacified himself, however, with the conclusion that it must have been youthful impatience which had induced him thus to spur on sooner than his attendants.

"I am sorry," said the stranger, "to break in upon you thus unseasonably—"

Here the baron interrupted him with a world of compliments and greetings, for, to tell the truth, he prided himself upon his courtesy and eloquence. The stranger attempted, once or twice to stem the torrent of words, but in vain, so he bowed his head and suffered it to flow on. By the time the baron had come to a pause, they had reached the inner court of the castle, and the stranger was again about to speak when he was once more interrupted by the appearance of the female part of the family, leading forth the shrinking and blushing bride. He gazed on her for a moment as one entranced; it seemed as if his whole soul beamed forth in the gaze, and rested upon that lovely form. One of the maiden aunts whispered something in her ear; she made an effort to speak; her moist blue eye was timidly raised, gave a shy glance of inquiry on the stranger, and was cast again to the ground. The words died away, but there was a sweet smile playing about her lips and a soft dimpling of the cheek that showed her glance had not been unsatisfactory. It was impossible for a girl of the fond age of eighteen, highly predisposed for love and matrimony, not to be pleased with so gallant a cavalier.

The late hour at which the guest had arrived left no time for parley. The baron was peremptory, and deferred all particular conversation until the morning, and led the way to the untasted banquet.

It was served up in the great hall of the castle. Around the walls hung the hard-favored portraits of the heroes of the house of Katzenellenbogen and the trophies which they had gained in the field and in the chase. Hacked corslets, splintered jousting spears, and tattered banners were mingled with the spoils of sylvan warfare; the jaws of the wolf and the tusks of the boar grinned horribly among cross-bows and battle-axes, and a huge pair of antlers branched immediately over the head of the youthful bridegroom.

The cavalier took but little notice of the company or the entertainment. He scarcely tasted the banquet, but seemed absorbed in admiration of his bride. He conversed in a low tone that could not be overheard —for the language of love is never loud; but where is the female ear so dull that it cannot catch the softest whisper of the lover? There was a mingled tenderness and gravity in his manner that appeared to have a powerful effect upon the young lady. Her color came and went as she listened with deep attention. Now and then she made some blushing reply, and when his eye was turned away, she would steal a sidelong glance at his romantic countenance and heave a gentle sigh of tender happiness. It was evident that the young couple were completely enamored. The aunts, who were deeply versed in the mysteries of the heart, declared that they had fallen in love with each other at first sight.

The feast went on merrily, or at least noisily, for the guests were all blessed with those keen appetites that attend upon light purses and mountain air. The baron told his best and longest stories, and never had he told them so well or with such great effect. If there was anything marvelous, his auditors were lost in astonishment; and if anything facetious, they were sure to laugh exactly in the right place. The baron, it is true, like most great men, was too dignified to utter any joke but a dull one; it was always enforced, however, by a bumper of excellent Hockheimer, and even a dull joke, at one's own table, served up with jolly old wine, is irresistible. Many good things were said by poorer and keener wits that would not bear repeating, except on similar occasions; many sly speeches whispered in ladies ears that almost convulsed them with suppressed laughter; and a song or two roared out by a poor but merry and broad-faced cousin of the baron that absolutely made the maiden aunts hold up their fans.

Amidst all this revelry, the stranger guest maintained a most singular and unseasonable gravity. His countenance assumed a deeper cast of dejection as the evening advanced; and, strange as it may appear, even the baron's jokes seemed only to render him the more melancholy. At times he was lost in thought, and at times there was a perturbed and restless wandering of the eye that bespoke a mind but ill at ease. His conversations with the bride became more and more earnest and mysterious. Lowering clouds began to steal over the fair serenity of her brow, and tremors to run through her tender frame.

All this could not escape the notice of the company. Their gaiety was chilled by the unaccountable gloom of the bridegroom; their spirits were infected; whispers and glances were interchanged, accompanied by shrugs and dubious shakes of the head. The song and the laugh grew less and less frequent; there were dreary pauses in the conversation, which were at length succeeded by wild tales and supernatural legends. One dismal story produced another still more dismal, and the baron nearly frightened some of the ladies into hysterics with the history of the goblin horseman that carried away the fair Leonora; a dreadful story, which has since been put into excellent verse, and is read and believed by all the world.

The bridegroom listened to this tale with profound attention. He kept his eyes steadily fixed on the baron, and, as the story drew to a close, began gradually to rise from his seat, growing taller and taller, until, in the baron's entranced eye, he seemed almost to tower into a giant. The moment the tale was finished, he heaved a deep sigh, and took a solemn farewell of the company. They were all amazement. The baron was perfectly thunderstruck.

"What! Going to leave the castle at midnight? Why, everything was prepared for his reception; a chamber was ready for him if he wished to retire."

The stranger shook his head mournfully and mysteriously. "I must lay my head in a different chamber tonight!"

There was something in this reply and the tone in which it was uttered that made the baron's heart misgive him, but he rallied his forces and repeated his hospitable entreaties.

The stranger shook his head silently, but positively, at every offer; and, waving his farewell to the company, stalked slowly out of the hall. The maiden aunts were absolutely petrified—the bride hung her head, and a tear stole to her eye.

The baron followed the stranger to the great court of the castle, where the black charger stood pawing the earth, and snorting with impatience. When they had reached the portal, whose deep archway was dimly lighted by a cresset, the stranger paused, and addressed the baron in a hollow tone of voice, which the vaulted roof rendered still more sepulchral.

"Now that we are alone," said he, "I will impart to you the reason of my going. I have a solemn, an indispensable engagement——"

"Why," said the baron, "cannot you send someone in your place?"

"It admits of no substitute—I must attend it in person—I must away to Würzburg cathedral——"

"Ay," said the baron, plucking up spirit, "but not until tomorrow—tomorrow you shall take your bride there."

"No! no!" replied the stranger, with tenfold solemnity, "my engagement is with no bride—the worms! The worms expect me! I am a dead man—I have been slain by robbers—my body lies at Würzburg—at midnight I am to be buried—the grave is waiting for me—I must keep my appointment!"

He sprang on his black charger, dashed over the drawbridge, and the clattering of his horse's hoofs was lost in the whistling of the night blast.

The baron returned to the hall in the utmost consternation and related what had passed. Two ladies fainted outright, others sickened at the idea of having banqueted with a specter. It was the opinion of some that this might be the wild huntsman, famous in German legend. Some talked of mountain sprites, of wood demons, and of other supernatural beings, with which the good people of Germany have been so grievously harassed since time immemorial. One of the poor relations ventured to suggest that it might be some sportive evasion of the young cavalier, and that the very gloominess of the caprice seemed to accord with so melancholy a personage. This, however, drew on him the indignation of the whole company, and especially of the baron, who looked upon him as little better than an infidel, so that he was fain to abjure his heresy as speedily as possible and come into the faith of the true believers.

But whatever may have been the doubts entertained, they were completely put to an end by the arrival, next day, of regular missives, confirming the intelligence of the young count's murder, and his interment in Würzburg cathedral.

The dismay at the castle may well be imagined.

The baron shut himself up in his chamber. The guests, who had come to rejoice with him, could not think of abandoning him in his distress. They wandered about the courts, or collected in groups in the hall, shaking their heads and shrugging their shoulders at the troubles of so good a man; and sat longer than ever at table, and ate and drank more stoutly than ever, by way of keeping up their spirits. But the situation of the widowed bride was the most pitiable. To have lost a husband before she had even embraced him—and such a husband! If the very specter could be so gracious and noble, what must have been the living man? She filled the house with lamentations.

On the night of the second day of her widowhood, she had retired to her chamber, accompanied by one of her aunts, who insisted on sleeping with her. The aunt, who was one of the best tellers of ghost stories in all Germany, had just been recounting one of her longest, and had fallen asleep in the very midst of it. The chamber was remote, and overlooked a small garden. The niece lay pensively gazing at the beams of the rising moon, as they trembled on the leaves of an aspen tree before the lattice. The castle clock had just tolled midnight when a soft strain of music stole up from the garden. She rose hastily from her bed, and stepped lightly to the window. A tall figure stood among the shadows of the trees. As it raised its head, a beam of moonlight fell upon the countenance. Heaven on earth! She beheld the Specter Bridegroom! A loud shriek at that moment burst upon her ear, and her aunt, who had been awakened by the music and had followed her silently to the window, fell into her arms. When she looked again, the specter had disappeared.

Of the two females, the aunt now required the more soothing, for she was perfectly beside herself with terror. As to the young lady, there was something, even in the specter of her lover, that seemed endearing. There was still the semblance of manly beauty; and though the shadow of a man is but little calculated to satisfy the affections of a lovesick girl, yet, where the substance is not to be had, even that is consoling. The aunt declared she would never sleep in that chamber again; the niece, for once, was refractory, and declared as strongly that she would sleep in no other in the castle. The consequence was that she had to sleep in it alone; but she drew a promise from her aunt not to relate the story of the specter, lest she should be denied the only melancholy pleasure left her on earth—that of inhabiting the chamber over which the guardian shade of her lover kept its nightly vigils.

How long the good old lady would have observed this promise is uncertain, for she dearly loved to talk of the marvelous, and there is a triumph in being the first to tell a frightful story; it is, however, still quoted in the neighborhood, as a memorable instance of female secrecy, that she kept it to herself for a whole week, when she was suddenly absolved from all further restraint by intelligence brought to the breakfast table one morning that the young lady was not to be found. Her room was empty—the bed had not been slept in—the window was open, and the bird had flown!

The astonishment and concern with which the intelligence was received can only be imagined by those who have witnessed the agitation which the mishaps of a great man cause among his friends. Even the poor relations paused for a moment from the indefatigable labors of the trencher, when the aunt, who had at first been struck speechless, wrung her hands, and shrieked out, "The goblin! The goblin! She's carried away by the goblin."

In a few words she related the fearful scene of the garden, and concluded that the specter must have carried off his bride. Two of the domestics corroborated the opinion, for they had heard the clattering of a horse's hoofs down the mountain about midnight, and had no doubt that it was the specter on his black charger, bearing her away to the tomb. All present were struck with the direful probability, for events of the kind are extremely common in Germany, as many well-authenticated histories bear witness.

What a lamentable situation was that of the poor baron! What a heart-rending dilemma for a fond father, and a member of the great family of Katzenellenbogen! His only daughter had either been rapt away to the grave, or he was to have some wood demon for a son-in-law, and, perchance, a troop of goblin grandchildren. As usual, he was completely bewildered, and all the castle in an uproar. The men were ordered to take horse and scour every road and path and glen of the Odenwald. The baron himself had just drawn on his jack boots, girded on his sword, and was about to mount his steed to sally forth on the doubtful quest when he was brought to a pause by a new apparition. A lady was seen approaching the castle, mounted on a palfrey, attended by a cavalier on horseback. She galloped up to the gate, sprang from her horse, and, falling at the baron's feet, embraced his knees. It was his lost daughter and her companion—the Spector Bridegroom! The baron was astounded. He looked at his daughter, then at the specter, and almost doubted the evidence of his senses. The latter, too, was wonderfully improved in his appearance since his visit to the world of spirits. His dress was splendid, and set off a noble figure of manly symmetry. He was no longer pale and melancholy. His fine countenance was flushed with the glow of youth, and joy rioted in his large dark eye.

The mystery was soon cleared up. The cavalier (for, in truth, as you must have known all the while, he was no goblin) announced himself as Sir Herman Von Starkenfaust. He related his adventure with the young count. He told how he had hastened to the castle to deliver the unwelcome tidings, but that the eloquence of the baron had interrupted him in every attempt to tell his tale. How the sight of the bride had completely captivated him, and that to pass a few hours near her he had tacitly suffered the mistake to continue. How he had been sorely perplexed in what way to make a decent retreat, until the baron's goblin stories had suggested his eccentric exit. How, fearing the feudal hostility of the family, he had repeated his visits by stealth—had haunted the garden beneath the young lady's window—had wooed—had won— had borne away in triumph—and, in a word, had wedded the fair.

Under any other circumstances the baron would have been inflexible, for he was tenacious of paternal authority and devoutly obstinate in all family feuds; but he loved his daughter; he had lamented her as lost; he rejoiced to find her still alive; and, though her husband was of a hostile house, yet, thank Heaven, he was not a goblin. There was something, it must be acknowledged, that did not exactly accord with his notions of strict veracity, in the joke the knight had passed upon him of his being a dead man; but several old friends present, who had served in the wars, assured him that every stratagem was excusable in love, and that the cavalier was entitled to especial privilege, having lately served as a trooper.

Matters, therefore, were happily arranged. The baron pardoned the young couple on the spot. The revels at the castle were resumed. The poor relations overwhelmed this new member of the family with loving kindness; he was so gallant, so generous—and so rich. The aunts, it is true, were somewhat scandalized that their system of strict seclusion and passive obedience should be so badly exemplified, but attributed it all to their negligence in not having the windows grated. One of them was particularly mortified at having her marvelous story marred, and that the only specter she had ever seen should turn out a counterfeit; but the niece seemed perfectly happy at having found him substantial flesh and blood—and so the story ends.

THE BROKEN HEART

> *I never heard*
> *Of any true affection, but 'twas nipt*
> *With care, that, like the caterpillar, eats*
> *The leaves of the spring's sweetest book, the rose.*
>   MIDDLETON

It is a common practice with those who have outlived the susceptibility of early feeling, or have been brought up in the gay heartlessness of dissipated life, to laugh at all love stories and to treat the tales of romantic passion as mere fictions of novelists and poets. My observations on human nature have induced me to think otherwise. They have convinced me that, however the surface of the character may be chilled and frozen by the cares of the world, or cultivated into mere smiles by the arts of society, still there are dormant fires lurking in the depths of the coldest bosom, which, when once enkindled, become impetuous and are sometimes desolating in their effects. Indeed, I am a true believer in the blind deity and go to the full extent of his doctrines. Shall I confess it? I believe in broken hearts and the possibility of dying of disappointed love. I do not, however, consider it a malady often fatal to my own sex; but I firmly believe that it withers down many a lovely woman into an early grave.

Man is the creature of interest and ambition. His nature leads him forth into the struggle and bustle of the world. Love is but the embellishment of his early life, or a song piped in the intervals of the acts. He seeks for fame, for fortune, for space in the world's thought, and dominion over his fellow men. But a woman's whole life is a history of the affections. The heart is her world: it is there her ambition strives for empire; it is there her avarice seeks for hidden treasures. She sends forth her sympathies on adventure; she embarks her whole soul in the traffic of affection; and if shipwrecked, her case is hopeless —for it is a bankruptcy of the heart.

To a man, the disappointment of love may occasion some bitter pangs; it wounds some feelings of tenderness; it blasts some prospects of felicity. But he is an active being—he may dissipate his thoughts in the whirl of varied occupation, or may plunge into the tide of pleasure; or, if the scene of disappointment be too full of painful associations, he can shift his abode at will, and, taking as it were the wings of the morning, can "fly to the uttermost parts of the earth, and be at rest."

But woman's is comparatively a fixed, a secluded, and a meditative life. She is more the companion of her own thoughts and feelings; and if they are turned to ministers of sorrow, where shall she look for consolation? Her lot is to be wooed and won; and if unhappy in her love, her heart is like some fortress that has been captured, and sacked, and abandoned, and left desolate.

How many bright eyes grow dim—how many soft cheeks grow pale—how many lovely forms fade away into the tomb, and none can tell the cause that blighted their loveliness! As the dove will clasp its wings to its side and cover and conceal the arrow that is preying on its vitals, so is it the nature of woman to hide from the world the pangs of wounded affection. The love of a delicate female is always shy and silent. Even when fortunate, she scarcely breathes it to herself; but when otherwise, she buries it in the recesses of her bosom, and there lets it cower and brood among the ruins of her peace. With her the desire of the heart has failed. The great charm of existence is at an end. She neglects all the cheerful exercises which gladden the spirits, quicken the pulses, and send the tide of life in healthful currents through the veins. Her rest is broken—the sweet refreshment of sleep is poisoned by melancholy dreams—"dry sorrow drinks her blood," until her enfeebled frame sinks under the slightest external injury. Look for her, after a little while, and you find friendship weeping over her untimely grave and wondering that one who but lately glowed with all the radiance of health and beauty should so speedily be brought down to "darkness and the worm." You will be told of some wintry chill, some casual indisposition, that laid her low—but no one knows of the mental malady which previously sapped her strength and made her so easy a prey to the spoiler.

She is like some tender tree, the pride and beauty of the grove, graceful in its form, bright in its foliage, but with the worm preying at its heart. We find it suddenly withering when it should be most fresh and luxuriant. We see it drooping its branches to the earth and shedding leaf by leaf until, wasted and perished away, it falls even in the stillness of the forest; and as we muse over the beautiful ruin, we strive in vain to recollect the blast or thunderbolt that could have smitten it with decay.

I have seen many instances of women running to waste and self-neglect, and disappearing gradually from the earth almost as if they had been exhaled to heaven; and have repeatedly fancied that I could trace their death through the various declensions of consumption, cold, debility, languor, melancholy, until I reached the first symptom of disappointed love. But an instance of the kind was lately told to me; the circumstances are well known in the country where they happened, and I shall but give them in the manner in which they were related.

Everyone must recollect the tragical story of young E——, the Irish patriot; it was too touching to be soon forgotten. During the troubles in Ireland, he was tried, condemned, and executed on a charge of treason. His fate made a deep impression on public sympathy. He was so young, so intelligent, so generous, so brave, so everything that we are apt to like in a young man. His conduct under trial, too, was so lofty and intrepid. The noble indignation with which he repelled the charge of treason against his country, the eloquent vindication of his name, and his pathetic appeal to posterity, in the hopeless hour of condemnation, all these entered deeply into every generous bosom, and even his enemies lamented the stern policy that dictated his execution

But there was one heart whose anguish it would be impossible to describe. In happier days and fairer fortunes, he had won the affections of a beautiful and interesting girl, the daughter of a late, celebrated Irish barrister. She loved him with the disinterested fervor of a woman's first and early love. When every worldly maxim arrayed itself against him, when blasted in fortune and disgrace and danger darkened around his name, she loved him the more ardently for his very sufferings. If, then, his fate could awaken the sympathy even of his foes, what must have been the agony of her whose whole soul was occupied by his image! Let those tell who have had the portals of the tomb suddenly closed between them and the being they most loved on earth, who have sat at its threshold, as one shut out in a cold and lonely world, whence all that was most lovely and loving had departed.

But then the horrors of such a grave! So frightful, so dishonored! There was nothing for memory to dwell on that could soothe the pang of separation —none of those tender though melancholy circumstances which endear the parting scene, nothing to melt sorrow into those blessed tears, sent like the dews of heaven to revive the heart in the parting hour of anguish.

To render her widowed situation more desolate, she had incurred her father's displeasure by her unfortunate attachment, and was an exile from the paternal roof. But could the sympathy and kind offices of friends have reached a spirit so shocked and driven in by horror, she would have experienced no want of consolation, for the Irish are a people of quick and generous sensibilities. The most delicate and cherishing attentions were paid her by families of wealth and distinction. She was led into society, and they tried by all kinds of occupation and amusement to dissipate her grief and wean her from the tragic story of her loves. But it was all in vain. There are some strokes of calamity which scathe and scorch the soul—which penetrate to the vital seat of happiness—and blast it, never again to put forth bud or blossom. She never objected to frequent the haunts of pleasure, but was as much alone there as in the depths of solitude, walking about in a sad reverie, apparently unconscious of the world around her. She carried with her an inward woe that mocked at all the blandishments of friendship and "heeded not the song of the charmer, charm he never so wisely."

The person who told me her story had seen her at a masquerade. There can be no exhibition of fargone wretchedness more striking and painful than to meet it in such a scene. To find it wandering like a specter, lonely and joyless, where all around is gay—to see it dressed out in the trappings of mirth and looking so wan and woebegone, as if it had tried in vain to cheat the poor heart into a momentary forgetfulness of sorrow. After strolling through the splendid rooms and giddy crowd with an air of utter abstraction, she sat herself down on the steps of an orchestra, and, looking about for some time with a vacant air that showed her insensibility to the garish scene, she began, with the capriciousness of a sickly heart, to warble a little plaintive air. She had an exquisite voice, but on this occasion it was so simple, so touching, it breathed forth such a soul of wretchedness that she drew a crowd mute and silent around her, and melted everyone into tears.

The story of one so true and tender could not but excite great interest in a country remarkable for enthusiasm. It completely won the heart of a brave officer, who paid his addresses to her, and thought that one so true to the dead could not but prove affectionate to the living. She declined his attentions, for her thoughts were irrevocably engrossed by the memory of her former lover. He, however, persisted in his suit. He solicited not her tenderness, but her esteem. He was assisted by her conviction of his worth, and her sense of her own destitute and dependent situation, for she was existing on the kindness of friends. In a word, he at length succeeded in gaining her hand, though with the solemn assurance that her heart was unalterably another's.

He took her with him to Sicily, hoping that a change of scene might wear out the remembrance of early woes. She was an amiable and exemplary wife and made an effort to be a happy one, but nothing could cure the silent and devouring melancholy that had entered into her very soul. She wasted away in a slow but hopeless decline, and at length sunk into the grave, the victim of a broken heart.

It was on her that Moore, the distinguished Irish poet, composed the following lines:

She is far from the land where her young hero sleeps,
  And lovers around her are sighing;
But coldly she turns from their gaze, and weeps,
  For her heart in his grave is lying.

She sings the wild songs of her dear native plains,
  Every note which he loved awaking—
Ah! little they think, who delight in her strains,
  How the heart of the minstrel is breaking!

He had lived for his love—for his country he died,
  They were all that to life had entwined him—
Nor soon shall the tears of his country be dried,
  Nor long will his love stay behind him!

Oh! make her a grave where the sunbeams rest,
  When they promise a glorious morrow;
They'll shine o'er her sleep, like a smile from the west,
  From her own loved island of sorrow!

THE WIFE

The treasures of the deep are not so precious
As are the conceal'd comforts of a man
Locked up in woman's love. I scent the air
Of blessings, when I come but near the house.
What a delicious breath marriage sends forth . . .
The violet bed's not sweeter.

MIDDLETON

I have often had occasion to remark the fortitude with which women sustain the most overwhelming reverses of fortune. Those disasters which break down the spirit of a man and prostrate him in the dust seem to call forth all the energies of the softer sex, and give such intrepidity and elevation to their character that at times it approaches to sublimity. Nothing can be more touching than to behold a soft and tender female, who had been all weakness and dependence and alive to every trivial roughness while treading the prosperous paths of life, suddenly rising in mental force to be the comforter and support of her husband under misfortune, and abiding with unshrinking firmness the bitterest blasts of adversity.

As the vine, which has long twined its graceful foliage about the oak and been lifted by it into sunshine, will, when the hardy plant is rifted by the thunderbolt, cling around it with its caressing tendrils and bind up its shattered boughs, so is it beautifully ordered by Providence, that woman, who is the mere dependent and ornament of man in his happier hours, should be his stay and solace when smitten with sudden calamity, winding herself into the rugged recesses of his nature, tenderly supporting the drooping head, and binding up the broken heart.

I was once congratulating a friend, who had around him a blooming family, knit together in the strongest affection. "I can wish you no better lot," said he, with enthusiasm, "than to have a wife and children. If you are prosperous, there they are to share your prosperity; if otherwise, there they are to comfort you." And, indeed, I have observed that a married man falling into misfortune is more apt to retrieve his situation in the world than a single one, partly because he is more stimulated to exertion by the necessities of the helpless and beloved beings who depend upon him for subsistence, but chiefly because his spirits are soothed and relieved by domestic endearments, and his self-respect kept alive by finding that, though all abroad is darkness and humiliation, yet there is still a little world of love at home, of which he is the monarch. Whereas a single man is apt to run to waste and self-neglect, to fancy himself lonely and abandoned, and his heart to fall to ruin like some deserted mansion for want of an inhabitant.

These observations call to mind a little domestic story, of which I was once a witness. My intimate friend, Leslie, had married a beautiful and accomplished girl who had been brought up in the midst of fashionable life. She had, it is true, no fortune, but that of my friend was ample; and he delighted in the anticipation of indulging her in every elegant pursuit and administering to those delicate tastes and fancies that spread a kind of witchery about the sex. "Her life," said he, "shall be like a fairy tale."

The very difference in their characters produced a harmonious combination: he was of a romantic and somewhat serious cast; she was all life and gladness. I have often noticed the mute rapture with which he would gaze upon her in company, of which her sprightly powers made her the delight; and how, in the midst of applause, her eye would still turn to him, as if there alone she sought favor and acceptance. When leaning on his arm, her slender form contrasted finely with his tall, manly person. The fond confiding air with which she looked up to him seemed to call forth a flush of triumphant pride and cherishing tenderness, as if he doted on his lovely burden for its very helplessness. Never did a couple set forward on the flowery path of early and well-suited marriage with a fairer prospect of felicity.

It was the misfortune of my friend, however, to have embarked his property in large speculations; and he had not been married many months when, by a succession of sudden disasters, it was swept from him, and he found himself reduced almost to penury. For a time he kept his situation to himself, and went about with a haggard countenance and a breaking heart. His life was but a protracted agony; and what rendered it more insupportable was the necessity of keeping up a smile in the presence of his wife, for he could not bring himself to overwhelm her with the news. She saw, however, with the quick eyes of affection that all was not well with him. She marked his altered looks and stifled sighs, and was not to be deceived by his sickly and vapid attempts at cheerfulness. She tasked all her sprightly powers and tender blandishments to win him back to happiness, but she only drove the arrow deeper into his soul. The more he saw cause to love her, the more torturing was the thought that he was soon to make her wretched. A little while, thought he, and the smile will vanish from that cheek—the song will die away from those lips—the luster of those eyes will be quenched with sorrow; and the happy heart, which now beats lightly in that bosom, will be weighed down like mine, by the cares and miseries of the world.

At length he came to me one day and related his whole situation in a tone of the deepest despair. When I heard him through, I inquired, "Does your wife know all this?" At the question he burst into an agony of tears. "For God's sake!" cried he, "if you have any pity on me, don't mention my wife; it is the thought of her that drives me almost to madness!"

"And why not?" said I. "She must know it sooner

or later; you cannot keep it long from her, and the intelligence may break upon her in a more startling manner than if imparted by yourself, for the accents of those we love soften the hardest tidings. Besides, you are depriving yourself of the comforts of her sympathy; and not merely that, but also endangering the only bond that can keep hearts together—an unreserved community of thought and feeling. She will soon perceive that something is secretly preying upon your mind; and true love will not brook reserve; it feels undervalued and outraged when even the sorrows of those it loves are concealed from it."

"Oh, but, my friend! To think what a blow I am to give to all her future prospects—how I am to strike her very soul to the earth by telling her that her husband is a beggar! That she is to forego all the elegancies of life—all the pleasures of society—to shrink with me into indigence and obscurity! To tell her that I have dragged her down from the sphere in which she might have continued to move in constant brightness—the light of every eye—the admiration of every heart! How can she bear poverty? She has been brought up in all the refinements of opulence. How can she bear neglect? She has been the idol of society. Oh! It will break her heart—it will break her heart!"

I saw his grief was eloquent, and I let it have its flow, for sorrow relieves itself by words. When his paroxysm had subsided and he had relapsed into moody silence, I resumed the subject gently, and urged him to break his situation at once to his wife. He shook his head mournfully but positively.

"But how are you to keep it from her? It is necessary she should know it, that you may take the steps proper to the alteration of your circumstances. You must change your style of living—nay," observing a pang to pass across his countenance, "don't let that afflict you. I am sure you have never placed your happiness in outward show—you have yet friends, warm friends, who will not think the worse of you for being less splendidly lodged; and surely it does not require a palace to be happy with Mary——"

"I could be happy with her," cried he, convulsively, "in a hovel! I could go down with her into poverty and the dust! I could—I could—God bless her! God bless her!" cried he, bursting into a transport of grief and tenderness.

"And believe me, my friend," said I, stepping up and grasping him warmly by the hand, "believe me, she can be the same with you. Aye, more: it will be a source of pride and triumph to her—it will call forth all the latent energies and fervent sympathies of her nature, for she will rejoice to prove that she loves you for yourself. There is in every true woman's heart a spark of heavenly fire, which lies dormant in the broad daylight of prosperity, but which kindles up, and beams and blazes in the dark hour of adversity. No man knows what the wife of his bosom is—no man knows what a ministering angel she is—until he has gone with her through the fiery trials of this world."

There was something in the earnestness of my manner and the figurative style of my language that caught the excited imagination of Leslie. I knew the auditor I had to deal with; and following up the impression I had made, I finished by persuading him to go home and unburden his sad heart to his wife.

I must confess, notwithstanding all I had said, I felt some little solicitude for the result. Who can calculate on the fortitude of one whose life has been a round of pleasures? Her gay spirits might revolt at the dark downward path of low humility suddenly pointed out before her, and might cling to the sunny regions in which they had hitherto reveled. Besides, ruin in fashionable life is accompanied by so many galling mortifications, to which in other ranks it is a stranger. In short, I could not meet Leslie the next morning without trepidation. He had made the disclosure.

"And how did she bear it?"

"Like an angel! It seemed rather to be a relief to her mind, for she threw her arms around my neck and asked if this was all that had lately made me unhappy. But, poor girl," added he, "she cannot realize the change we must undergo. She has no idea of poverty but in the abstract; she has only read of it in poetry, where it is allied to love. She feels as yet no privation; she suffers no loss of accustomed conveniences nor elegancies. When we come practically to experience its sordid cares, its paltry wants, its petty humiliations—then will be the real trial."

"But," said I, "now that you have got over the severest task, that of breaking it to her, the sooner you let the world into the secret the better. The disclosure may be mortifying, but then it is a single misery, and soon over; whereas you otherwise suffer it, in anticipation, every hour in the day. It is not poverty so much as pretense that harasses a ruined man—the struggle between a proud mind and an empty purse—the keeping up a hollow show that must soon come to an end. Have the courage to appear poor and you disarm poverty of its sharpest sting." On this point I found Leslie perfectly prepared. He had no false pride himself, and as to his wife, she was only anxious to conform to their altered fortunes.

Some days afterward he called upon me in the evening. He had disposed of his dwelling house and taken a small cottage in the country, a few miles from town. He had been busied all day in sending out furniture. The new establishment required few articles, and those of the simplest kind. All the splendid furniture of his late residence had been sold, excepting his wife's harp. That, he said, was too closely associated with the idea of herself; it belonged to the little story of their loves, for some of the sweetest moments of their courtship were those when he had leaned over that instrument and listened to the melting tones of her voice. I could not but smile at this instance of romantic gallantry in a doting husband.

He was now going out to the cottage, where his wife had been all day superintending its arrangement. My feelings had become strongly interested in the progress of this family story, and, as it was a fine evening, I offered to accompany him.

He was wearied with the fatigues of the day, and

as he walked out fell into a fit of gloomy musing.

"Poor Mary!" at length broke, with a heavy sigh, from his lips.

"And what of her?" asked I. "Has anything happened to her?"

"What," said he, darting an impatient glance. "Is it nothing to be reduced to this paltry situation—to be caged in a miserable cottage—to be obliged to toil almost in the menial concerns of her wretched habitation?"

"Has she then repined at the change?"

"Repined! She has been nothing but sweetness and good humor. Indeed, she seems in better spirits than I have ever known her; she has been to me all love, and tenderness, and comfort!"

"Admirable girl!" exclaimed I. "You call yourself poor, my friend; you never were so rich—you never knew the boundless treasures of excellence you possess in that woman."

"Oh! But, my friend, if this first meeting at the cottage were over, I think I could then be comfortable. But this is her first day of real experience; she has been introduced into a humble dwelling, she has been employed all day in arranging its miserable equipments, she has for the first time known the fatigues of domestic employment, she has for the first time looked around her on a home destitute of everything elegant—almost of everything convenient—and may now be sitting down, exhausted and spiritless, brooding over a prospect of future poverty."

There was a degree of probability in this picture that I could not gainsay, so we walked on in silence.

After turning from the main road up a narrow lane so thickly shaded with forest trees as to give it a complete air of seclusion, we came in sight of the cottage. It was humble enough in its appearance for the most pastoral poet, and yet it had a pleasing rural look. A wild vine had overrrun one end with a profusion of foliage; a few trees threw their branches gracefully over it, and I observed several pots of flowers tastefully disposed about the door and on the grass plot in front. A small wicket gate opened upon a footpath that wound through some shrubbery to the door. Just as we approached, we heard the sound of music—Leslie grasped my arm; we paused and listened. It was Mary's voice singing, in a style of the most touching simplicity, a little air of which her husband was peculiarly fond.

I felt Leslie's hand tremble on my arm. He stepped forward to hear more distinctly. His step made a noise on the gravel walk. A bright, beautiful face glanced out at the window and vanished, a light footstep was heard, and Mary came tripping forth to meet us; she was in a pretty rural dress of white, a few wild flowers were twisted in her fine hair, a fresh bloom was on her cheek, her whole countenance beamed with smiles— I had never seen her look so lovely.

"My dear George," cried she, "I am so glad you are come! I have been watching and watching for you, and running down the lane, and looking out for you. I've set out a table under a beautiful tree behind the cottage, and I've been gathering some of the most delicious strawberries, for I know you are fond of them—and we have such excellent cream—and everything is so sweet and still here. . . . Oh!" said she, putting her arm within his and looking up brightly in his face. "Oh, we shall be so happy!"

Poor Leslie was overcome. He caught her to his bosom, he folded his arms around her, he kissed her again and again—he could not speak, but the tears gushed into his eyes; and he has often assured me that, though the world has since gone prosperously with him, and his life has, indeed, been a happy one, yet never has he experienced a moment of more exquisite felicity.

THE VOYAGE

> *Ships, ships, I will descrie you*
>   *Amidst the main,*
> *I will come and try you,*
> *What you are protecting,*
>   *And projecting,*
>   *Whats your end and aim.*
> *One goes abroad for merchandise and trading,*
> *Another stays to keep his country from invading,*
> *A third is coming home with rich and wealthy lading.*
>   *Halloo! my fancie, whither wilt thou go?*
>
> OLD POEM

To an American visiting Europe, the long voyage he has to make is an excellent preparative. The temporary absence of worldly scenes and employments produces a state of mind peculiarly fitted to receive new and vivid impressions. The vast space of waters that separates the hemispheres is like a blank page in existence. There is no gradual transition, by which, as in Europe, the features and population of one country blend almost imperceptibly with those of another. From the moment you lose sight of the land you have left, all is vacancy until you step on the opposite shore and are launched at once into the bustle and novelties of another world.

In traveling by land, there is a continuity of scene and a connected succession of persons and incidents that carry on the story of life and lessen the effect of absence and separation. We drag, it is true, "a lengthening chain" at each remove of our pilgrimage; but the chain is unbroken: we can trace it back link by link, and we feel that the last still grapples us to home. But a wide sea voyage severs us at once. It makes us conscious of being cast loose from the secure anchorage of settled life, and sent adrift upon a doubtful world. It interposes a gulf, not merely imaginary but real, between us and our homes— a gulf subject to tempest and fear and uncertainty, rendering distance palpable and return precarious.

Such, at least, was the case with myself. As I saw the last blue line of my native land fade away like a cloud in the horizon, it seemed as if I had closed one volume of the world and its concerns, and had time for meditation before I opened another. That land, too, now vanishing from my view, which contained all most dear to me in life; what vicissitudes might occur in it, what changes might take place in me before I should visit it again! Who can tell, when he sets forth to wander, whither he may be driven by the uncertain currents of existence, or when he may return, or whether it may be his lot to revisit the scenes of his childhood?

I said that at sea all is vacancy; I should correct the expression. To one given to daydreaming and fond of losing himself in reveries, a sea voyage is full of subjects for meditation; but then they are the wonders of the deep and of the air, and rather tend to abstract the mind from worldly themes. I delighted to loll over the quarter railing, or climb to the maintop, of a calm day, and muse for hours together on the tranquil bosom of a summer's sea; to gaze upon the piles of golden clouds just peering above the horizon, fancy them some fairy realms, and people them with a creation of my own; to watch the gentle undulating billows, rolling their silver volumes, as if to die away on those happy shores.

There was a delicious sensation of mingled security and awe with which I looked down from my giddy height on the monsters of the deep at their uncouth gambols. Shoals of porpoises tumbling about the bow of the ship, the grampus slowly heaving his huge form above the surface, or the ravenous shark, darting, like a specter, through the blue waters. My imagination would conjure up all that I had heard or read of the watery world beneath me, of the finny herds that roam its fathomless valleys, of the shapeless monsters that lurk among the very foundations of the earth, and of those wild phantasms that swell the tales of fishermen and sailors.

Sometimes a distant sail, gliding along the edge of the ocean, would be another theme of idle speculation. How interesting this fragment of a world, hastening to rejoin the great mass of existence! What a glorious monument of human invention, which has in a manner triumphed over wind and wave; has brought the ends of the world into communion; has established an interchange of blessings, pouring into the sterile regions of the north all the luxuries of the south; has diffused the light of knowledge and the charities of cultivated life; and has thus bound together those scattered portions of the human race, between which nature seemed to have thrown an insurmountable barrier.

We one day descried some shapeless object drifting at a distance. At sea, everything that breaks the monotony of the surrounding expanse attracts attention. It proved to be the mast of a ship that must have been completely wrecked, for there were the remains of handkerchiefs by which some of the crew had fastened themselves to this spar to prevent their being washed off by the waves. There was no trace by which the name of the ship could be ascertained. The wreck had evidently drifted about for many months; clusters of shellfish had fastened about it, and long seaweeds flaunted at its sides. But where, thought I, is the crew? Their struggle has long been over—they have gone down amidst the roar of the tempest—their bones lie whitening among the caverns of the deep. Silence, oblivion, like the waves, have closed over them, and no one can tell the story of their end. What sighs have been wafted after that ship! What prayers offered up at the deserted fireside of home! How often has the mistress, the wife, the mother, pored over the daily news, to catch some casual intelligence of this rover of the deep! How has expectation darkened into anxiety—anxiety into dread—and dread into despair! Alas! Not one memento may ever return for love to cherish. All that may ever be known is that she sailed from her port, "and was never heard of more!"

The sight of this wreck, as usual, gave rise to many dismal anecdotes. This was particularly the case in the evening, when the weather, which had hitherto been fair, began to look wild and threatening, and gave indications of one of those sudden storms which will sometimes break in upon the serenity of a summer voyage. As we sat around the dull light of a lamp in the cabin that made the gloom more ghastly, everyone had his tale of shipwreck and disaster. I was particularly struck with a short one related by the captain.

"As I was once sailing," said he, "in a fine, stout ship across the banks of Newfoundland, one of those heavy fogs which prevail in those parts rendered it impossible for us to see far ahead even in the daytime; but at night the weather was so thick that we could not distinguish any object at twice the length of the ship. I kept lights at the masthead, and a constant watch forward to look out for fishing smacks, which are accustomed to lie at anchor on the banks. The wind was blowing a smacking breeze, and we were going at a great rate through the water. Suddenly the watch gave the alarm of 'a sail ahead!' It was scarcely uttered before we were upon her. She was a small schooner, at anchor, with her broadside toward us. The crew were all asleep, and had neglected to hoist a light. We struck her just amidships. The force, the size, the weight of our vessel bore her down below the waves; we passed over her and were hurried on our course. As the crashing wreck was sinking beneath us, I had a glimpse of two or three half-naked wretches rushing from her cabin; they just started from their beds to be swallowed shrieking by the waves. I heard their drowning cry mingling with the wind. The blast that bore it to our ears swept us out of all farther hearing. I shall never forget that cry! It was some time before we could put the ship about, she was under such headway. We returned, as nearly as we could guess, to the place where the smack had anchored. We cruised about for several hours in the dense fog. We fired signal guns and listened if we might hear the halloo of any survivors, but all was silent—we never saw or heard anything of them more."

I confess these stories, for a time, put an end to all my fine fancies. The storm increased with the night. The sea was lashed into tremendous confusion. There was a fearful, sullen sound of rushing waves and broken surges. Deep called unto deep. At times the black column of clouds overhead seemed rent asunder by flashes of lightning, which quivered along the foaming billows and made the succeeding darkness doubly terrible. The thunders bellowed over the wild waste of waters, and were echoed and prolonged by the mountain waves. As I saw the ship staggering and plunging among these roaring caverns, it seemed miraculous that she regained her balance or preserved her buoyancy. Her yards would dip into the water: her bow was almost buried beneath the waves. Sometimes an impending surge appeared ready to overwhelm her, and nothing but a dexterous movement of the helm preserved her from the shock.

When I retired to my cabin, the awful scene still followed me. The whistling of the wind through the rigging sounded like funereal wailings. The creaking of the masts, the straning and groaning of bulkheads as the ship labored in the weltering sea were frightful. As I heard the waves rushing along the sides of the ship and roaring in my very ear, it seemed as if Death were raging around this floating prison, seeking for his prey: the mere starting of a nail, the yawning of a seam, might give him entrance.

A fine day, however, with a tranquil sea and favoring breeze, soon put all these dismal reflections to flight. It is impossible to resist the gladdening influence of fine weather and fair wind at sea. When the ship is decked out in her canvas, every sail swelled, and careering gaily over the curling waves, how lofty, how gallant she appears—how she seems to lord it over the deep!

I might fill a volume with the reveries of a sea voyage, for with me it is almost a continual reverie —but it is time to get to shore.

It was a fine sunny morning when the thrilling cry of "land!" was given from the masthead. None but those who have experienced it can form an idea of the delicious throng of sensations which rush into an American's bosom when he first comes in sight of Europe. There is a volume of associations with the very name. It is the land of promise, teeming with everything of which his childhood has heard or on which his studious years have pondered.

From that time until the moment of arrival, it was all feverish excitement. The ships of war that prowled like guardian giants along the coast; the headlands of Ireland, stretching out into the channel; the Welsh mountains, towering into the clouds; all were objects of intense interest. As we sailed up the Mersey, I reconnoitered the shores with a telescope. My eye dwelt with delight on neat cottages, with their trim shrubberies and green grass plots. I saw the moldering ruin of an abbey overrun with ivy, and the taper spire of a village church rising from the brow of a neighboring hill—all were characteristic of England.

The tide and wind were so favorable that the ship was enabled to come at once to the pier. It was thronged with people; some, idle lookers-on, others, eager expectants of friends or relatives. I could distinguish the merchant to whom the ship was consigned. I knew him by his calculating brow and restless air. His hands were thrust into his pockets; he was whistling thoughtfully, and walking to and fro, a small space having been accorded him by the crowd, in deference to his temporary importance. There were repeated cheerings and salutations interchanged between the shore and the ship as friends happened to recognize each other. I particularly noticed one young woman of humble dress but interesting demeanor. She was leaning forward from among the crowd; her eye hurried over the ship as it neared the shore to catch some wished-for countenance. She seemed disappointed and agitated, when I heard a faint voice call her name. It was from a poor sailor who had been ill all the voyage and had excited the sympathy of everyone on board. When the weather was fine, his messmates had spread a mattress for him on deck in the shade, but of late his illness had so increased that he had taken to his hammock, and only breathed a wish that he might see his wife before he died. He had been helped on deck as we came up the river, and was no leaning against the shrouds, with a countenance so wasted, so pale, so ghastly that it was no wonder even the eye of affection did not recognize him. But at the sound of his voice, her eye darted on his features; it read, at once, a whole volume of sorrow; she clasped her hands, uttered a faint shriek, and stood wringing them in silent agony.

All now was hurry and bustle. The meetings of acquaintances—the greetings of freinds—the consultations of men of business. I alone was solitary and idle. I had no friend to meet, no cheering to receive. I stepped upon the land of my forefathers—but felt that I was a stranger in the land.

TRAITS OF INDIAN CHARACTER

"I appeal to any white man if ever he entered Logan's cabin hungry, and he gave him not to eat; if ever he came cold and naked, and he clothed him not."

SPEECH OF AN INDIAN CHIEF

There is something in the character and habits of the North American savage, taken in connection with the scenery over which he is accustomed to range, its vast lakes, boundless forests, majestic rivers, and trackless plains, that is, to my mind, wonderfully striking and sublime. He is formed for the wilderness as the Arab is for the desert. His nature is stern, simple, and enduring; fitted to grapple with difficulties, and to support privations. There seems but little soil in his heart for the support of the kindly virtues, and yet, if we would but take the trouble to penetrate through that proud stoicism and habitual taciturnity which lock up his character from casual

observation we should find him linked to his fellow-
and affectations than are usually ascribed to him.

It has been the lot of the unfortunate aborigines
of America, in the early periods of colonization, to
be doubly wronged by the white men. They have
been dispossessed of their hereditary possessions by
mercenary and frequently wanton warfare, and their
characters have been traduced by bigoted and interested writers. The colonist often treated them like
beasts of the forest, and the author has endeavored to justify him in his outrages. The former found
it easier to exterminate than to civilize, the latter
to vilify than to discriminate. The appellations of
savage and pagan were deemed sufficient to sanction
the hostilities of both; and thus the poor wand-
erers of the forest were persecuted and defamed, not
because they were guilty, but because they were ignorant.

The rights of the savage have seldom been properly appreciated or respected by the white man. In
peace he has too often been the dupe of artful
traffic; in war he has been regarded as a ferocious
animal, whose life or death was a question of mere
precaution and convenience. Man is cruelly waste-
ful of life when his own safety is endangered, and
he is sheltered by impunity; and little mercy is to be
expected from him when he feels the sting of the
reptile and is conscious of the power to destroy.

The same prejudices, which were indulged thus
early, exist in common circulation at the present day.
Certain learned societies have, it is true, with laud-

able diligence endeavored to investigate and record
the real characters and manners of the Indian tribes;
the American government, too, has wisely and hu-
manely exerted itself to inculcate a friendly and for-
bearing spirit toward them and to protect them from
fraud and injustice.* The current opinion of the Indian character, however, is too apt to be formed
from the miserable hordes which infest the frontiers
and hang on the skirts of the settlements. These are
too commonly composed of degenerate beings, corrupted and enfeebled by the vices of society without being benefited by its civilization. That proud in-
dependence, which formed the main pillar of savage
virtue, has been shaken down, and the whole moral
fabric lies in ruins. Their spirits are humiliated and
debased by a sense of inferiority, and their native
courage cowed and daunted by the superior knowledge and power of their enlightened neighbors. Society has advanced upon them like one of those withering airs that will sometimes breed desolation over
a whole region of fertility. It has enervated their
strength, multiplied their diseases and superinduced
upon their original barbarity the low vices of arti-
ficial life. It has given them a thousand superfluous

* The American government has been indefatigable in
its exertions to ameliorate the situation of the Indians, and
to introduce among them the arts of civilization, and civil
and religious knowledge. To protect them from the frauds
of the white traders, no purchase of land from them by in-
dividuals is permitted; nor is any person allowed to receive
lands from them as a present, without the express sanction
of government. These precautions are strictly enforced.

wants, while it has diminished their means of mere existence. It has driven before it the animals of the chase, who fly from the sound of the axe and the smoke of the settlement and seek refuge in the depths of remoter forests and yet untrodden wilds. Thus do we too often find the Indians on our frontiers to be the mere wrecks and remnants of once powerful tribes who have lingered in the vicinity of the settlements and sunk into precarious and vagabond existence. Poverty, repining and hopeless poverty, a canker of the mind unkown in savage life, corrodes their spirits and blights every free and noble quality of their natures. They become drunken, indolent, feeble, thievish, and pusillanimous. They loiter like vagrants about the settlements, among spacious dwellings replete with elaborate comforts which only render them sensible of the comparative wretchedness of their own condition. Luxury spreads its ample board before their eyes; but they are excluded from the banquet. Plenty revels over the fields; but they are starving in the midst of its abundance: the whole wilderness has blossomed into a garden; but they feel as reptiles that infest it.

How different was their state while yet the undisputed lords of the soil! Their wants were few, and the means of gratification within their reach. They saw everyone around them sharing the same lot, enduring the same hardships, feeding on the same aliments, arrayed in the same rude garments. No roof then rose but was open to the homeless stranger; no smoke curled among the trees but he was welcome to sit down by its fire and join the hunter in his repast. "For," says an old historian of New England, "their life is so void of care, and they are so loving also that they make use of those things they enjoy as common goods, and are therein so compassionate that rather than one should starve through want, they would starve all; thus they pass their time merrily, not regarding our pomp, but are better content with their own, which some men esteem so meanly of." Such were the Indians while in the pride and energy of their primitive natures; they resembled those wild plants which thrive best in the shades of the forest but shrink from the hand of cultivation and perish beneath the influence of the sun.

In discussing the savage character, writers have been too prone to indulge in vulgar prejudice and passionate exaggeration, instead of the candid temper of true philosophy. They have not sufficiently considered the peculiar circumstances in which the Indians have been placed, and the peculiar principles under which they have been educated. No being acts more rigidly from rule than the Indian. His whole conduct is regulated according to some general maxims early implanted in his mind. The moral laws that govern him are, to be sure, but few, but then he conforms to them all; the white man abounds in laws of religion, morals, and manners, but how many does he violate?

A frequent ground of accusation against the Indians is their disregard of treaties, and the treachery and wantonness with which, in time of apparent peace, they will suddenly fly to hostilities. The intercourse of the white men with the Indians, however, is too apt to be cold, distrustful, oppressive and insulting. They seldom treat them with that confidence and frankness which are indispensable to real friendship; nor is sufficient caution observed not to offend against those feelings of pride or superstition which often prompt the Indian to hostility quicker than mere considerations of interest. The solitary savage feels silently, but acutely. His sensibilities are not diffused over so wide a surface as those of the white man, but they run in steadier and deeper channels. His pride, his affections, his superstitions, are all directed toward fewer objects; but the wounds inflicted on them are proportionably severe, and furnish motives of hostility which we cannot sufficiently appreciate. Where a community is also limited in number, and forms one great patriarchal family, as in an Indian tribe, the injury of an individual is the injry of the whole, and the sentiment of vengeance is almost instantaneously diffused. One council fire is sufficient for the discussion and arrangement of a plan of hostilities. Here all the fighting men and sages assemble. Eloquence and superstition combine to inflame the minds of the warriors. The orator awakens their martial ardor, and they are wrought up to a kind of religious desperation by the visions of the prophet and the dreamer.

An instance of one of those sudden exasperations, arising from a motive peculiar to the Indian character, is extant in an old record of the early settlement of Massachusetts. The planters of Plymouth had defaced the monuments of the dead at Passonagessit, and had plundered the grave of the Sachem's mother of some skins with which it had been decorated. The Indians are remarkable for the reverence which they entertain for the sepulchres of their kindred. Tribes that have passed generations exiled from the abodes of their ancestors, when by chance they have been traveling in the vicinity, have been known to turn aside from the highway, and, guided by wonderfully accurate tradition, have crossed the country for miles to some tumulus, buried perhaps in woods, where the bones of their tribe were anciently deposited, and there have passed hours in silent meditation. Influenced by this sublime and holy feeling, the Sachem, whose mother's tomb had been violated, gathered his men together, and addressed them in the following beautifully simple and pathetic harangue, a curious specimen of Indian eloquence and an affecting instance of filial piety in a savage.

"When last the glorious light of all the sky was underneath this globe, and birds grew silent, I began to settle, as my custom is, to take repose. Before mine eyes were fast closed, methought I saw a vision, at which my spirit was much troubled; and trembling at that doleful sight, a spirit cried aloud, 'Behold, my son, whom I have cherished, see the breasts that gave thee suck, the hands that lapped thee warm, and fed thee oft. Canst thou forget to take revenge of those wild people who have defaced my monument in a despiteful manner, disdaining our antiquities and honorable customs? See, now, the Sachem's grave lies like the common people, defaced by an ignoble race. Thy mother doth complain, and implores thy aid against this thievish people, who have newly intruded on our land. If this be suffered, I shall not rest quiet in my everlasting habitation.' This said, the spirit vanished, and I, all in a sweat, not able scarce to speak, began to get some strength and recollect my spirits that were fled, and determined to demand your counsel and assistance."

I have adduced this anecdote at some length, as it tends to show how these sudden acts of hostility, which have been attributed to caprice and perfidy, may often arise from deep and generous motives, which our inattention to Indian character and customs prevents our properly appreciating.

Another ground of violent outcry against the Indians is their barbarity to the vanquished. This had its origin partly in policy and partly in superstition. The tribes, though sometimes called nations, were never so formidable in their numbers but that the loss of several warriors was sensibly felt; this was particularly the case when they had frequently been engaged in warfare; and many an instance occurs in Indian history where a tribe that had long been formidable to its neighbors has been broken up and driven away by the capture and massacre of its principal fighting men. There was a strong temptation, therefore, to the victor to be merciless, not so much to gratify any cruel revenge as to provide for future security. The Indians had also the superstitious belief, frequent among barbarous nations and prevalent also among the ancients, that the manes of their friends who had fallen in battle were soothed by the blood of the captives. The prisoners, however, who are not thus sacrificed are adopted into their families in the place of the slain and are treated with the confidence and affection of relatives and friends; nay, so hospitable and tender is their entertainment that when the alternative is offered them, they will often prefer to remain with their adopted brethren rather than return to the home and the friends of their youth.

The cruelty of the Indians toward their prisoners has been heightened since the colonization of the whites. What was formerly a compliance with policy and superstition has been exasperated into a gratification of vengeance. They cannot but be sensible that the white men are the usurpers of their ancient dominion, the cause of their degradation, and the gradual destroyers of their race. They go forth to battle, smarting with injuries and indignities which they have individually suffered, and they are driven to madness and despair by the wide-spreading desolation and the overwhelming ruin of European warfare. The whites have too frequently set them an example of violence by burning their villages and laying waste their slender means of subsistence; and yet they wonder that savages do not show moderation and magnanimity toward those who have left them nothing but mere existence and wretchedness.

We stigmatize the Indians, also, as cowardly and treacherous because they use stratagem in warfare in preference to open force; but in this they are fully justified by their rude code of honor. They are early taught that stratagem is praiseworthy; the bravest warrior thinks it no disgrace to lurk in silence and take every advantage of his foe; he triumphs in the superior craft and sagacity by which he has been enabled to surprise and destroy an enemy. Indeed, man is naturally more prone to subtilty than open valor, owing to his physical weakness in comparison with other animals. They are endowed with natural weapons of defense: with horns, with tusks, with hoofs, and talons; but man has to depend on his superior sagacity. In all his encounters with these, his proper enemies, he resorts to stratagem; and when he perversely turns his hostility against his fellow-man, he at first continues the same subtle mode of warfare.

The natural principle of war is to do the most harm to our enemy with the least harm to ourselves, and this of course is to be effected by statagem. That chivalrous courage which induces us to despise the suggestions of prudence and to rush in the face of certain danger is the offspring of society and produced by education. It is honorable because it is in fact the triumph of lofty sentiment over an instinctive repugnance to pain and over those yearnings after personal ease and security whch society has condemned as ignoble. It is kept alive by pride and the fear of shame; and thus the dread of real evil is overcome by the superior dread of an evil which exists but in the imagination. It has been cherished and stimulated also by various means. It has been the theme of spirit-stirring song and chivalrous story. The poet and minstrel have delighted to shed round it the splendors of fiction; and even the historian has forgotten the sober gravity of narration and broken forth into enthusiasm and rhapsody in its praise. Triumphs and gorgeous pageants have been its reward; monuments, on which art has exhausted its skill and

opulence its treasures, have been erected to perpetu-
ate a nation's gratitude and admiration. Thus arti-
ficially excited, courage has risen to an extraordinary
and factitious degree of heroism; and arrayed in all
the glorious "pomp and circumstance of war," this
turbulent quality has even been able to eclipse many
of those quiet but invaluable virtues which silently
ennoble the human character and swell the tide of
human happiness.

But if courage intrinsically consists in the defiance
of danger and pain, the life of the Indian is a continual exhibition of it. He lives in a state of perpetual
hostility and risk. Peril and adventure are congenial
to his nature, or rather seem necessary to arouse his
faculties and to give an interest to his existence. Surrounded by hostile tribes, whose mode of warfare is
by ambush and surprisal, he is always prepared for
fight, and lives with his weapons in his hands. As the
ship careers in fearful singleness through he solitudes
of ocean; as the bird mingles among clouds and
storms, and wings its way, a mere speck, across the
pathless fields of air; so the Indian holds his course,
silent, solitary, but undaunted, through the boundless bosom of the wilderness. His expeditions may
vie in distance and danger with the pilgrimage of
the devotee, or the crusade of the knight-errant. He
traverses vast forests, exposed to the hazards of
lonely sickness, of lurking enemies, and pining famine. Stormy lakes, those great inland seas, are no obstacles to his wanderings; in his light canoe of bark
he sports, like a feather, on their waves, and darts,
with the swiftness of an arrow, down the roaring

rapids of the rivers. His very subsistence is snatched from the midst of toil and peril. He gains his food by the hardships and dangers of the chase; he wraps himself in the spoils of the bear, the panther, and the buffalo, and sleeps among the thunders of the cataract.

No hero of ancient or modern days can surpass the Indian in his lofty contempt of death, and the fortitude with which he sustains its cruelest infliction. Indeed we here behold him rising superior to the white man, in consequence of his peculiar education. The latter rushes to glorious death at the cannon's mouth; the former calmly contemplates its approach, and triumphantly endures it, amid the varied torments of surrounding foes and the protracted agonies of fire. He even takes a pride in taunting his persecutors and provoking their ingenuity of torture; and as the devouring flames prey on his very vitals, and the flesh shrinks from the sinews, he raises his last song of triumph, breathing the defiance of an unconquered heart and invoking the spirits of his fathers to witness that he dies without a groan.

Notwithstanding the obloquy with which the early historians have overshadowed the characters of the unfortunate natives, some bright gleams occasionally break through, which throw a degree of melancholy luster on their memories. Facts are occasionally to be met with in the rude annals of the eastern provinces, which, though recorded with the coloring of prejudice and bigotry, yet speak for themselves, and will be dwelt on with applause and sympathy when prejudice shall have passed away.

In one of the homely narratives of the Indian wars
in New England, there is a touching account of the
desolation carried into the tribe of the Pequod Indians. Humanity shrinks from the cold-blooded de-
tail of indiscriminate butchery. In one place we read
of the surprisal of an Indian fort in the night, when
the wigwams were wrapped in flames, and the miserable inhabitants shot down and slain in attempting
to escape, "all being despatched and ended in the
course of an hour." After a series of similar trans-
actions, "our soldiers," as the historian piously observes, "being resolved by God's assistance to make
a final destruction of them," the unhappy savages being hunted from their homes and fortresses and pursued with fire and sword, a scanty but gallant band,
the sad remnant of the Pequod warriors, with their
wives and children, took refuge in a swamp.

Burning with indignation and rendered sullen by
despair, with hearts bursting with grief at the destruction of their tribe and spirits galled and sore at the
fancied ignominy of their defeat, they refused to ask
their lives at the hands of an insulting foe, and preferred death to submission.

As the night drew on they were surrounded in
their dismal retreat, so as to render escape imprac-
ticable. Thus situated, their enemy "plied them with
shot all the time, by which means many were killed
and buried in the mire." In the darkness and fog that
preceded the dawn of day some few broke through
the besiegers and escaped into the woods; "the rest
were left to the conquerors, of which many were
killed in the swamp, like sullen dogs who would

rather, in their self-willedness and madness, sit still and be shot through, or cut to pieces," than implore for mercy. When the day broke upon this handful of forlorn but dauntless spirits, the soldiers, we are told, entering the swamp, "saw several heaps of them sitting close together, upon whom they discharged their pieces, laden with ten or twelve pistol bullets at a time, putting the muzzles of the pieces under the boughs, within a few yards of them; so as, besides those that were found dead, many more were killed and sunk into the mire, and never were minded more by friend or foe."

Can anyone read this plain unvarnished tale without admiring the stern resolution, the unbending pride, the loftiness of spirit that seemed to nerve the hearts of these self-taught heroes and to raise them above the instinctive feelings of human nature? When the Gauls laid waste the city of Rome, they found the senators clothed in their robes, and seated with stern tranquillity in their curule chairs; in this manner they suffered death without resistance or even supplication. Such conduct was, in them, applauded as noble and magnanimous; in the hapless Indian it was reviled as obstinate and sullen! How truly are we the dupes of show and circumstance! How different is virtue, clothed in purple and enthroned in state, from virtue, naked and destitute and perishing obscurely in a wilderness!

But I forbear to dwell on these gloomy pictures. The eastern tribes have long since disappeared; the forests that sheltered them have been laid low, and scarcely any traces remain of them in the thickly settled states of New England, excepting here and there the Indian name of a village or a stream. And such must, sooner or later, be the fate of those other tribes which skirt the frontiers, and have occasionally been inveigled from their forests to mingle in the wars of white men. In a little while, and they will go the way that their brethren have gone before. The few hordes which still linger about the shores of Huron and Superior and the tributary streams of the Mississippi will share the fate of those tribes that once spread over Massachusetts and Connecticut and lorded it along the proud banks of the Hudson, of that gigantic race said to have existed on the borders of the Susquehanna, and of those various nations that flourished about the Potomac and the Rappahannock and that peopled the forests of the vast valley of Shenandoah. They will vanish like a vapor from the face of the earth; their very history will be lost in forgetfulness, and "the places that now know them will know them no more for ever." Or, if perchance, some dubious memorial of them should survive, it may be in the romantic dreams of the poet, to people in imagination his glades and groves, like the fauns and satyrs and sylvan deities of antiquity. But should he venture upon the dark story of their wrongs and wretchedness; should he tell how they were invaded, corrupted, despoiled, driven from their native abodes and the sepulchres of their fathers, hunted like wild beasts about the earth, and sent down with violence and butchery to the grave, posterity will either turn with horror and incredulity from the tale, or blush with indignation at the inhumanity of their forefathers. "We are driven back," said an old warrior, "until we can retreat no farther—our hatchets are broken, our bows are snapped, our fires are nearly extinguished; a little longer and the white man will cease to persecute us—for we shall cease to exist!"

THE PRIDE OF THE VILLAGE

May no wolfe howle; no screech owle stir
A wing about thy sepulchre!
No boysterous winds or stormes come hither,
        To starve or wither
Thy soft sweet earth! but, like a spring,
Love kept it ever flourishing.

HERRICK

In the course of an excursion through one of the remote counties of England, I had struck into one of those crossroads that lead through the more secluded parts of the country, and stopped one afternoon at a village, the situation of which was beautifully rural and retired. There was an air of primitive simplicity about its inhabitants, not to be found in the villages which lie on the great coach roads. I determined to pass the night there, and, having taken an early dinner, strolled out to enjoy the neighboring scenery.

My ramble, as is usually the case with travelers, soon led me to the church, which stood at a little distance from the village. Indeed, it was an object of some curiosity, its old tower being completely overrun with ivy, so that only here and there a jutting buttress, an angle of gray wall, or a fantastically carved ornament peered through the verdant covering. It was a lovely evening. The early part of the day had been dark and showery, but in the afternoon it had cleared up; and though sullen clouds still hung overhead, yet there was a broad tract of golden sky in the west from which the setting sun gleamed through the dripping leaves, and lit up all nature with a melancholy smile. It seemed like the parting hour of a good Christian, smiling on the sins and sorrows of the world, and giving, in the serenity of his decline, an assurance that he will rise again in glory.

I had seated myself on a half-sunken tombstone, and was musing, as one is apt to do at this sober-thoughted hour, on past scenes and early friends—on those who were distant and those who were dead—and indulging in that kind of melancholy fancying which has in it something sweeter even than pleasure. Every now and then the stroke of a bell from the neighboring tower fell on my ear; its tones were in unison with the scene, and, instead of jarring, chimed in with my feelings, and it was some time before I recollected that it must be tolling the knell of some new tenant of the tomb.

Presently I saw a funeral train moving across the village green; it wound slowly along a lane, was lost, and reappeared through the breaks of the hedges, until it passed the place where I was sitting. The pall was supported by young girls, dressed in white; and another, about the age of seventeen, walked before, bearing a chaplet of white flowers, a token that the deceased was a young and unmarried female. The corpse was followed by the parents. They were a venerable couple of the better order of peasantry. The father seemed to repress his feelings, but his fixed eye contracted brow, and deeply—furrowed face showed the struggle that was passing within. His wife hung on his arm, and wept aloud with the convulsive bursts of a mother's sorrow.

I followed the funeral into the church. The bier was placed in the center aisle, and the chaplet of white flowers, with a pair of white gloves, was hung over the seat which the deceased had occupied.

Everyone knows the soul-subduing pathos of the funeral service, for who is so fortunate as never to have followed someone he has loved to the tomb? But when performed over the remains of innocence and beauty, thus laid low in the bloom of existence— what can be more affecting? At that simple but most solemn consignment of the body to the grave— "Earth to earth—ashes to ashes—dust to dust!"—the tears of the youthful companions of the deceased flowed unrestrained. The father still seemed to struggle with his feelings, and to comfort himself with the assurance that the dead are blessed which die in the Lord; but the mother only thought of her child as a flower of the field cut down and withered in the midst of its sweetness; she was like Rachel, "mourning over her children, and would not be comforted."

On returning to the inn, I learned the whole story

of the deceased. It was a simple one, and such as has often been told. She had been the beauty and pride of the village. Her father had once been an opulent farmer, but was reduced in circumstances. This was an only child, and brought up entirely at home, in the simplicity of rural life. She had been the pupil of the village pastor, the favorite lamb of his little flock. The good man watched over her education with paternal care; it was limited, and suitable to the sphere in which she was to move, for he only sought to make her an ornament to her station in life, not to raise her above it. The tenderness and indulgence of her parents and the exemption from all ordinary occupations had fostered a natural grace and delicacy of character that accorded with the fragile loveliness of her form. She appeared like some tender plant of the garden, blooming accidentally amid the hardier natives of the fields.

The superiority of her charms was felt and acknowledged by her companions, but without envy, for it was surpassed by the unassuming gentleness and winning kindness of her manners. It might be truly said of her:

This is the prettiest low-born lass, that ever
Ran on the green-sward; nothing she does or seems,
But smacks of something greater than herself;
Too noble for this place.

The village was one of those sequestered spots which still retain some vestiges of old English customs. It had its rural festivals and holiday pastimes, and still kept up some faint observance of the once-popular rites of May. These, indeed, had been promoted by its present pastor, who was a lover of old customs and one of those simple Christians that think their mission fulfilled by promoting joy on earth and good will among mankind. Under his auspices the Maypole stood from year to year in the center of the village green; on May Day it was decorated with garlands and streamers, and a queen or lady of the May was appointed, as in former times, to preside at the sports and distribute the prizes and rewards. The picturesque situation of the village and the fancifulness of its rustic fetes would often attract the notice of casual visitors. Among these, on one May Day, was a young officer whose regiment had been recently quartered in the neighborhood. He was charmed with the native taste that pervaded this village pageant, but, above all, with the dawning loveliness of the queen of May. It was the village favorite, who was crowned with flowers, and blushing and smiling in all the beautiful confusion of girlish diffidence and delight. The artlessness of rural habits enabled him readily to make her acquaintance; he gradually won his way into her intimacy; and paid his court to her in that unthinking way in which young officers are too apt to trifle with rustic simplicity.

There was nothing in his advances to startle or alarm. He never even talked of love; but there are modes of making it more eloquent than language, and which convey it subtilely and irresistibly to the heart. The beam of the eye, the tone of voice, the thousand tendernesses which emanate from every word and look and action—these form the true eloquence of love, and can always be felt and understood, but never described. Can we wonder that they should readily win a heart, young, guileless, and susceptible? As to her, she loved almost unconsciously; she scarcely inquired what was the growing passion that was absorbing every thought and feeling, or what were to be its consequences. She, indeed, looked not to the future. When present, his looks and words occupied her whole attention; when absent, she thought but of what had passed at their recent interview. She would wander with him through the green lanes and rural scenes of the vicinity. He taught her to see new beauties in nature; he talked in the language of polite and cultivated life, and breathed into her ear the witcheries of romance and poetry.

Perhaps there could not have been a passion between the sexes more pure than this innocent girl's. The gallant figure of her youthful admirer and the splendor of his military attire might at first have charmed her eye; but it was not these that had captivated her heart. Her attachment had something in it of idolatry. She looked up to him as to a being of a superior order. She felt in his society the enthusiasm of a mind naturally delicate and poetical, and now first awakened to a keen perception of the beautiful and grand. Of the sordid distinctions of rank and fortune she thought nothing; it was the difference of intellect, of demeanor, of manners from those of the rustic society to which she had been accustomed that elevated him in her opinion. She would listen to him with charmed ear and downcast look of mute delight, and her cheek would mantle with enthusiasm; or if ever she ventured a shy glance of timid admiration, it was as quickly withdrawn, and she would sigh and blush at the idea of her comparative unworthiness.

Her lover was equally impassioned; but his passion was mingled with feelings of a coarser nature. He had begun the connection in levity, for he had often heard his brother officers boast of their village conquests, and thought some triumph of the kind necessary to his reputation as a man of spirit. But he was too full of youthful fervor. His heart had not yet been rendered sufficiently cold and selfish by a wandering and dissipated life; it caught fire from the very flame it sought to kindle, and before he was aware of the nature of his situation he became really in love.

What was he to do? There were the old obstacles which so incessantly occur in these heedless attachments. His rank in life—the prejudices of titled connections—his dependence upon a proud and unyielding father—all forbade him to think of matrimony: but when he looked down upon this innocent being, so tender and confiding, there was a purity in her manners, a blamelessness in her life, and a beseeching modesty in her looks that awed down every licentious feeling. In vain did he try to fortify himself by a thousand heartless examples of men of fashion, and to chill the glow of generous sentiment with that cold derisive levity with which he had heard them talk of female virtue; whenever he came into her presence, she was still surrounded by that mysterious but impassive charm of virgin purity in whose hallowed sphere no guilty thought can live.

The sudden arrival of orders for the regiment to repair to the continent completed the confusion of his mind. He remained for a short time in a state of the most painful irresolution; he hesitated to communicate the tidings until the day for marching was at hand, when he gave her the intelligence in the course of an evening ramble.

The idea of parting had never before occurred to her. It broke in at once upon her dream of felicity; she looked upon it as a sudden and insurmountable evil, and wept with the guileless simplicity of a child. He drew her to his bosom, and kissed the tears from her soft cheek; nor did he meet with a repulse, for there are moments of mingled sorrow and tenderness which hallow the caresses of affection. He was naturally impetuous; and the sight of beauty, apparently yielding in his arms, the confidence of his power over her, and the dread of losing her for ever, all conspired to overwhelm his better feelings—he ventured to propose that she should leave her home and be the companion of his fortunes.

He was quite a novice in seduction, and blushed and faltered at his own baseness; but so innocent of mind was his intended victim that she was at first at a loss to comprehend his meaning; and why she should leave her native village, and the humble roof of her parents. When at last the nature of his proposal flashed upon her pure mind, the effect was withering. She did not weep—she did not break forth into re- proach—she said not a word—but she shrunk back aghast as from a viper; gave him a look of anguish that pierced to his very soul; and, clasping her hands in agony, fled, as if for refuge, to her father's cottage.

The officer retired, confounded, humiliated, and repentant. It is uncertain what might have been the result of the conflict of his feelings had not his thoughts been diverted by the bustle of departure. New scenes, new pleasures, and new companions soon dissipated his self-reproach and stifled his ten- derness; yet, amidst the stir of camps, the revelries of garrisons, the array of armies, and even the din of battles, his thoughts would sometimes steal back to the scenes of rural quiet and village simplicity— the white cottage—the footpath along the silver brook and up the hawthorn hedge, and the little village maid loitering along it, leaning on his arm, and listening to him with eyes beaming with uncon- scious affection.

The shock which the poor girl had received, in the destruction of all her ideal world, had indeed been cruel. Faintings and hysterics had at first shaken her tender frame, and were succeeded by a settled and pin- ing melancholy. She had beheld from her window the march of the departing troops. She had seen her faithless lover borne off, as if in triumph, amidst the sound of drum and trumpet and the pomp of arms. She strained a last aching gaze after him, as the morning sun glittered about his figure, and his plume waved in the breeze; he passed away like a bright vision from her sight, and left her all in darkness.

It would be trite to dwell on the particulars of her after story. It was, like other tales of love, melancholy. She avoided society, and wandered out alone in the walks she had most frequented with her lover. She sought, like the stricken deer, to weep in silence and loneliness, and brood over the barbed sorrow that rankled in her soul. Sometimes she would be seen late of an evening sitting in the porch of the village church; and the milkmaids, returning from the fields, would now and then overhear her singing some plaintive ditty in the hawthorn walk. She became fervent in her devotions at church; and as the old people saw her approach, so wasted away, yet with a hectic bloom, and that hallowed air which melancholy diffuses around the form, they would make way for her, as for something spiritual, and, looking after her, would shake their heads in gloomy foreboding.

She felt a conviction that she was hastening to the tomb, but looked forward to it as a place of rest. The silver cord that had bound her to existence was loosed, and there seemed to be no more pleasure under the sun. If ever her gentle bosom had entertained resentment against her lover, it was extinguished. She was incapable of angry passions; and in a moment of saddened tenderness, she penned him a farewell letter. It was couched in the simplest language, but touching from its very simplicity. She told him that she was dying, and did not conceal from him that his conduct was the cause. She even depicted the sufferings which she had experienced, but concluded with saying that she could not die in peace until she had sent him her forgiveness and her blessing.

By degrees her strength declined, that she could no longer leave the cottage. She could only totter to the window, where, propped up in her chair, it was her enjoyment to sit all day and look out upon the landscape. Still she uttered no complaint, nor imparted to anyone the malady that was preying on her heart. She never even mentioned her lover's name, but would lay her head on her mother's bosom and weep in silence. Her poor parents hung, in mute anxiety, over this fading blossom of their hopes, still flattering themselves that it might again revive to freshness, and that the bright unearthly bloom which sometimes flushed her cheek might be the promise of returning health.

In this way she was seated between them one Sunday afternoon; her hands were clasped in theirs, the lattice was thrown open, and the soft air that stole in brought with it the fragrance of the clustering honeysuckle which her own hands had trained around the window.

Her father had just been reading a chapter in the Bible; it spoke of the vanity of worldly things, and of the joys of heaven; it seemed to have diffused comfort and serenity through her bosom. Her eye was fixed on the distant village church; the bell had tolled for the evening service; the last villager was lagging into the porch; and everything had sunk into that hallowed stillness peculiar to the day of rest. Her parents were gazing on her with yearning hearts. Sickness and sorrow, which pass so roughly over some faces, had given to hers the expression of a seraph's. A tear trembled in her soft blue eye. Was she thinking of her faithless lover? Or were her thoughts wandering to that distant churchyard, into whose bosom she might soon be gathered?

Suddenly the clang of hoofs was heard—a horseman galloped to the cottage—he dismounted before the window—the poor girl gave a faint exclamation, and sank back in her chair: it was her repentant lover! He rushed into the house and flew to clasp her to his bosom; but her wasted form—her deathlike countenance—so wan, yet so lovely in its desolation—smote him to the soul, and he threw himself in agony at her feet. She was too faint to rise—she attempted to extend her trembling hand—her lips moved as if she spoke, but no word was articulated —she looked down upon him with a smile of unutterable tenderness—and closed her eyes for ever!

Such are the particulars which I gathered of this village story. They are but scanty, and I am conscious have little novelty to recommend them. In the present rage also for strange incident and high-seasoned narrative they may appear trite and insignificant, but they interested me strongly at the time; and, taken in connection with the affecting ceremony which I had just witnessed, left a deeper impression on my mind than many circumstances of a more striking nature. I have passed through the place since, and visited the church again, from a better motive than mere curiosity. It was a wintry evening; the trees were stripped of their foliage; the churchyard looked naked and mournful, and the wind rustled coldly through the dry grass. Evergreens, however, had been planted about the grave of the village favorite, and osiers were bent over it to keep the turf uninjured.

The church door was open, and I stepped in. There hung the chaplet of flowers and the gloves, as on the day of the funeral; the flowers were withered, it is true, but care seemed to have been taken that no dust should soil their whiteness. I have seen many monuments where art has exhausted its powers to awaken the sympathy of the spectator, but I have met with none that spoke more touchingly to my heart than this simple but delicate memento of departed innocence.

THE ANGLER

This day dame Nature seem'd in love,
The lusty sap began to move,
Fresh juice did stir th' embracing vines
And birds had drawn their valentines.
The jealous trout that low did lie,
Rose at a well-dissembled flie.
There stood my friend, with patient skill,
Attending of his trembling quill.

SIR H. WOTTON

It is said that many an unlucky urchin is induced to run away from his family, and betake himself to a seafaring life, from reading the history of Robinson Crusoe; and I suspect that, in like manner, many of those worthy gentlemen who are given to haunt the sides of pastoral streams with angle rods in hand may trace the origin of their passion to the seductive pages of honest Izaak Walton. I recollect studying his *Compleat Angler* several years since, in company with a knot of friends in America, and moreover that we were all completely bitten with the angling mania. It was early in the year; but as soon as the weather was auspicious, and that the spring began to melt into the verge of summer, we took rod in hand and sallied into the country, as stark mad as was ever Don Quixote from reading books of chivalry.

One of our party had equaled the Don in the fullness of his equipments, being attired cap-a-pie for the enterprise. He wore a broad-skirted fustian coat perplexed with half a hundred pockets; a pair of stout shoes, and leathern gaiters; a basket slung on one side for fish; a patent rod, a landing net, and a score of other inconveniences only to be found in the true angler's armory. Thus harnessed for the field, he was as great a matter of stare and wonderment among the country folk, who had never seen a regular angler, as was the steel-clad hero of La Mancha among the goatherds of the Sierra Morena.

Our first assay was along a mountain brook, among the highlands of the Hudson, a most unfortunate place for the execution of those piscatory tactics which had been invented along the velvet margins of quiet English rivulets. It was one of those wild streams that lavish among our romantic solitudes unheeded beauties, enough to fill the sketch book of a hunter of the picturesque. Sometimes it would leap down rock shelves, making small cascades, over which the trees threw their broad balancing sprays, and long nameless weeds hung in fringes from the impending banks, dripping with diamond drops. Sometimes it would brawl and fret along a ravine in the matted shade of a forest, filling it with murmurs; and, after this termagant career, would steal forth into open day with the most placid demure face imaginable, as I have seen some pestilent shrew of a housewife, after filling her home with uproar and ill-humor, come dimpling out of doors, swimming and courtesying, and smiling upon' all the world.

How smoothly would this vagrant brook glide, at such times, through some bosom of green meadow land among the mountains, where the quiet was only interrupted by the occasional tinkling of a bell from the lazy cattle among the clover, or the sound of a woodcutter's axe from the neighboring forest.

For my part, I was always a bungler at all kinds of sport that required either patience or adroitness, and had not angled above half an hour before I had completely "satisfied the sentiment," and convinced myself of the truth of Izaak Walton's opinion that angling is something like poetry—a man must be born to it. I hooked myself instead of the fish; tangled my line in every tree; lost my bait; broke my rod; until I gave up the attempt in despair, and passed the day under the trees, reading old Izaak, satisfied that it was his fascinating vein of honest simplicity and rural feeling that had bewitched me and not the passion for angling. My companions, however, were more persevering in their delusion. I have them at this moment before my eyes, stealing along the border of the brook, where it lay open to the day or was merely fringed by shrubs and bushes. I see the bittern rising with hollow scream as they break in upon his rarely invaded haunt; the kingfisher watching them suspiciously from his dry tree that overhangs the deep black millpond, in the gorge of the hills; the tortoise letting himself slip sideways from off the stone or log on which he is sunning himself; and the panic-struck frog plumping in headlong as they approach, and spreading an alarm throughout the watery world around.

I recollect also, that, after toiling and watching and creeping about for the greater part of a day with scarcely any success in spite of all our admirable apparatus, a lubberly country urchin came down from the hills with a rod made from a branch of a tree, a few yards of twine, and, as Heaven shall help me, I believe, a crooked pin for a hook, baited with a vile earthworm—and in half an hour caught more fish than we had nibbles throughout the day!

But, above all, I recollect the "good, honest, wholesome, hungry" repast which we made under a beech tree, just by a spring of pure sweet water that stole out of the side of a hill; and how, when it was over, one of the party read old Izaak Walton's scene with the milkmaid, while I lay on the grass and built castles in a bright pile of clouds until I fell asleep. All this may appear like mere egotism; yet I cannot refrain from uttering these recollections, which are passing like a strain of music over my mind, and have been called up by an agreeable scene which I witnessed not long since.

In a morning's stroll along the banks of the Alun, a beautiful little stream which flows down from the Welsh hills and throws itself into the Dee, my attention was attracted to a group seated on the margin.

On approaching, I found it to consist of a veteran angler and two rustic disciples. The former was an old fellow with a wooden leg, with clothes very much but very carefully patched, betokening poverty, honestly come by, and decently maintained. His face bore the marks of former storms but present fair weather; its furrows had been worn into an habitual smile; his iron-gray locks hung about his ears, and he had altogether the good-humored air of a constitutional philosopher who was disposed to take the world as it went. One of his companions was a ragged wight, with the skulking look of an arrant poacher, and I'll warrant could find his way to any gentleman's fish pond in the neighborhood in the darkest night. The other was a tall, awkward country lad, with a lounging gait, and apparently somewhat of a rustic beau. The old man was busy in examining the maw of a trout which he had just killed, to discover by its contents what insects were seasonable for bait, and was lecturing on the subject to his companions, who appeared to listen with infinite deference. I have a kind feeling toward all "brothers of the angle" ever since I read Izaak Walton. They are men, he affirms, of a "mild, sweet, and peaceable spirit"; and my esteem for them has been increased since I met with an old *Tretyse of Fishing with the Angle,* in which are set forth many of the maxims of their inoffensive fraternity. "Take good hede," sayeth this honest little tretyse, "that in going about your disportes ye open no man's gates but that ye shet them again. Also ye shall not use this forsayd crafti disport for no covetousness to the increasing and spar-ing of your money only, but principally for your solace, and to cause the helth of your body and specyally of your soule."*

I thought that I could perceive in the veteran angler before me an exemplification of what I had read, and there was a cheerful contentedness in his looks that quite drew me toward him. I could not but remark the gallant manner in which he stumped from one part of the brook to another, waving his rod in the air to keep the line from dragging on the ground or catching among the bushes, and the adroitness with which he would throw his fly to any particular place, sometimes skimming it lightly along a little rapid, sometimes casting it into one of those dark holes made by a twisted root or overhanging bank, in which the large trout are apt to lurk. In the meanwhile he was giving instructions to his two disciples, showing them the manner in which they should handle their rods, fix their flies, and play them along the surface of the stream. The scene brought to my mind the instructions of the sage Piscator to his scholar. The country around was of that pastoral kind which Walton is fond of describing. It was a part

* From this same treatise, it would appear that angling is a more industrious and devout employment than it is generally considered. "For when ye purpose to go on your disportes in fishynge ye will not desyre greatlye many persons with you, which might let you of your game. And that ye may serve God devoutly in sayinge effectually your customable prayers. And thus doying, ye shall eschew and also avoyde many vices, as ydelnes, which is principall cause to induce man to many other vices, as it is right well known."

of the great plain of Cheshire, close by the beautiful vale of Gessford, and just where the inferior Welsh hills begin to swell up from among fresh-smelling meadows. The day, too, like that recorded in his work, was mild and sunshiny, with now and then a soft-dropping shower that sowed the whole earth with diamonds.

I soon fell into conversation with the old angler, and was so much entertained that, under pretext of receiving instructions in his art, I kept company with him almost the whole day, wandering along the banks of the stream and listening to his talk. He was very communicative, having all the easy garrulity of cheerful old age, and I fancy was a little flattered by having an opportunity of displaying his piscatory lore, for who does not like now and then to play the sage?

He had been much of a rambler in his day, and had passed some years of his youth in America, particularly in Savannah, where he had entered into trade, and had been ruined by the indiscretion of a partner. He had afterward experienced many ups and down in life, until he got into the navy, where his leg was carried away by a cannon ball at the battle of Camperdown. This was the only stroke of real good fortune he had ever experienced, for it got him a pension, which, together with some small paternal property, brought him in a revenue of nearly forty pounds. On this he retired to his native village, where he lived quietly and independently, and devoted the remainder of his life to the "noble art of angling."

I found that he had read Izaak Walton attentively, and he seemed to have imbibed all his simple frankness and prevalent good humor. Though he had been sorely buffeted about the world, he was satisfied that the world, in itself, was good and beautiful. Though he had been as roughly used in different countries as a poor sheep that is fleeced by every hedge and thicket, yet he spoke of every nation with candor and kindness, appearing to look only on the good side of things; and, above all, he was almost the only man I had ever met with who had been an unfortunate adventurer in America, and had honesty and magnanimity enough to take the fault of his own door, and not to curse the country. The lad that was receiving his instructions, I learned, was the son and heir apparent of a fat old widow who kept the village inn, and of course a youth of some expectation, and much courted by the idle gentlemanlike personages of the place. In taking him under his care, therefore, the old man had probably an eye to a privileged corner in the taproom, and an occasional cup of cheerful ale free of expense.

There is certainly something in angling (if we could forget, which anglers are apt to do, the cruelties and tortures inflicted on worms and insects) that tends to produce a gentleness of spirit, and a pure serenity of mind. As the English are methodical, even in their recreations, and are the most scientific of sportsmen, it has been reduced among them to perfect rule and system. Indeed it is an amusement peculiarly adpated to the mild and highly cultivated scenery of England, where every roughness has been softened away from the landscape. It is delightful to saunter along those limpid streams which wander, like veins of silver, through the bosom of this beautiful country, leading one through a diversity of small home scenery, sometimes winding through ornamented grounds, sometimes brimming along through rich pasturage where the fresh green is mingled with sweet-smelling flowers, sometimes venturing in sight of villages and hamlets, and then running capriciously away into shady retirements. The sweetness and serenity of nature and the quiet watchfulness of the sport gradually bring on pleasant fits of musing, which are now and then agreeably interrupted by the song of a bird, the distant whistle of the peasant, or perhaps the vagary of some fish, leaping out of the still water and skimming transiently about its glassy surface. "When I would beget content," says Izaak Walton, "and increase confidence in the power and wisdom and providence of Almighty God, I will walk the meadows by some gliding stream, and there contemplate the lilies that take no care, and those very many other little living creatures that are not only created, but fed (man knows not how) by the goodness of the God of nature, and therefore trust in him."

I cannot forbear to give another quotation from one of those ancient champions of angling, which breathes the same innocent and happy spirit:

Let me live harmlessly, and near the brink
    Of Trent or Avon have a dwelling-place,
Where I may see my quill, or cork, down sink,

With eager bite of pike, or bleak, or dace;
And on the world and my Creator think:
    Whilst some men strive ill-gotten goods t' embrace;
And others spend their time in base excess
    Of wine, or worse, in war, or wantonness.

Let them that will, these pastimes still pursue,
    And on such pleasing fancies feed their fill;
So I the fields and meadows green may view,
    And daily by fresh rivers walk at will,
Among the daisies and the violets blue,
    Red hyacinth and yellow daffodil.*

On parting with the old angler I inquired after his
place of abode, and happening to be in the neighborhood of the village a few evenings afterward, I had
the curiosity to seek him out. I found him living in
a small cottage, containing only one room, but a
perfect curiosity in its method and arrangement. It
was on the skirts of the village, on a green bank, a little back from the road, with a small garden in
front, stocked with kitchen herbs, and adorned
with a few flowers. The whole front of the cottage
was overrun with a honeysuckle. On the top was a
ship for a weathercock. The interior was fitted up
in a truly nautical style, his ideas of comfort and
convenience having been acquired on the berth deck
of a man-of-war. A hammock was slung from the
ceiling, which, in the daytime, was lashed up so as to
take but little room. From the center of the chamber

* J. Davors.

hung a model of a ship, of his own workmanship. Two or three chairs, a table, and a large sea chest formed the principal movables. About the wall were stuck up naval ballads, such as *Admiral Hosier's Ghost, All in the Downs,* and *Tom Bowline,* intermingled with pictures of sea fights, among which the battle of Camperdown held a distinguished place. The mantelpiece was decorated with seashells, over which hung a quadrant, flanked by two woodcuts of most bitter-looking naval commanders. His implements for angling were carefully disposed on nails and hooks about the room. On a shelf was arranged his library, containing a work on angling, much worn, a Bible covered with canvas, an odd volume or two of voyages, a nautical almanac, and a book of songs.

His family consisted of a large black cat with one eye, and a parrot which he had caught and tamed and educated himself, in the course of one of his voyages, and which uttered a variety of sea phrases with the hoarse brattling tone of a veteran boatswain. The establishment reminded me of that of the renowed Robinson Crusoe; it was kept in neat order, everything being "stowed away" with the regularity of a ship of war; and he informed me that he "scoured the deck every morning, and swept it between meals."

I found him seated on a bench before the door, smoking his pipe in the soft evening sunshine. His cat was purring soberly on the threshold, and his parrot describing some strange evolutions in an iron ring that swung in the center of his cage. He had been angling all day, and gave me a history of his sport with as much minuteness as a general would talk over a campaign, being particularly animated in relating the manner in which he had taken a large trout, which had completely tasked all his skill and wariness, and which he had sent as a trophy to mine hostess of the inn.

How comforting it is to see a cheerful and contented old age; and to behold a poor fellow, like this, after being tempest-tossed through life, safely moored in a snug and quiet harbor in the evening of his days! His happiness, however, sprung from within himself, and was independent of external circumstances; for he had that inexhaustible good nature, which is the most precious gift of Heaven, spreading itself like oil over the troubled sea of thought and keeping the mind smooth and equable in the roughest weather.

On inquiring further about him, I learned that he was a universal favorite in the village, and the oracle of the taproom, where he delighted the rustics with his songs, and, like Sinbad, astonished them with his stories of strange lands, and shipwrecks, and sea fights. He was much noticed too by gentlemen sportsmen of the neighborhood; had taught several of them the art of angling; and was a privileged visitor to their kitchens. The whole tenor of his life was quiet and inoffensive, being principally passed about the neighboring streams, when the weather and season were favorable; and at other times he employed himself at home, preparing his fishing tackle for the next campaign, or manufacturing rods, nets, and flies for his patrons and pupils among the gentry.

He was a regular attendant at church on Sundays, though he generally fell asleep during the sermon. He had made it his particular request that when he died he should be buried in a green spot, which he could see from his seat in church, and which he had marked out ever since he was a boy, and had thought of when far from home on the raging sea, in danger of being food for the fishes—it was the spot where his father and mother had been buried.

I have done, for I fear that my reader is growing weary, but I could not refrain from drawing the picture of this worthy "brother of the angle," who has made me more than ever in love with the theory, though I fear I shall never be adroit in the practice of his art; and I will conclude this rambling sketch in the words of honest Izaak Walton, by craving the blessing of St. Peter's master upon my reader, "and upon all that are true lovers of virtue; and dare trust in his providence; and be quiet; and go a-angling."

THE ADVENTURE
OF THE GERMAN STUDENT

On a stormy night, in the tempestuous times of the French revolution, a young German was returning to his lodgings, at a late hour, across the old part of Paris. The lightning gleamed, and the loud claps of thunder rattled through the lofty narrow streets—but I should first tell you something about this young German.

Gottfried Wolfgang was a young man of good family. He had studied for some time at Göttingen, but being of a visionary and enthusiastic character, he had wandered into those wild and speculative doctrines which have so often bewildered German students. His secluded life, his intense application, and the singular nature of his studies, had an effect on both mind and body. His health was impaired; his imagination diseased. He had been indulging in fanciful speculations on spiritual essences, until, like Swedenborg, he had an ideal world of his own around him. He took up a notion, I do not know from what cause, that there was an evil influence

hanging over him; an evil genius or spirit seeking to
ensnare him and ensure his perdition. Such an idea
working on his melancholy temperament, produced
the most gloomy effects. He became haggard and
desponding. His friends discovered the mental malady preying upon him, and determined that the best
cure was a change of scene; he was sent, therefore,
to finish his studies amidst the splendors and gayeties
of Paris.

Wolfgang arrived at Paris at the breaking out of
the revolution. The popular delirium at first caught
his enthusiastic mind, and he was captivated by the
political and philosophical theories of the day:
but the scenes of blood which followed shocked his
sensitive nature, and made him more than ever a
recluse. He shut himself up in a solitary apartment in
the *Pays Latin*, the quarter of students. There, in a
gloomy street not far from the monastic walls of the
Sorbonne, he pursued his favorite speculations.
Sometimes he spent hours together in the great librar-
ies of Paris, those catacombs of departed authors,
rummaging among their hordes of dusty and obsolete
works in quest of food for his unhealthy appetite.
He was, in a manner, a literary ghoul, feeding in the
charnel-house of decayed literature.

Wolfgang, though solitary and recluse, was of
an ardent temperament, but for a time it operated
merely upon his imagination. He was too shy and
ignorant of the world to make any advances to the
fair, but he was a passionate admirer of female
beauty, and in his lonely chamber would often lose
himself in reveries on forms and faces which he had

seen, and his fancy would deck out images of loveliness far surpassing the reality.

While his mind was in this excited and sublimated state, a dream produced an extraordinary effect upon him. It was of a female face of transcendent beauty. So strong was the impression made, that he dreamt of it again and again. It haunted his thoughts by day, his slumbers by night; in fine, he became passionately enamoured of this shadow of a dream. This lasted so long that it became one of those fixed ideas which haunt the minds of melancholy men, and are at times mistaken for madness.

Such was Gottfried Wolfgang, and such his situation at the time I mentioned. He was returning home late one stormy night, through some of the old and gloomy streets of the *Marais,* the ancient part of Paris. The loud claps of thunder rattled among the high houses of the narrow streets. He came to the Place de Grève, the square where public executions are performed. The lightning quivered about the pinnacles of the ancient Hôtel de Ville, and shed flickering gleams over the open space in front. As Wolfgang was crossing the square, he shrank back with horror at finding himself close by the guillotine. It was the height of the reign of terror, when this dreadful instrument of death stood ever ready, and its scaffold was continually running with the blood of the virtuous and the brave. It had that very day been actively employed in the work of carnage, and there it stood in grim array, amidst a silent and sleeping city, waiting for fresh victims.

Wolfgang's heart sickened within him, and he was

turning shuddering from the horrible engine, when he beheld a shadowy form, cowering as it were at the foot of the steps which led up to the scaffold. A succession of vivid flashes of lightning revealed it more distinctly. It was a female figure, dressed in black. She was seated on one of the lower steps of the scaffold, leaning forward, her face hid in her lap; and her long dishevelled tresses hanging to the ground, streaming with the rain which fell in torrents. Wolfgang paused. There was something awful in this solitary monument of woe. The female had the appearance of being above the common order. He knew the times to be full of vicissitude, and that many a fair head, which had once been pillowed on down, now wandered houseless. Perhaps this was some poor mourner whom the dreadful axe had rendered desolate, and who sat here heart-broken on the strand of existence, from which all that was dear to her had been launched into eternity.

He approached, and addressed her in the accents of sympathy. She raised her head and gazed wildly at him. What was his astonishment at beholding, by the bright glare of the lightning, the very face which had haunted him in his dreams. It was pale and disconsolate, but ravishingly beautiful.

Trembling with violent and conflicting emotions, Wolfgang again accosted her. He spoke something of her being exposed at such an hour of the night, and to the fury of such a storm, and offered to conduct her to her friends. She pointed to the guillotine with a gesture of dreadful signification.

"I have no friend on earth!" said she.

"But you have a home," said Wolfgang.

"Yes—in the grave!"

The heart of the student melted at the words.

"If a stranger dare make an offer," said he, "without danger of being misunderstood, I would offer my humble dwelling as a shelter; myself as a devoted friend. I am friendless myself in Paris, and a stranger in the land; but if my life could be of service, it is at your disposal, and should be sacrificed before harm or indignity should come to you."

There was an honest earnestness in the young man's manner that had its effect. His foreign accent, too, was in favor; it showed him not to be a hackneyed inhabitant of Paris. Indeed, there is an eloquence in true enthusiasm that is not to be doubted. The homeless stranger confided herself implicitly to the protection of the student.

He supported her faltering steps across the Pont Neuf, and by the place where the statue of Henry the Fourth had been overthrown by the populace. The storm had abated and the thunder rumbled at a distance. All Paris was quiet; that great volcano of human passion slumbered for a while, to gather fresh strength for the next day's eruption. The student conducted his charge through the ancient streets of the *Pays Latin,* and by the dusky walls of the Sorbonne, to the great dingy hotel which he inhabited. The old portress who admitted them stared with surprise at the unusual sight of the melancholy Wolfgang with a female companion.

On entering his apartment, the student, for the first time, blushed at the scantiness and indifference of his dwelling. He had but one chamber—an old-fashioned saloon—heavily carved, and fantastically furnished with the remains of former magnificence, for it was one of those hotels in the quarter of the Luxembourg palace, which had once belonged to nobility. It was lumbered with books and papers, and all the usual apparatus of a student, and his bed stood in a recess at one end.

When lights were brought, and Wolfgang had a better opportunity of contemplating the stranger, he was more than ever intoxicated by her beauty. Her face was pale, but of a dazzling fairness, set off by a profusion of raven hair that hung clustering about it. Her eyes were large and brilliant, with a singular expression approaching almost to wildness. As far as her black dress permitted her shape to be seen, it was of perfect symmetry. Her whole appearance was highly striking, though she was dressed in the simplest style. The only thing approaching to an ornament which she wore, was a broad black band round her neck, clasped by diamonds.

The perplexity now commenced with the student how to dispose of the helpless being thus thrown upon his protection. He thought of abandoning his chamber to her, and seeking shelter for himself elsewhere. Still he was so fascinated by her charms, there seemed to be such a spell upon his thoughts and senses, that he could not tear himself from her presence. Her manner, too, was singular and unaccountable. She spoke no more of the guillotine. Her grief had abated. The attentions of the student had first won her confidence, and then, apparently, her heart. She was evidently an enthusiast like himself, and enthusiasts soon understand each other.

In the infatuation of the moment, Wolfgang avowed his passion for her. He told her the story of his mysterious dream, and how she had possessed his heart before he had even seen her. She was strangely affected by his recital, and acknowledged to have felt an impulse towards him equally unaccountable. It was the time for wild theory and wild actions. Old prejudices and superstitions were done away; everything was under the sway of the "Goddess of Reason." Among other rubbish of the old times, the forms and ceremonies of marriage began to be considered superfluous bonds for honorable minds. Social compacts were the vogue. Wolfgang was too much of a theorist not to be tainted by the liberal doctrines of the day.

"Why should we separate?" said he; "our hearts are united; in the eye of reason and honor we are as one. What need is there of sordid forms to bind high souls together?"

The stranger listened with emotion: she had evidently received illumination at the same school.

"You have no home or family," continued he, "let me be everything to you, or rather let us be everything to one another. If form is necessary, form shall be observed—there is my hand. I pledge myself to you forever."

"Forever?" said the stranger, solemnly.

"Forever!" repeated Wolfgang.

The stranger clasped the hand extended to her: "Then I am yours," murmured she, and sank upon his bosom.

The next morning the student left his bride sleeping, and sallied forth at an early hour to seek more spacious apartments suitable to the change in his situation. When he returned, he found the stranger lying with her head hanging over the bed, and one arm thrown over it. He spoke to her, but received no reply. He advanced to awaken her from her uneasy posture. On taking her hand, it was cold—there was no pulsation—her face was pallid and ghastly. In a word, she was a corpse.

Horrified and frantic, he alarmed the house. A scene of confusion ensued. The police was summoned. As the officer of police entered the room, he started back on beholding the corpse.

"Great heaven!" cried he, "how did this woman come here?"

"Do you know anything about her?" said Wolfgang eagerly.

"Do I?" exclaimed the officer: "she was guillotined yesterday."

He stepped forward; undid the black collar round the neck of the corpse, and the head rolled on the floor!

The student burst into a frenzy. "The fiend! the fiend has gained possession of me!" shrieked he; "I am lost forever."

They tried to soothe him, but in vain. He was possessed with the frightful belief that an evil spirit had reanimated the dead body to ensnare him. He went distracted, and died in a madhouse.

Here the old gentleman with the haunted head finished his narrative.

"And is this really a fact?" said the inquisitive gentleman.

"A fact not to be doubted," replied the other. "I had it from the best authority. The student told it to me himself. I saw him in a mad-house in Paris."

THE DEVIL AND TOM WALKER

A few miles from Boston in Massachusetts, there is a deep inlet, winding several miles into the interior of the country from Charles Bay, and terminating in a thickly-wooded swamp or morass. On one side of this inlet is a beautiful dark grove; on the opposite side the land rises abruptly from the water's edge into a high ridge, on which grow a few scattered oaks of great age and immense size. Under one of these gigantic trees, according to old stories, there was a great amount of treasure buried by Kidd the priate. The inlet allowed a facility to bring the money in a boat secretly and at night to the very foot of the hill; the elevation of the place permitted a good lookout to be kept that no one was at hand; while the remarkable trees formed good landmarks by which the place might easily be found again. The old stories add, moreover, that the devil presided at the hiding of the money, and took it under his guardianship; but this, it is well known, he always does with buried treasure, particularly when it has been ill-gotten. Be that as it may, Kidd never returned to recover his wealth; being shortly after seized at Boston, sent out to England, and there hanged for a pirate.

About the year 1727, just at the time that earthquakes were prevalent in New England, and shook many tall sinners down upon their knees, there lived near this place a meagre, miserly fellow, of the name of Tom Walker. He had a wife as miserly as himself: they were so miserly that they even conspired to cheat each other. Whatever the woman could lay hands on, she hid away; a hen could not cackle but she was on the alert to secure the new-laid egg. Her husband was continually prying about to detect her secret hoards, and many and fierce were the conflicts that took place about what ought to have been common property. They lived in a forlorn-looking house that stood alone, and had an air of starvation. A few straggling savin-trees, emblems of sterility, grew near it; no smoke ever curled from its chimney; no traveller stopped at its door. A miserable horse, whose ribs were as articulate as the bars of a gridiron, stalked about a field, where a thin carpet of moss, scarcely covering the ragged beds of puddingstone, tantalized and balked his hunger; and sometimes he would lean his head over the fence, look piteously at the passerby, and seem to petition deliverance from this land of famine.

The house and its inmates had altogether a bad name. Tom's wife was a tall termagant, fierce of temper, loud of tongue, and strong of arm. Her voice was often heard in wordy warfare with her husband; and his face sometimes showed signs that their conflicts were not confined to words. No one ventured, however, to interfere between them. The lonely wayfarer shrunk within himself at the horrid clamor and clapper-clawing; eyed the den of discord askance; and hurried on his way, rejoicing, if a bachelor, in his celibacy.

One day that Tom Walker had been to a distant part of the neighborhood, he took what he considered a short cut homeward, through the swamp. Like most short cuts, it was an ill-chosen route. The swamp was thickly grown with great gloomy pines and hemlocks, some of them ninety feet high, which made it dark at noonday, and a retreat for all the owls of the neighborhood. It was full of pits and quagmires, partly covered with weeds and mosses, where the green surface often betrayed the traveller into a gulf of black, smothering mud: there were also dark and stagnant pools, the abodes of the tadpole, the bull-frog, and the water-snake; where the trunks of pines and hemlocks lay half drowned, half rotting, looking like alligators sleeping in the mire.

Tom had long been picking his way cautiously through this treacherous forest; stepping from tuft to tuft of rushes and roots, which afforded precarious footholds among deep sloughs; or pacing carefully, like a cat, along the prostrate trunks of trees; startled now and then by the sudden screaming of the bittern, or the quacking of wild duck rising on the wind from some solitary pool. At length he arrived at a firm piece of ground, which ran out like a peninsula into the deep bosom of the swamp. It had been one of the strongholds of the Indians during their wars with the first colonists. Here they had thrown up a kind of fort, which they had looked upon as almost impregnable and had used as a place of refuge for their squaws and children. Nothing remained of the old Indian fort but a few embankments, gradually sinking to the level of the surrounding earth, and already overgrown in part by oaks and other forest trees, the foliage of which formed a contrast to the dark pines and hemlocks of the swamp.

It was late in the dusk of evening when Tom Walker reached the old fort, and he paused there awhile to rest himself. Any one but he would have felt unwilling to linger in this lonely, melancholy place, for the common people had a bad opinion of it, from the stories handed down from the time of the Indian wars; when it was asserted that the savages held incantations here, and made sacrifices to the evil spirit.

Tom Walker, however, was not a man to be troubled with any fears of the kind. He reposed himself for some time on the trunk of a fallen hemlock, listening to the boding cry of the tree-toad, and delving with his walking-staff into a mound of black mould at his feet. As he turned up the soil unconsciously, his staff struck against something hard. He raked it out of the vegetable mould, and lo! a cloven skull, with an Indian tomahawk buried deep in it, lay before him. The rust on the weapon showed the time that had elapsed since this death-blow had been given. It was a dreary memento of the fierce struggle that had taken place in this last foothold of the Indian warriors.

"Humph!" said Tom Walker, as he gave it a kick to shake the dirt from it.

"Let that skull alone!" said a gruff voice. Tom lifted up his eyes, and beheld a great black man seated directly opposite him, on the stump of a tree. He was exceedingly surprised, having neither heard nor seen any one approach; and he was still more perplexed on observing, as well as the gathering gloom would permit, that the stranger was neither Negro nor Indian. It is true he was dressed in a rude half Indian garb, and had a red belt or sash swathed round his body! but his face was neither black nor copper-color, but swarthy and dingy, and begrimed with soot, as if he had been accustomed to toil among fires and forges. He had a shock of coarse black hair, that stood out from his head in all directions, and bore an axe on his shoulder.

He scowled for a moment at Tom with a pair of great red eyes.

"What are you doing on my grounds?" said the black man, with a hoarse, growling voice.

"Your grounds!" said Tom, with a sneer, "no more your grounds than mine; they belong to Deacon Peabody."

"Deacon Peabody be d———d," said the stranger, "as I flatter myself he will be, if he does not look more to his own sins and less to those of his neighbors. Look yonder, and see how Deacon Peabody is faring."

Tom looked in the direction that the stranger pointed, and beheld one of the great trees, fair and flourishing without, but rotten at the core, and saw that it had been nearly hewn through, so that the first high wind was likely to blow it down. On the bark of the tree was scored the name of Deacon Peabody, an eminent man, who had waxed wealthy by driving shrewd bargains with the Indians. He now looked around, and found most of the tall trees marked with the name of some great man of the colony, and all more or less scored by the axe. The one on which he had been seated, and which had evidently just been hewn down, bore the name of Crowninshield; and he recollected a mighty rich man of that name, who made a vulgar display of wealth, which it was whispered he had acquired by buccaneering.

"He's just ready for burning!" said the black man, with a growl of triumph. "You see I am likely to have a good stock of firewood for winter."

"But what right have you," said Tom, "to cut down Deacon Peabody's timber?"

"The right of a prior claim," said the other. "This woodland belonged to me long before one of your white-faced race put foot upon the soil."

"And pray, who are you, if I may be so bold?" said Tom.

"Oh, I go by various names. I am the wild huntsman in some countries; the black miner in others.

In this neighborhood I am he to whom the red men consecrated this spot, and in honor of whom they now and then roasted a white man, by way of sweet-smelling sacrifice. Since the red men have been exterminated by you white savages, I amuse myself by presiding at the persecutions of Quakers and Anabaptists; I am the great patron and prompter of slave-dealers, and the grand-master of the Salem witches."

"The upshot of all which is, that, if I mistake not," said Tom, sturdily, "you are he commonly called Old Scratch."

"The same, at your service!" replied the black man, with a half civil nod.

Such was the opening of this interview, according to the old story; though it has almost too familiar an air to be credited. One would think that to meet with such a singular personage, in this wild, lonely place, would have shaken any man's nerves; but Tom was a hard-minded fellow, not easily daunted, and he had lived so long with a termagant wife, that he did not even fear the devil.

It is said that after this commencement they had a long and earnest conversation together, as Tom returned homeward. The black man told him of great sums of money buried by Kidd the pirate, under the oak-trees on the high ridge, not far from the morass. All these were under his command, and protected by his power, so that none could find them but such as propitiated his favor. These he offered to place within Tom Walker's reach, having conceived an especial kindness for him; but they were to be had only on certain conditions. What these conditions were may be easily surmised, though Tom never disclosed them publicly. They must have been very hard, for he required time to think of them, and he was not a man to stick at trifles when money was in view. When they had reached the edge of the swamp, the stranger paused. "What proof have I that all you have been telling me is true?" said Tom. "There's my signature," said the black man, pressing his finger on Tom's forehead. So saying, he turned off among the thickest of the swamp, and seemed, as Tom said, to go down, down, down, into the earth, until nothing but his head and shoulders could be seen, and so on, until he totally disappeared.

When Tom reached home, he found the black print of a finger burnt, as it were, into his forehead, which nothing could obliterate.

The first news his wife had to tell him was the sudden death of Absalom Crowninshield, the rich buccaneer. It was announced in the papers with the usual flourish, that "A great man had fallen in Israel."

Tom recollected the tree which his black friend had just hewn down, and which was ready for burning. "Let the freebooter roast," said Tom; "who cares!" He now felt convinced that all he had heard and seen was no illusion.

He was not prone to let his wife into his confidence; but as this was an uneasy secret, he willingly shared it with her. All her avarice was awakened at the mention of hidden gold, and she urged her husband to comply with the black man's terms, and secure what would make them wealthy for life. However Tom might have felt disposed to sell himself to the devil, he was determined not to do so to oblige his wife; so he flatly refused, out of the mere spirit of contradiction. Many and bitter were the quarrels they had on the subject; but the more she talked, the more resolute was Tom not to be damned to please her.

At length she determined to drive the bargain on her own account, and if she succeeded, to keep all the gain to herself. Being of the same fearless temper as her husband, she set off for the old Indian fort towards the close of a summer's day. She was many hours absent. When she came back, she was reserved and sullen in her replies. She spoke something of a black man, whom she met about twilight hewing at the root of a tall tree. He was sulky, however, and would not come to terms; she was to go again with a propitiatory offering, but what it was she forbore to say.

The next evening she set off again for the swamp, with her apron heavily laden. Tom waited and waited for her, but in vain; midnight came, but she did not make her appearance: morning, noon, night returned, but still she did not come. Tom now grew uneasy for her safety, especially as he found she had carried off in her apron the silver tea-pot and spoons, and every portable article of value. Another night elapsed, another morning came; but no wife. In a word, she was never heard of more.

What was her real fate nobody knows, in consequence of so many pretending to know. It is one of those facts which have become confounded by a variety of historians. Some asserted that she lost her way among the tangled mazes of the swamp, and sank into some pit or slough; others, more uncharitable, hinted that she had eloped with the household booty, and made off to some other province; while others surmised that the tempter had decoyed her into a dismal quagmire, on the top of which her hat was found lying. In confirmation of this, it was said a great black man, with an axe on his shoulder, was seen late that very evening coming out of the swamp, carrying a bundle tied in a check apron, with an air of surly triumph.

The most current and probable story, however, observes, that Tom Walker grew so anxious about the fate of his wife and his property, that he set out at length to seek them both at the Indian fort. During a long summer's afternoon he searched about the gloomy place, but no wife was to be seen. He called her name repeatedly, but she was nowhere to be heard. The bittern alone responded to his voice, as he flew screaming by; or the bullfrog croaked dolefully from a neighboring pool. At length, it is said, just in the brown hour of twilight, when the owls began to hoot, and the bats to flit about, his attention was attracted by the clamor of carrion crows hovering about a cypress-tree. He looked up, and beheld a bundle tied in a check apron, and hanging in the branches of the tree, with a great vulture perched hard by, as if keeping watch upon it. He leaped with joy; for he recognized his wife's apron, and supposed it to contain the household valuables.

"Let us get hold of the property," said he, consolingly to himself, "and we will endeavor to do without the woman."

As he scrambled up the tree, the vulture spread its wide wings, and sailed off screaming, into the deep shadows of the forest. Tom seized the checked apron, but, woful sight! found nothing but a heart and liver tied up in it!

Such, according to this most authentic old story, was all that was to be found of Tom's wife. She had probably attempted to deal with the black man as she had been accustomed to deal with her husband; but though a female scold is generally considered a match for the devil, yet in this instance she appears to have had the worst of it. She must have died game, however; for it is said Tom noticed many prints of cloven feet stamped upon the tree, and found handfuls of hair, that looked as if they had been plucked from the coarse black shock of the woodman. Tom knew his wife's prowess by experience. He shrugged his shoulders, as he looked at the signs of a fierce, clapper-clawing. "Egad," said he to himself, "Old Scratch must have had a tough time of it!"

Tom consoled himself for the loss of his property with the loss of his wife, for he was a man of fortitude. He even felt something like gratitude towards the black woodman, who, he considered, had done him a kindness. He sought, therefore, to cultivate a further acquaintance with him, but for some time without success; the old black-legs played shy, for whatever people may think, he is not always to be had for calling for: he knows how to play his cards when pretty sure of his game.

At length, it is said, when delay had whetted Tom's eagerness to the quick, and prepared him to agree to anything rather than not gain the promised treasure, he met the black man one evening in his usual woodman's dress, with his axe on his shoulder, sauntering along the swamp, and humming a tune. He affected to receive Tom's advances with great indifference, made brief replies, and went on humming his tune.

By degrees, however, Tom brought him to business, and they began to haggle about the terms on which the former was to have the pirate's treasure. There was one condition which need not be mentioned, being generally understood in all cases where the devil grants favors; but there were others about which, though of less importance, he was inflexibly obstinate. He insisted that the money found through his means should be employed in his service. He proposed, therefore, that Tom should employ it in the black traffic; that is to say, that he should fit out a slave-ship. This, however, Tom resolutely refused: he was bad enough in all conscience; but the devil himself could not tempt him to turn slave-trader.

Finding Tom so squeamish on this point, he did not insist upon it, but proposed, instead, that he should turn usurer; the devil being extremely anxious for the increase of usurers, looking upon them as his peculiar people.

To this no objections were made, for it was just to Tom's taste.

"You shall open a broker's shop in Boston next month," said the black man.

"I'll do it to-morrow if you wish," said Tom Walker.

"You shall lend money at two per cent a month."

"Egad, I'll charge four!" replied Tom Walker.

"You shall extort bonds, foreclose mortgages, drive the merchants to bankruptcy"——

"I'll drive them to the d——l," cried Tom Walker.

"You are the usurer for my money!" said black-legs with delight. "When will you want the rhino?"

"This very night."

"Done!" said the devil.

"Done!" said Tom Walker.—So they shook hands and struck a bargain.

A few days time saw Tom Walker seated behind his desk in a counting-house in Boston.

His reputation for a ready-moneyed man, who would lend money out for a good consideration, soon spread abroad. Everybody remembers the time of Governor Belcher, when money was particularly scarce. It was a time of paper credit. The country had been deluged with government bills, the famous Land Bank had been established; there had been a rage for speculating; the people had run mad with schemes for new settlements; for building cities in the wilderness; land-jobbers went about with maps of grants, and townships, and Eldorados, lying nobody knew where, but which everybody was ready to purchase. In a word, the great speculating fever which breaks out every now and then in the country, had raged to an alarming degree, and everybody was dreaming of making sudden fortunes from nothing. As usual the fever had subsided; the dream had gone off, and the imaginary fortunes with it; the patients were left in doleful plight, and the whole country resounded with the consequent cry of "hard times."

At this propitious time of public distress did Tom Walker set up as usurer in Boston. His door was soon thronged by customers. The needy and adventurous; the gambling speculator; the dreaming land-jobber; the thriftless tradesman; the merchant with cracked credit; in short, every one driven to raise money by desperate means and desperate sacrifices, hurried to Tom Walker.

Thus Tom was the universal friend of the needy, and acted like a "friend in need"; that is to say, he always exacted good pay and good security. In proportion to the distress of the applicant was the hardness of his terms. He accumulated bonds and mortgages; gradually squeezed his customers closer and closer: and sent them at length, dry as a sponge, from his door.

In this way he made money hand over hand; became a rich and mighty man, and exalted his cocked hat upon 'Change. He built himself, as usual, a vast house, out of ostentation; but left the greater part of it unfinished and unfurnished, out of parsimony. He even set up a carriage in the fullness of his vain-glory, though he nearly starved the horses which drew it; and as the ungreased wheels groaned and screeched on the axle-trees, you would have thought you heard the souls of the poor debtors he was squeezing.

As Tom waxed old, however, he grew thoughtful. Having secured the good things of this world, he began to feel anxious about those of the next. He thought with regret on the bargain he had made with his black friend, and set his wits to work to cheat him out of the conditions. He became, therefore, all of a sudden, a violent church-goer. He prayed loudly and strenuously, as if heaven were to be taken by force of lungs. Indeed, one might always tell when he had sinned most during the week, by the clamor of his Sunday devotion. The quiet Christians who had been modestly and steadfastly traveling Zionward, were struck with self-reproach at seeing themselves so sud-denly outstripped in their career by this new-made convert. Tom was as rigid in religious as in money matters; he was a stern supervisor and censurer of his neighbors, and seemed to think every sin entered up to their account became a credit on his own side of the page. He even talked of the expediency of reviv-ing the persecution of Quakers and Anabaptists. In a word, Tom's zeal became as notorious as his riches.

Still, in spite of all this strenuous attention to forms, Tom had a lurking dread that the devil, after all, would have his due. That he might not be taken unawares, therefore, it is said he always carried a small Bible in his coat-pocket. He had also a great folio Bible on his counting house desk, and would frequently be found reading it when people called on business; on such occasions he would lay his green spectacles in the book, to mark the place, while he turned round to drive some usurious bargain.

Some say that Tom grew a little crack-brained in his old days, and that, fancying his end approaching, he had his horse new shod, saddled and bridled, and buried with his feet uppermost; because he supposed that at the last day the world would be turned upside-down; in which case he should find his horse standing ready for mounting, and he was determined at the worst to give his old friend a run for it. This, however, is probably a mere old wives' fable. If he really did take such a precaution, it was totally superfluous; at least so says the authentic old legend, which closes his story in the following manner:

One hot summer afternoon in the dog-days, just as a terrible black thunder gust was coming up, Tom sat in his counting-house, in his white cap and India silk morning gown. He was on the point of foreclosing a mortgage, by which he would complete the ruin of an unlucky land-speculator for whom he had professed the greatest friendship. The poor land-jobber begged him to grant a few months' indulgence. Tom had grown testy and irritated, and refused another day.

"My family will be ruined and brought upon the parish," said the land-jobber. "Charity begins at home," replied Tom; "I must take care of myself in these hard times."

"You have made so much money out of me," said the speculator.

Tom lost his patience and his piety. "The devil take me," said he, "if I have made a farthing!"

Just then there were three loud knocks at the street door. He stepped out to see who was there. A black man was holding a black horse, which neighed and stamped with impatience.

"Tom, you're come for," said the black fellow, gruffly. Tom shrank back, but too late. He had left his little Bible at the bottom of his coat-pocket, and his big Bible on the desk buried under the mortgage he was about to foreclose; never was a sinner taken more unawares. The black man whisked him like a child into the saddle, gave the horse the lash, and away he galloped, with Tom on his back, in the midst of the thunderstorm. The clerks stuck their pens behind their ears, and stared after him from the windows. Away went Tom Walker, dashing down the streets; his white cap bobbing up and down; his morning-gown fluttering in the wind, and his steed striking fire out of the pavement at every bound.

When the clerks turned to look for the black man, he had disappeared.

Tom Walker never returned to foreclose the mortgage. A countryman, who lived on the border of the swamp, reported that in the height of the thundergust he had heard a great clattering of hoofs and a howling along the road, and running to the window caught sight of a figure, such as I have described, on a horse that galloped like mad across the fields, over the hills, and down into the black hemlock swamp towards the old Indian fort; and that shortly after a thunder-bolt falling in that direction seemed to set the whole forest in a blaze.

The good people of Boston shook their heads and shrugged their shoulders, but had been so much accustomed to witches and goblins, and tricks of the devil, in all kinds of shapes, from the first settlement of the colony, that they were not so much horror-struck as might have been expected. Trustees were appointed to take charge of Tom's effects. There was nothing, however, to administer upon. On searching his coffers, all his bonds and mortgages were found reduced to cinders. In place of gold and silver, his iron chest was filled with chips and shavings; two skeletons lay in his stable instead of his half-starved horses, and the very next day his great house took fire and burnt to the ground.

Such was the end of Tom Walker and his ill-gotten wealth. Let all griping money-brokers lay this story to heart. The truth of it is not to be doubted. The very hole under the oak-trees whence he dug Kidd's money is to be seen to this day; and the neighboring swamp and old Indian fort are often haunted in stormy nights by a figure on horseback, in morning-gown and white cap, which is doubtless the troubled spirit of the usurer. In fact the story has resolved itself into a proverb; prevalent throughout New England, of "The Devil and Tom Walker."

THE ADVENTURE OF THE MASON

"There was once upon a time a poor mason, or bricklayer, in Granada, who kept all the saints' days and holidays, and Saint Monday into the bargain, and yet, with all his devotion, he grew poorer and poorer, and could scarcely earn bread for his numerous family. One night he was roused from his first sleep by a knocking at his door. He opened it, and beheld before him a tall, meagre, cadaverous-looking priest.

" 'Hark ye, honest friend!'said the stranger; 'I have observed that you are a good Christian, and one to be trusted; will you undertake a job this very night?'

" 'With all my heart, Señor Padre, on condition that I am paid accordingly.'

" 'That you shall be; but you must suffer yourself to be blindfolded.'

"To this the mason made no objection. So, being hoodwinked, he was led by the priest through various rough lanes and winding passages, until they stopped before the portal of a house. The priest then applied a key, turned a creaking lock, and opened what sounded like a ponderous door. They entered, the door was closed and bolted, and the mason was conducted through an echoing corridor and a spacious hall to an interior part of the building. Here the bandage was removed from his eyes, and he found himself in a *patio,* or court, dimly lighted by a single lamp. In the centre was the dry basin of an old Moorish fountain, under which the priest requested him to form a small vault, bricks and mortar being at hand for the purpose. He accordingly worked all night, but without finishing the job. Just before daybreak the priest put a piece of gold into his hand, and having again blindfolded him, conducted him back to his dwelling.

" 'Are you willing,' said he, 'to return and complete your work?'

" 'Gladly, Señor Padre, provided I am so well paid.'

" 'Well, then, to-morrow at midnight I will call again.'

"He did so, and the vault was completed.

" 'Now,' said the priest, 'you must help me to bring forth the bodies that are to be buried in this vault.'

"The poor mason's hair rose on his head at these words: he followed the priest, with trembling steps, into a retired chamber of the mansion, expecting to behold some ghastly spectacle of death, but was relieved on perceiving three or four portly jars standing in one corner. They were evidently full of money, and it was with great labor that he and the priest carried them forth and consigned them to their tomb. The vault was then closed, the pavement replaced, and all traces of the work were obliterated. The mason was again hoodwinked and led forth by a route different from that by which he had come. After they had wandered for a long time through a perplexed maze of lanes and alleys, they halted. The priest then put two pieces of gold into his hand: 'Wait here,' said he, 'until you hear the cathedral bell toll for matins. If you presume to uncover your eyes before that time, evil will befall you': so saying, he departed. The mason waited faithfully, amusing himself, by weighing the gold pieces in his hand, and clinking them against each other. The moment the cathedral bell rang its matin peal, he uncovered his eyes, and found himself on the banks of the Xenil, whence he made the best of his way home, and revelled with his family for a whole fortnight on the profits of his two nights' work; after which he was as poor as ever.

"He continued to work a little, and pray a good deal, and keep saints' days and holidays, from year to year, while his family grew up as gaunt and ragged as a crew of gypsies. As he was seated one evening at the door of his hovel, he was accosted by a rich old curmudgeon, who was noted for owning many houses, and being a griping landlord. The man of money eyed him for a moment from beneath a pair of anxious shagged eyebrows.

" 'I am told, friend, that you are very poor.'

" 'There is no denying the fact, Señor,—it speaks for itself.'

" 'I presume, then, that you will be glad of a job, and will work cheap.'

" 'As cheap, my master, as any mason in Granada.'

" 'That's what I want. I have an old house fallen

into decay, which costs me more money than it is worth to keep it in repair, for nobody will live in it; so I must contrive to patch it up and keep it together at as small expense as possible.'

"The mason was accordingly conducted to a large deserted house that seemed going to ruin. Passing through several empty halls and chambers, he entered an inner court, where his eye was caught by an old Moorish fountain. He paused for a moment, for a dreaming recollection of the place came over him.

" 'Pray,' said he, 'who occupied this house formerly?'

" 'A pest upon him!' cried the landlord; 'it was an old miserly priest, who cared for nobody but himself. He was said to be immensely rich, and, having no relations, it was though, he would leave all his treasures to the Church. He died suddenly, and the priests and friars thronged to take possession of his wealth, but nothing could they find but a few ducats in a leathern purse. The worst luck has fallen on me, for, since his death, the old fellow continued to occupy my house without paying rent, and there is no taking the law of a dead man. The people pretend to hear the clinking of gold all night in the chamber where the old priest slept, as if he were counting over his money, and sometimes a groaning and moaning about the court. Whether true or false, these stories have brought a bad name on my house, and not a tenant will remain in it.'

" 'Enough,' said the mason sturdily; 'let me live in your house rent-free until some better tenant present and I will engage to put it in repair, and to quiet the troubled spirit that disturbs it. I am a good Christian and a poor man, and am not to be daunted by the Devil himself, even though he should come in the shape of a big bag of money!'

"The offer of the honest mason was gladly accepted; he moved with his family into the house, an fulfilled all his engagements. By little and little he restored it to its former state; the clinking of gold was no more heard at night in the chamber of the defunct priest, but began to be heard by day in the pocket of the living mason. In a word, he increased rapidly in wealth, to the admiration of all his neighbors, and became one of the richest men in Granada: he gave large sums to the Church, by way, no doubt, of satisfying his conscience, and never revealed the secret of the vault until on his deathbed to his son and heir."

THE GOVERNOR
AND THE NOTARY

In former times there ruled, as governor of the Alhambra, a doughty old cavalier, who, from having lost one arm in the wars, was commonly known by the name of El Gobernador Manco, or "the one-armed governor." He in fact prided himself upon being an old soldier, wore his moustaches curled up to his eyes, a pair of campaigning boots, and a toledo as long as a spit, with his pocket-handkerchief in the basket-hilt.

He was, moreover, exceedingly proud and punctilious, and tenacious of all his privileges and dignities. Under his sway the immunities of the Alhambra, as a royal residence and domain, were rigidly exacted. No one was permitted to enter the fortress with firearms, or even with a sword or staff, unless he were of a certain rank; and every horseman was obliged to dismount at the gate, and lead his horse by the bridle. Now as the hill of the Alhambra rises from the very midst of the city of Granada, being, as it were, an excrescence of the capital, it must at all times be some-

212

what irksome to the captain-general, who commands the province, to have thus an *imperium in imperio,* a petty independent post in the very centre of his domains. It was rendered the more galling, in the present instance, from the irritable jealousy of the old governor, that took fire on the least question of authority and jurisdiction; and from the loose vagrant character of the people who had gradually nestled themselves within the fortress, as in a sanctuary, and thence carried on a system of roguery and depredation at the expense of the honest inhabitants of the city.

Thus there was a perpetual feud and heart-burning between the captain-general and the governor, the more virulent on the part of the latter, inasmuch as the smallest of two neighboring potentates is always the most captious about his dignity. The stately palace of the captain-general stood in the Plaza Nueva, immediately at the foot of the hill of the Alhambra; and here was always a bustle and parade of guards, and domestics, and city functionaries. A beetling bastion of the fortress overlooked the palace and public square in front of it; and on this bastion the old governor would occasionally strut backwards and forwards, with his toledo girded by his side, keeping a wary eye down upon his rival, like a hawk reconnoitring his quarry from his nest in a dry tree.

Whenever he descended into the city, it was in grand parade; on horseback, surrounded by his guards; or in his state coach, an ancient and unwieldy Spanish edifice of carved timber and gilt leather, drawn by eight mules, with running footmen, out-

riders, and lackeys; on which occasions he flattered
himself he impressed every beholder with awe and
admiration as viceregent of the king; though the wits
of Granada, particularly those who loitered about
the palace of the captain-general, were apt to sneer
at his petty parade, and, in allusion to the vagrant
character of his subjects, to greet him with the appellation of "the king of the beggars." One of the
most fruitful sources of dispute between these two
doughty rivals was the right claimed by the governor
to have all things passed free of duty through the
city that were intended for the use of himself or his
garrison. By degrees this privilege had given rise to
extensive smuggling. A nest of *contrabandistas* took
up their abode in the hovels of the fortress and the
numerous caves in its vicinity, and drove a thriving
business under the connivance of the soldiers of
the garrison.

The vigilance of the captain-general was aroused.
He consulted his legal adviser and factotum, a shrewd,
meddlesome *escribano,* or notary, who rejoiced in an
opportunity of perplexing the old potentate of the
Alhambra, and involving him in a maze of legal
subtleties. He advised the captain-general to insist
upon the right of examining every convoy passing
through the gates of his city, and penned a long letter
for him in vindication of the right. Governor Manco
was a straightforward cut-and-thrust old soldier, who
hated an *escribano worse than the devil, and this one*
in particular worse than all other *escribanos.*

"What!" said he, curling up his moustaches fiercely,
"does the captain-general set his man of the pen to

practise confusions upon me? I'll let him see an old soldier is not to be baffled by schoolcraft."

He seized his pen and scrawled a short letter in a crabbed hand, in which, without deigning to enter into argument, he insisted on the right of transit free of search, and denounced vengeance on any custom-house officer who should lay his unhallowed hand on any convoy protected by the flag of the Alhambra. While this question was agitated between the two pragmatical potentates, it so happened that a mule laden with supplies for the fortress arrived one day at the gate of Xenil, by which it was to traverse a suburb of the city on its way to the Alhambra. The convoy was headed by a testy old corporal, who had long served under the governor, and was a man after his own heart; as rusty and stanch as an old Toledo blade.

As they approached the gate of the city, the corporal placed the banner of the Alhambra on the pack-saddle of the mule, and drawing himself up to a perfect perpendicular, advanced with his head dressed to the front, but with the wary sideglance of a cur passing through hostile ground and ready for a snap and a snarl.

"Who goes there?" said the sentinel at the gate.

"Slodier of the Alhambra!" said the corporal, without turning his head.

"What have you in charge?"

"Provisions for the garrison."

"Proceed."

The corporal marched straight forward, followed by the convoy, but had not advanced many paces before a posse of custom-house officers rushed out of a small toll-house.

"Hallo there!" cried the leader. "Muleteer, halt, and open those packages."

The corporal wheeled round and drew himself up in battle array. "Respect the flag of the Alhambra," said he; "these things are for the governor."

"A *figo* for the governor and a *figo* for his flag. Muleteer, halt, I say."

"Stop the convoy at your peril!" cried the corporal, cocking his musket. "Muleteer, proceed."

The muleteer gave his beast a hearty thwack; the customhouse officer sprang forward and seized the halter; whereupon the corporal levelled his piece and shot him dead.

The street was immediately in an uproar.

The old corporal was seized, and after undergoing sundry kicks, and cuffs, and cudgellings, which are generally given impromptu by the mob in Spain as a foretaste of the after penalties of the law, he was loaded with irons and conducted to the city prison, while his comrades were permitted to proceed with the convoy, after it had been well rummaged, to the Alhambra.

The old governor was in a towering passion when he heard of this insult to his flag and capture of his corporal. For a time he stormed about the Moorish halls, and vapored about the bastions, and looked down fire and sword upon the palace of the captain-general. Having vented the first ebullition of his wrath, he despatched a message demanding the surrender of the corporal, as to him alone belonged the right of sitting in judgement of the offences of those under his command. The captain-general, aided by the pen of the delighted *escribano*, replied at great length, arguing that, as the offence had been committed within the walls of his city, and against one of his civil officers, it was clearly within his proper jurisdiction.

The governor rejoined by a repetition of his demand; the captain-general gave a surrejoinder of still greater length and legal acumen; the governor became hotter and more peremptory in his demands, and the captain-general cooler and more copious in his replies; unil the old lion-hearted soldier absolutely roared with fury at being thus entangled in the meshes of legal controversy.

While the subtle *escribano* was thus amusing himself at the expense of the governor, he was conducting the trial of the corporal, who, mewed up in a narrow dungeon of the prison, had merely a small grated window at which to show his iron-bound visage and receive the consolations of his friends.

A mountain of written testimony was diligently heaped up, according to Spanish form, by the indefatigable *escribano;* the corporal was completely overwhelmed by it. He was convicted of murder, and sentenced to be hanged.

It was in vain the governor sent down remonstrance and menace from the Alhambra. The fatal day was at hand, and the corporal was put *in capilla,* that is to say, in the chapel of the prison, as is always done with cuptrits the day before execution, that they may meditate on their approaching end and repent them of their sins.

Seeing things drawing to extremity, the old governor determined to attend to the affair in person. For this purpose he ordered out his carriage of state, and, surrounded by his guards, rumbled down the avenue of the Alhambra into the city. Driving to the house of the *escribano,* he summoned him to the portal.

The eye of the old governor gleamed like a coal at beholding the smirking man of the law advancing with an air of exultation.

"What is this I hear," cried he, "that you are about to put to death one of my soldiers?"

"All according to law—all in strict form of justice," said the self-sufficient *escribano,* chuckling and rubbing his hands; "I can show your Excellency the written testimony in the case."

"Fetch it hither," said the governor. The *escribano* bustled into his office, delighted with having another opportunity of displaying his ingenuity at the expense of the hard-headed veteran. He returned with a satchel full of papers, and began to read a long deposition with professional volubility. By this time a crowd had collected, listening with outstretched necks and gaping mouths.

"Prithee, man, get into the carriage, out of this pestilent throng, that I may the better hear thee," said the governor.

The *escribano* entered the carriage, when, in a twinkling, the door was closed, the coachman smacked his whip, —mules, carriage, guards, and all dashed off at a thundering rate, leaving the crowd in gaping wonderment; nor did the governor pause until he had lodged his prey in one of the strongest dungeons of the Alhambra.

He then sent down a flag of truce in military style, proposing a cartel, or exchange or prisoners, —the corporal for the notary. The pride of the captain-general was piqued; he returned a contemptuous refusal, and forthwith caused a gallows, tall and strong, to be erected in the centre of the Plaza Nueva for the execution of the corporal.

"Oho! is that the game?" said Governor Manco. He gave orders, and immediately a gibbet was reared on the verge of the great beetling bastion that overlooked the Plaza. "Now," said he, in a message to the captain-general, "hang my soldier when you please; but at the same time that he is swung off in the square, look up to see your *escribano* dangling against the sky."

The captain-general was inflexible; troops were paraded in the square; the drums beat, the bell tolled. An immense multitude of amateurs gathered together to behold the execution. On the other hand, the governor paraded his garrison on the bastion, and tolled the funeral dirge of the notary from the Torre de la campana, or Tower of the Bell.

The notary's wife pressed through the crowd, with a whole progeny of little embryo *escribanos* at her heels, and throwing herself at the feet of the captain-general, implored him not to sacrifice the life of her husband, and the welfare of herself and her numerous little ones, to a point of pride; "for you know the old governor too well," said she, "to doubt that he will put his threat into execution, if you hang the soldier."

The captain-general was overpowered by her tears and lamentations, and the clamors of her callow brood. The corporal was sent up to the Alhambra, under a guard, in his gallows garb, like a hooded friar, but with head erect and a face of iron. The *escribano* was demanded in exchange, according to the cartel. The once bustling and self-sufficient man of the law was drawn forth from his dungeon more dead than alive. All his flippany and conceit had evaporated; his hair, it is said, had nearly turned gray with affright, and he had a downcast, dogged look, as if he still felt the halter round his neck.

The old governor stuck his one arm akimbo, and for a moment surveyed him with an iron smile. "Henceforth, my friend," said he, "moderate your zeal in hurrying others to the gallows; be not too certain of your safety, even though you should have the law on your side; and above all, take care how you play off your schoolcraft another time upon an old soldier."

THE GRAND PRAIRIE—
A BUFFALO HUNT

After proceeding about two hours in a southerly direction, we emerged towards mid-day from the dreary belt of the Cross Timber, and to our infinite delight beheld "the Great Prairie," stretching to the right and left before us. We could distinctly trace the meandering course of the Main Canadian, and various smaller streams, by the strips of green forests that bordered them. The landscape was vast and beautiful. There is always an expansion of feeling in looking upon these boundless and fertile wastes; but I was doubly conscious of it after emerging from our "close dungeon of innumerous boughs."

From a rising ground Beatte pointed out the place he and his comrades had killed the buffaloes; and we beheld several black objects moving in the distance, which he said were part of the herd. The Captain determined to shape his course to a woody bottom about a mile distant, and to encamp there for a day for two, by way of having a regular buffalo-hunt, and getting a supply of provisions. As the troop defiled along the slope of the hill towards the camping ground, Beatte proposed to my messmates and myself, that we should put ourselves under his guidance, promising to take us where we should have plenty of sport. Leaving the line of march, therefore, we diverged towards the prairie; traversing a small valley, and ascending a gentle swell of land. As we reached the summit, we beheld a gang of wild horses about a mile off. Beattle was immediately on the alert, and no longer thought of buffalo hunting. He was mounted on his powerful half wild horse, with a lariat coiled at the saddle-bow, and set off in pursuit; while we remained on a rising ground watching his manœuvres with great solicitude. Taking advantage of a strip of woodland, he stole quietly along, so as to get close to them before he was perceived. The moment they caught sight of him a grand scamper took place. We watched him skirting along the horizon like a privateer in full chase of a merchantman; at length he passed over the brow of a ridge, and down a shallow valley; in a few moments he was on the opposite hill, and close upon one of the horses. He was soon head and head, and appeared to be trying to noose his prey; but they both disappeared again behind the hill, and we saw no more of them. It turned out afterwards that he had noosed a powerful horse, but could not hold him, and had lost his lariat in the attempt.

While we were waiting for his return, we perceived two buffalo descending a slope, towards a stream, which wound through a ravine fringed with trees.

The young Count and myself endeavored to get near them under covert of the trees. They discovered us while we were yet three or four hundred yards off, and turning about, retreated up the rising ground. We urged our horses across the ravine, and gave chase. The immense weight of head and shoulders causes the buffalo to labor heavily up-hill; but it accelerates his descent. We had the advantage, therefore, and gained rapidly upon the fugitives, though it was difficult to get our horses to approach them, their very scent inspiring them with terror. The Count, who had a double-barrelled gun loaded with ball, fired, but it missed. The bulls now altered their course, and galloped down-hill with headlong rapidity. As they ran in different directions, we each singled one and separated. I was provided with a brace of veteran brass-barrelled pistols, which I had borrowed at Fort Gibson, and which had evidently seen some service. Pistols are very effective in buffalo hunting, as the hunter can ride up close to the animal, and fire it while at full speed; whereas the long heavy rifles used on the frontier, cannot be easily managed, nor discharged with accurate aim from horseback. My object, therefore, was to get within pistol-shot of the buffalo. This was no very easy matter. I was well mounted on a horse of excellent speed and bottom, that seemed eager for the chase, and soon overtook the game; but the moment he came nearly parallel, he would keep sheering off, with ears forked and pricked forward, and every symptom of aversion and alarm. It was no wonder.

Of all animals, a buffalo, when close pressed by the hunter, has an aspect the most diabolical. His two short black horns curve out of a huge frontlet of shaggy hair; his eyes glow like coals; his mouth is open; his tongue parched and drawn up into a half crescent; his tail is erect, and tufted and whisking about in the air; he is a perfect picture of mingled rage and terror.

It was with difficulty I urged my horse sufficiently near, when, taking aim, to my chagrin both pistols missed fire. Unfortunately the locks of these veteran weapons were so much worn, that in the gallop the priming had been shaken out of the pans. At the snapping of the last pistol I was close upon the buffalo, when, in his despair, he turned round with a sudden snort, and rushed upon me. My horse wheeled about as if on a pivot, made a convulsive spring, and, as I had been leaning on one side with pistol extended, I came near being thrown at the feet of the buffalo.

Three or four bounds of the horse carried us out of the reach of the enemy, who, having merely turned in desperate self-defence, quickly resumed his flight. As soon as I could gather in my panic-stricken horse, and prime the pistols afresh, I again spurred in pursuit of the buffalo, who had slackened his speed to take breath. On my approach he again set off full tilt, heaving himself forward with a heavy rolling gallop, dashing with headlong precipitation through brakes and ravines, while several deer and wolves, startled from their coverts by his thundering career, ran helter-skelter to right and left across the waste.

A gallop across the prairies in pursuit of game is by no means so smooth a career as those may imagine who have only the idea of an open level plain. It is true, the prairies of the hunting ground are not so much entangled with flowering plants and long herbage as the lower prairies, and are principally covered with short buffalo-grass; but they are diversified by hill and dale, and where most level, are apt to be cut up by deep rifts and ravines, made by torrents after rains; and which, yawning from an even surface, are almost like pitfalls in the way of the hunter, checking him suddenly when in full career, or subjecting him to the risk of limb and life. The plains, too, are beset by burrowing-holes of small animals, in which the horse is apt to sink to the fetlock, and throw both himself and his rider. The late rain had covered some parts of the prairie, where the ground was hard, with a thin sheet of water, through which the horse had to splash his way. In other parts there were innumerable shallow hollows, eight or ten feet in diameter, made by the buffaloes, who wallow in sand and mud like swine. These being filled with water, shone like mirrors, so that the horse was continually leaping over them or springing on one side. We had reached, too, a rough part of the prairie, very much broken and cut up; the buffalo, who was running for life, took no heed to his course, plunging down break-neck ravines, where it was necessary to skirt the borders in search of a safer descent. At length we came to where a winter stream had torn a deep chasm across the whole prairie, leaving open jagged rocks, and forming a long glen bordered by steep crumbling cliffs of mingled stone and clay. Down one of these the buffalo flung himself, half tumbling, half leaping, and then scuttled along the bottom; while I, seeing all furher pursuit useless, pulled up, and gazed quietly after him from the border of the cliff, until he disappeared amidst the windings of the ravine.

Nothing now remained but to turn my steed and rejoin my companions. Here at first was some little difficulty. The ardor of the chase had betrayed me into a long, heedless gallop. I now found myself in the midst of a lonely waste, in which the prospect was bounded by undulating swells of land, naked and uniform, where, from the deficiency of landmarks and distinct features, an inexperienced man may become bewildered, and lose his way as readily as in the wastes of the ocean. The day, too, was overcast, so that I could not guide myself by the sun; my only mode was to retrace the track my horse had made in coming, though this I would often lose sight of, where the ground was covered with parched herbage.

To one unaccustomed to it, there is something inexpressibly lonely in the solitude of a prairie. The loneliness of a forest seems nothing to it. There the view is shut in by trees, and the imagination is left free to picture some livelier scene beyond. But here we have an immense extent of landscape without a sign of human existence. We have the consciousness of being far, far beyond the bounds of human habitation; we feel as if moving in the midst of a desert world. As my horse lagged slowly back over the scenes of our late scamper, and the delirium of the chase had passed away, I was peculiarly sensible to these circumstances. The silence of the waste was now and then broken by the cry of a distant flock of pelicans, stalking like spectres about a shallow pool; sometimes by the sinister croaking of a raven in the air, while occasionally a scoundrel wolf would scour off from before me, and, having attained a safe distance, would sit down and howl and whine with tones that gave a dreariness to the surrounding solitude.

After pursuing my way for some time, I descried a horseman on the edge of a distant hill, and soon recognized him to be the Count. He had been equally unsuccessful with myself; we were shortly after rejoined by our worthy comrade, the Virtuoso, who, with spectacle on nose, had made two or three ineffectual shots from horseback.

We determined not to seek the camp until we had made one more effort. Casting our eyes about the surrounding waste, we descried a herd of buffalo about two miles distant, scattered apart, and quietly grazing near a small strip of trees and bushes. It required but little stretch of fancy to picture them so many cattle grazing on the edge of a common, and that the grove might shelter some lonely farm-house.

We now formed our plan to circumvent the herd,

and by getting on the other side of them, to hunt
them in the direction where we knew our camp to be
situated: otherwise, the pursuit might take us to such
a distance as to render it impossible to find our way
back before nightfall. Taking a wide circuit, therefore, we moved slowly and cautiously, pausing occasionally when we saw any of the herd desist from
grazing. The wind fortunately set from them, otherwise they might have scented us and have taken the
alarm. In this way we succeeded in getting round the
herd without disturbing it. It consisted of about
forty head; bulls, cows, and calves. Separating to
some distance from each other, we now approached
slowly in a parallel line, hoping by degrees to steal
near without exciting attention. They began, however, to move off quietly, stopping at every step or
two to graze, when suddenly a bull, that, unobserved
by us, had been taking his siesta under a clump of
trees to our left, roused himself from his lair, and
hastened to join his companions. We were still at a
considerable distance, but the game had taken
the alarm. We quickened our pace; they broke
into a gallop, and now commenced a full chase.

As the ground was level, they shouldered along
with great speed, following each other in a line; two
or three bulls bringing up the rear, the last of whom,
from his enormous size and venerable frontlet, and
beard of sunburnt hair, looked like the patriarch of
the herd, and as if he might long have reigned the
monarch of the prairie.

There is a mixture of the awful and the comic in

the look of these huge animals, as they bear their
great bulk forwards, with an up and down motion of
the unwieldy head and shoulders, their tail cocked
up like the cue of a Pantaloon in a pantomime, the
end whisking about in a fierce yet whimsical style,
and their eyes glaring venomously with an expression
of fright and fury.

For some time I kept parallel with the line, without being able to force my horse within pistol-shot,
so much had he been alarmed by the assault of the
buffalo in the preceding chase. At length I succeeded,
but was again balked by my pistols missing fire. My
companions, whose horses were less fleet and more
wayworn, could not overtake the herd; at length Mr.
L., who was in the rear of the line, and losing
ground, levelled his double-barrelled gun, and fired
a long raking shot. It struck a buffalo just above the
loins, broke its backbone, and brought it to the
ground. He stopped and alighted to dispatch his prey,
when, borrowing his gun, which had yet a charge
remaining in it, I put my horse to his speed, again
overtook the herd which was thundering along, pursued by the Count. With my present weapon there
was no need of urging my horse to such close quarters; galloping along parallel, therefore, I singled out
a buffalo, and by a fortunate shot brought it down
on the spot. The ball had struck a vital part; it could
not move from the place where it fell, but lay there
struggling in mortal agony, while the rest of the herd
kept on their headlong career across the prairie.

Dismounting, I now fettered my horse to prevent

his straying, and advanced to contemplate my victim. I am nothing of a sportsman; I had been prompted to this unwonted exploit by the magnitude of the game and the excitement of an adventurous chase. Now that the excitement was over, I could not but look with commiseration upon the poor animal that lay struggling and bleeding at my feet. His very size and importance, which had before inspired me with eagerness, now increased my compunction. It seemed as if I had inflicted pain in proportion to the bulk of my victim, and as if there were a hundred-fold greater waste of life than there would have been in the destruction of an animal of inferior size.

To add to these after-qualms of conscience, the poor animal lingered in his agony. He had evidently received a mortal wound, but death might be long in coming. It would not do to leave him here to be torn piecemeal while yet alive, by the wolves that had already snuffed his blood, and were skulking and howling at a distance, and waiting for my departure; and by the ravens that were flapping about, croaking dismally in the air. It became now an act of mercy to give him his quietus, and put him out of his misery. I primed one of the pistols, therefore, and advanced close up to the buffalo. To inflict a wound thus in cold blood, I found a totally different thing from firing in the heat of the chase. Taking aim, however, just behind the fore-shoulder, my pistol for once proved true; the ball must have passed through the heart, for the animal gave one convulsive throe and expired.

While I stood meditating and moralizing over the wreck I had so wantonly produced, with my horse grazing near me, I was rejoined by my fellow-sportsman the Virtuoso, who, being a man of universal adroitness, and withal more experienced and hardened in the gentle art of "venerie," soon managed to carve out the tongue of the buffalo, and delivered it to me to bear back to the camp as a trophy.

THE FIELD OF WATERLOO

I have spoken heretofore with some levity of the contrast that exists between the English and French character; but it deserves more serious consideration. They are the two great nations of modern times most diametrically opposed, and most worthy of each other's rivalry; essentially distinct in their characters, excelling in opposite qualities, and reflecting lustre on each other by their very opposition. In noting is this contrast more strikingly evinced than in their military conduct. For ages have they been contending, and for ages have they crowded each other's history with acts of splendid heroism. Take the Battle of Waterloo, for instance, the last and most memorable trial of their rival prowess. Nothing could surpass the brilliant daring on the one side, and the steadfast enduring on the other. The French cavalry broke like waves on the compact squares of English infantry. They were seen galloping round those serried walls of men, seeking in vain for an entrance; tossing their arms in the air, in the heat of their enthusiasm, and braving the whole front of battle. The British troops, on the other hand, forbidden to move or fire, stood firm and enduring. Their columns were ripped up by cannonry; whole rows were swept down at a shot; the survivors closed their ranks, and stood firm. In this way many columns stood through the pelting of the iron tempest without firing a shot, without any action to stir their blood or excite their spirits. Death thinned their ranks, but could not shake their souls.

A beautiful instance of the quick and generous impulses to which the French are prone is given in the case of a French cavalier in the hottest of the action, charging furiously upon a British officer, but, perceiving in the moment of assault that his adversary had lost his sword-arm, dropping the point of his sabre, and courteously riding on. Peace be with that generous warrior, whatever were his fate! If he went down in the storm of battle, with the foundering fortunes of his chieftain, may the turf of Waterloo grow green above his grave!— and happier far would be the fate of such a spirit to sink amidst the tempest, unconscious of defeat, than to survive and mourn over the blighted laurels of his country.

In this way the two armies fought through a long and bloody day,—the French with enthusiastic valor, the English with cool, inflexible courage, until Fate, as if to leave the question of superiority still undecided between two such adversaries, brought up the Prussians to decide the fortunes of the field.

It was several years afterward that I visited the field of Waterloo. The ploughshare had been busy with its oblivious labors, and the frequent harvest had nearly obliterated the vestiges of war. Still the blackened ruins of Hougoumont stood, a monumental pile to mark the violence of this vehement struggle. Its broken walls, pierced by bullets and shattered by explosions, showed the deadly strife that had taken place within, when Gaul and Briton, hemmed in between narrow walls, hand to hand and foot to foot, fought from garden to court-yard, from court-yard to chamber, with intense and concentrated rivalship. Columns of smoke towered from this vortex of battle as from a volcano: "It was," said my guide, "like a little hell upon earth." Not far off, two or three broad spots of rank, unwholesome green still marked the places where these rival warriors, after their fierce and fitful struggle, slept quietly together in the lap of their common mother earth. Over all the rest of the field peace had resumed its sway. The thoughtless whistle of the peasant floated on the air instead of the trumpet's clangor; the team slowly labored up the hillside once shaken by the hoofs of rushing squadrons; and wide fields of corn waved peacefully over the soldier's grave, as summer seas dimple over the place where the tall ship lies buried.

To the foregoing desultory notes on the French military character, let me append a few traits which I picked up verbally in one of the French provinces. They may have already appeared in print, but I have never met with them.

At the breaking out of the revolution, when so

many of the old families emigrated, a descendant of the great Turenne, by the name of De Latour d'Auvergne, refused to accompany his relations, and entered into the republican army. He served in all the campaigns of the revolution, distinguished himself by his valor, his accomplishments, and his generous spirit, and might have risen to fortune and to the highest honors. He refused, however, all rank in the army above that of captain, and would receive no recompense for his achievements but a sword of honor. Napoleon, in testimony of his merits, gave him the title of *Premier Grenadier de France* (First Grenadier of France), which was the only title he would ever bear. He was killed in Germany at the battle of Neuburg. To honor his memory, his place was always retained in his regiment as if he still occupied it; and whenever the regiment was mustered, and the name of De Latour d'Auvergne was called out, the reply was: "Dead on the field of honor!"

THE CREOLE VILLAGE

A Sketch From a Steamboat

In travelling about our motley country, I am often reminded of Ariosto's account of the moon, in which the good paladin Astolpho found everything garnered up that had been lost on earth. So I am apt to imagine that many things lost in the Old World are treasured up in the New; having been handed down from generation to generation, since the early days of the colonies. A European antiquary, therefore, curious in his researches after the ancient and almost obliterated customs and usages of his country, would do well to put himself upon the track of some early band of emigrants, follow them across the Atlantic, and rummage among their descendants on our shores.

In the phraseology of New England might be found many an old English provincial phrase, long since obsolete in the parent country; with some quaint relics of the Roundheads; while Virginia cherishes peculiarities characteristic of the days of Elizabeth and Sir Walter Raleigh.

In the same way, the sturdy yeomanry of New Jersey and Pennsylvania keep up many usages fading away in ancient Germany; while many an honest, broad-bottomed custom, nearly extinct in venerable Holland, may be found flourishing in pristine vigor and luxuriance in Dutch villages, on the banks of the Mohawk and the Hudson.

In no part of our country, however, are the customs and peculiarities imported from the old world by the earlier settlers kept up with more fidelity than in the little, poverty-stricken villages of Spanish and French origin, which bordered the rivers of ancient Louisiana. Their population is generally made up of the descendants of those nations, married and interwoven together, and occasionally crossed with a slight dash of the Indian. The French character, however, floats on top, as, from its buoyant qualities, it is sure to do, whenever it forms a particle, however small, of an intermixture.

In these serene and dilapidated villages, art and nature stand still, and the world forgets to turn round. The revolutions that distract other parts of this mutable planet, reach not here, or pass over without leaving any trace. The fortunate inhabitants have none of that public spirit which extends its cares beyond its horizon, and imports trouble and perplexity from all quarters in newspapers. In fact, newspapers are almost unknown in these villages; and, as French is the current language, the inhabitants have little community of opinion with their republican neighbors. They retain, therefore, their old habits of passive obedience to the decrees of government, as though they still lived under the absolute sway of colonial commandments, instead of being part and parcel of the sovereign people, and having a voice in public legislation.

A few aged men, who have grown gray on their hereditary acres, and are of the good old colonial stock, exert a patriarchal sway in all matters of public and private import; their opinions are considered oracular, and their word is law.

The inhabitants, moreover, have none of that eagerness for gain, and rage for improvement, which keep our people continually on the move, and our country towns incessantly in a state of transition. There the magic phrases, "town lots," "water privileges," "railroads," and other comprehensive and soul-stirring words from the speculator's vocabulary, are never heard. The residents dwell in the houses built by their forefathers, without thinking of enlarging or modernizing them, or pulling them down and turning them into granite stores. The trees under which they have been born, and have played in infancy, flourish undisturbed; though, by cutting them down, they might open new streets, and put money in their pockets. In a word, the almighty dollar, that great object of universal devotion throughout our land, seems to have no genuine devotees in these peculiar villages; and unless some of its missionaries penetrate there, and erect banking-houses and other pious shrines, there is no knowing how long the inhabitants may remain in their present state of contented poverty.

In descending one of our great western rivers in a steamboat, I met with two worthies from one of these villages, who had been on a distant excursion, the longest they had ever made, as they seldom ventured far from home. One was the great man, or Grand Seigneur of the village; not that he enjoyed any legal privileges or power there, everything of the kind having been done away with when the province was ceded by France to the United States. His sway over his neighbors was merely one of custom and convention, out of deference to his family. Beside, he was worth full fifty thousand dollars, an amount almost equal, in the imaginations of the villagers, to the treasures of King Solomon.

This very substantial old gentleman, though of the fourth or fifth generation in this country, retained the true Gallic feature and deportment, and reminded me of one of those provincial potentates that are to be met with in the remote parts of France. He was of a large frame, a ginger-bread complexion, strong features, eyes that stood out like glass knobs, and a prominent nose, which he frequently regaled from a gold snuff-box, and occasionally blew with a colored handkerchief, until it sounded like a trumpet.

He was attended by an old Negro, as black as ebony, with a huge mouth, in a continual grin; evidently a privileged and favorite servant, who had grown up and grown old with him. He was dressed in creole style, with white jacket and trousers, a stiff

shirt-collar, what threatened to cut off his ears, a
bright Madras handkerchief tied round his head, and
large gold ear-rings. He was the politest Negro I
met within a western tour, and that is saying a great
deal, for, excepting the Indians, the Negroes are the
most gentlemanlike personages to be met with in
those parts. It is true they differ from the Indians in
being a little extra polite and complimentary. He was
also one of the merriest; and here, too, the Negroes,
however we may deplore their unhappy condition,
have the advantage of their masters. The whites are,
in general, too free and prosperous to be merry. The
cares of maintaining their rights and liberties, adding
to their wealth, and making presidents, engross all
their thoughts and dry up all the moisture of their
souls. If you hear a broad, hearty, devil-may-care
laugh, be assured it is a Negro's.

Beside this African domestic, the seigneur of the
village had another no less cherished and privileged
attendant. This was a huge dog, of the mastiff breed,
with a deep, hanging mouth, and a look of surly
gravity. He walked about the cabin with the air of a
dog perfectly at home, and who had paid for his
passage. At dinner-time he took his seat beside his
master, giving him a glance now and then out of a
corner of his eye, which bespoke perfect confidence
that he would not be forgotten. Nor was he. Every
now and then a huge morsel would be thrown to
him, peradventure the half-picked leg of a fowl,
which he would receive with a snap like the springing of a steel trap,—one gulp, and all was down;

and a glance of the eye told his master that he was ready for another consignment.

The other village worthy, travelling in company with the seigneur, was of a totally different stamp; small, thin, and weazen-faced, as Frenchmen are apt to be represented in caricature, with a bright, squirrel-like eye, and a gold ring in his ear. His dress was flimsy, and sat loosely on his frame, and he had altogether the look of one with but little coin in his pocket. Yet, though one of the poorest, I was assured he was one of the merriest and most popular personages in his native village.

Compére Martin, as he was commonly called, was the factotum of the place—sportsman, shoolmaster, and land-surveyor. He could sing, dance, and, above all, play on the fiddle, an invaluable accomplishment in an old French creole village, for the inhabitants have a hereditary love for balls and *fétes*. If they work but little they dance a great deal; and a fiddle is the joy of their heart.

What had sent Compére Martin travelling with the Grand Seigneur I could not learn. He evidently looked up to him with great deference, and was assiduous in rendering him petty attentions; from which I concluded that he lived at home upon the crumbs which fell from his table. He was gayest when out of his sight, and had his song and his joke when forward among the deck passengers; but, altogether, Compére Martin was out of his element on board of a steamboat. He was quite another being I am told, when at home in his own village.

Like his opulent fellow-traveller, he too had his canine follower and retainer—and one suited to his different fortunes—one of the civilest, most unoffending little dogs in the world. Unlike the lordly mastiff, he seemed to think he had no right on board of the steamboat; if you did but look hard at him, he would throw himself upon his back, and lift up his legs, as if imploring mercy.

At table he took his seat a little distance from his master; not with the bluff, confident air of the mastiff, but quietly and diffidently; his head on one side, with one ear dubiously slouched, the other hopefully cocked up; his under-teeth projecting beyond his black nose, and his eye wistfully following each morsel that went into his master's mouth.

If Compére Martin now and then should venture to abstract a morsel from his plate, to give to his humble companion, it was edifying to see with what diffidence the exemplary little animal would take hold of it, with the very tip of his teeth, as if he would almost rather not, or was fearful of taking too great a liberty. And then with what decorum would he eat it! How many efforts would he make in swallowing it, as if it stuck in his throat; with what daintiness would he lick his lips; and then with what an air of thankfulness would he resume his seat, with his teeth once more projecting beyond his nose, and an eye of humble expectation fixed upon his master.

It was late in the afternoon when the steamboat stopped at the village which was the residence of these worthies. It stood on the high bank of the river, and bore traces of having been a frontier trading-post. There were the remains of stockades that once protected it from the Indians, and the houses were in the ancient Spanish and French colonial taste, the place having been successively under the domination of both those nations prior to the cession of Louisiana to the United States.

The arrival of the seigneur of fifty thousand dollars, and his humble companion, Compére Martin, had evidently been looked forward to as an event in the village. Numbers of men, women, and children, white, yellow, and black, were collected on the river bank; most of them clad in old-fashioned French garments, and their heads decorated with colored handkerchiefs or white nightcaps. The moment the steamboat came within sight and hearing, there was a waving of handkerchiefs, and a screaming and bawling of salutations and felicitations, that baffle all description.

The old gentleman of fifty thousand dollars was received by a train of relatives, and friends, and children, and grandchildren, whom he kissed on each cheek, and who formed a procession in his rear, with a legion of domestics, of all ages, following him to a large, old-fashioned French house, that domineered over the village.

His black *valet de chambre,* in white jacket and trousers, and gold ear-rings, was met on the shore by a boon, though rustic companion, a tall Negro fellow, with a long good-humored face, and the profile of a horse, which stood out from beneath a narrow-rimmed straw hat, stuck on the back of his head. The explosions of laughter of these two varlets on

meeting and exchanging compliments, were enough
to electrify the country round.

The most hearty reception, however, was that given
to Compére Martin. Everybody, young and old,
hailed him before he got to land. Everybody had a
joke for Compére Martin, and Compére Martin had
a joke for everybody. Even his little dog appeared to
partake of his popularity, and to be caressed by
every hand. Indeed, he was quite a different animal
the moment he touched the land. Here he was at
home; here he was of consequence. He barked, he
leaped, he frisked about his old friends, and then
would skim round the place in a wide circle, as if
mad.

I traced Compére Martin and his little dog to their
home. It was an old ruinous Spanish house, of large
dimensions, with verandas overshadowed by ancient
elms. The house had probably been the residence, in
old times, of the Spanish commandant. In one wing
of his crazy, but aristocratical abode, was nestled the
family of my fellow-traveller; for poor devils are apt
to be magnificently clad and lodged, in the cast-off
clothes and abandoned palaces of the great and
wealthy.

The arrival of Compére Martin was welcomed by
legion of women, children, and mongrel curs; and,
as poverty and gayety generally go hand-in-hand
among the French and their descendants, the crazy
mansion soon resounded with loud gossip and lighthearted laughter.

As the steamboat paused a short time at the village, I took occasion to stroll about the place. Most

of the houses were in the French taste, with case-
ments and rickety verandas, but most of them in
flimsy and ruinous condition. All the wagons,
ploughs, and other utensils about the place were of
ancient and inconvenient Gallic construction, such as
had been brought from France in the primitive days
of the colony. The very looks of the people reminded me of the villages of France .

From one of the houses came the hum of a spin-
ning-wheel, accompanied by a scrap of an old
French *chanson,* which I have heard many a time
among the peasantry of Languedoc, doubtless a tra-
ditional song, brought over by the first French emigrants, and handed down from generation to generation.

Half a dozen young lasses emerged from the adjacent dwellings, reminding me, by their light step and
gay costume, of scenes in ancient France, where taste
in dress comes natural to every class of females.
The trim bodice and colored petticoat, and little apron, with its pockets to receive the hands when in an
attitude for conversation; the colored kerchief wound
tastefully round the head, with a coquettish knot
perking above one ear; and the neat slipper and
tight-drawn stocking, with its braid of narrow ribbon embracing the ankle where it peeps from its
mysterious curtain. It is from this ambush that Cu-
pid sends his most inciting arrows.

While I was musing upon the recollections thus
accidentally summoned up, I heard the sound of a
fiddle from the mansion of Compère Martin, the signal, no doubt, for a joyous gathering. I was dis-

posed to turn my steps thither, and witness festivities of one of the very few villages I had met with in my wide tour that was yet poor enough to be merry; but the bell of the steamboat summoned me to reembark.

As we swept away from the shore, I cast back a wistful eye upon the moss-grown roofs and ancient elms of the village, and prayed that the inhabitants might long retain their happy ignorance, their absence of all enterprise and improvement, their respect for the fiddle, and their contempt for the almighty dollar.* I fear, however, my prayer is doomed to be of no avail. In a little while the steamboat whirled me to an American town, just springing into bustling and prosperous existence.

The surrounding forest had been laid out in town lots; frames of wooden buildings were rising from among stumps and burnt trees. The place already boasted a court-house, a jail, and two banks, all built of pine boards, on the model of Grecian temples. There were rival hotels, rival churches, and rival newspapers; together with the usual number of judges and generals and governors; not to speak of doctors by the dozen and lawyers by the score.

The place, I was told, was in an astonishing career of improvement, with a canal and two railroads in

* This phrase, used for the first time in this sketch, has since passed into current circulation, and by some has been questioned as savoring of irreverence. The author, therefore, owes it to his orthodoxy to declare that no irreverence was intended even to the dollar itself; which he is aware is daily becoming more and more an object of worship.

embryo. Lots doubled in price every week; everybody was speculating in land; everybody was rich; and everybody was growing richer. The community, however, was torn to pieces by new doctrines in religion and in political economy; there were camp-meetings, and agrarian meetings; and an election was at hand, which, it was expected, would throw the whle country into a paroxysm.

Alas! with such an enterprising neighbor, what is to become of the poor little creole village!

THE CHRONICLES OF THE
REIGN OF WILLIAM THE TESTY

1. Showing the nature of history in general; containing furthermore the universal acquirements of William the Testy, and how a man may learn so much as to render himself good for nothing.

When the lofty Thucydides is about to enter upon his description of the plague that desolated Athens, one of his modern commentators assures the reader, that the history is now going to be exceeding solemn, serious and pathetic, and hints, with that air of chuckling gratulation with which a good dame draws forth a choice morsel from a cupboard to regale a favorite, that this plague will give his history a most agreeable variety.

In like manner did my heart leap within me, when I came to the dolorous dilemma of Fort Goed Hoop, which I at once perceived to be the forerunner of a series of great events and entertaining disasters. Such are the true subjects for the historic pen. For what is history, in fact, but a kind of Newgate calendar, a register of the crimes and miseries that man has inflicted on his fellowman? It is a huge libel on human nature, to which we industriously add page after page, volume after volume, as if we were building up a monument to the honor, rather than the infamy of our species. If we turn over the pages of these chronicles that man has written of himself, what are the characters dignified by the appellation of great, and held up to the admiration of posterity? Tyrants, robbers, conquerors, renowned only for the magnitude of this misdeeds and the stupendous wrongs and miseries they have inflicted on mankind—warriors, who have hired themselves to the trade of blood, not from motives of virtuous patriotism, or to protect the injured and defenceless, but merely to gain the vaunted glory of being adroit and successful in massacring their fellow-beings! What are the great events that constitute a glorious era?—The fall of empires; the desolation of happy countries; splendid cities smoking in their ruins; the proudest works of art tumbled in the dust; the shrieks and groans of whole nations ascending unto heaven!

It is thus the historian may be said to thrive on the miseries of mankind, like birds of prey which hover over the field of battle to fatten on the mighty dead. It was observed by a great projector of inland lock-navigation, that rivers, lakes, and oceans were only formed to feed canals. In like manner I am tempted to believe that plots, conspiracies, wars, victories, and massacres are ordained by Providence only as food for the historian.

It is a source of great delight to the philosopher, in studying the wonderful economy of nature, to trace the mutual dependencies of things, how they are created reciprocally for each other, and how the most noxious and apparently unnecessary animal has its uses. Thus those swarms of flies, which are so often execrated as useless vermin, are created for the sustenance of spiders; and spiders, on the other hand, are evidently made to devour flies. So those heroes, who have been such scourges to the world, were bounteously provided as themes for the poet and historian while the poet and the historian were destined to record the achievements of heroes!

These, and many similar reflections, naturally arose in my mind as I took up my pen to commence the reign of William Kieft: for now the stream of our history, which hitherto has rolled in a tranquil current, is about to depart forever from its peaceful haunts, and brawl through many a turbulent and rugged scene.

As some sleek ox, sunk in the rich repose of a clover-field, dozing and chewing the cud, will bear repeated blows before it raises itself, so the province of Nieuw Nederlandts, having waxed fat under the drowsy reign of the Doubter, needed cuffs and kicks to rouse it into action. The reader will now witness the manner in which a peaceful community advances towards a state of war; which is apt to be like the approach of a horse to a drum, with much prancing and little progress, and too often with the wrong end foremost.

Wilhelmus Kieft, who in 1634 ascended the gubernatorial chair (to borrow a favorite though clumsy appellation of modern phraseologists), was of a lofty descent, his father being inspector of windmills in the ancient town of Saardam; and our hero, we are told, when a boy, made very curious investigations into the nature and operation of these machines, which was one reason why he afterwards came to be so ingenious a governor. His name, according to the most authentic etymologists, was a corruption of Kyver, that is to say, a *wrangler or scolder,* and expressed the characteristic of his family, which for nearly two centuries, had kept the windy town of Saardam in hot water, and produced more tartars and brimstones than any ten families in the place; and so truly did he inherit this family peculiarity, that he had not been a year in the government of the province, before he was universally denominated William the Testy. His appearance answered to his name. He was a brisk, wiry, waspish little old gentleman; such a one as may now and then be seen stumping about our city in a broad-skirted coat with huge buttons, a cocked hat stuck on the back of his head, and a cane as high as his chin. His face was broad, but his features were sharp; his cheeks were scorched into a dusky red by two fiery little gray eyes; his nose turned up, and the corners of his mouth turned down, pretty much like the muzzle of an irritable pug-dog.

I have heard it observed by a profound adept in human physiology, that if a woman waxes fat with the progress of years, her tenure of life is somewhat precarious, but if haply she withers as she grows old, she lives forever. Such promised to be the case with William the Testy, who grew tough in proportion as he dried. He had withered, in fact, not through the process of years, but through the tropical fervor of his soul, which burnt like a vehement rush-light in his bosom, inciting him to incessant broils and bickerings. Ancient traditions speak much of his learning, and of the gallant inroads he had made into the dead languages, in which he had made captive a host of Greek nouns and Latin verbs, and brought off rich booty in ancient saws and apothegms, which he was wont to parade in his public harangues, as a triumphant general of yore his *spoila opima*. Of metaphysics he knew enough to confound all hearers and himself into the bargain. In logic, he knew the whole family of syllogisms and dilemmas, and was so proud of his skill that he never suffered even a self-evident fact to pass unargued. It was observed, however, that he seldom got into an argument without getting into a perplexity, and then into a passion with his adversary for not being convinced gratis.

He had, moreover, skirmished smartly on the frontiers of several of the sciences, was fond of experimental philosophy, and prided himself upon inven-

tions of all kinds. His abode, which he had fixed at
a Bowerie or country-seat at a short distance from
the city, just at what is now called Dutch Street, soon
abounded with proofs of his ingenuity: patent smoke-
jacks that required a horse to work them; Dutch ovens
that roasted meat without fire; carts that went before
the horses; weather-cocks that turned against the
wind; and other wrong-headed contrivances that astonished and confounded all beholders. The house,
too, was beset with paralytic cats and dogs, the subjects of his experimental philosophy; and the yell-
ing and yelping of the latter unhappy victims of science, while aiding in the pursuit of knowledge, soon
gained for the place the name of "Dog's Misery,"
by which it continues to be known at the present
day.

It is in knowledge as in swimming; he who floun-
ders and splashes on the surface makes more noise,
and attracts more attention, than the pearl-diver who
quietly dives in quest of treasures at the bottom.
The vast acquirements of the new governor were the
theme of marvel among the simple burghers of New
Amsterdam; he figured about the place as learned a
man as a Bonze at Pekin, who has mastered one half
of the Chinese alphabet, and was unanimously pro-
nounced a "universal genius."

I have known in my time many a genius of this
stamp; but, to speak my mind freely, I never knew
one who, for the ordinary purposes of life, was
worth his weight in straw. In this respect, a little

sound judgment and plain common-sense is worth all
the sparkling genius that ever wrote poerty or invented theories. Let us see how the universal acquirements of William the Testy aided him in the affairs of government.

2. How William the Testy undertook to conquer
   by proclamation—How he was a great man
   abroad, but a little man in his own house.

No sooner had this bustling little potentate been
blown by a whiff of fortune into the seat of government than he called his council together to make
them a speech on the state of affairs.

Caius Gracchus, it is said, when he harangued the
Roman populace, modulated his tone by an ora-
torical flute or pitchpipe; Wilhelmus Kieft, not having such an instrument at hand, availed himself of
that musical organ or trump which nature has implanted in the midst of a man's face: in other words,
he preluded his address by a sonorous blast of the
nose,—a preliminary flourish much in vogue among
public orators.

He then commenced by expressing his humble sense

of his utter unworthiness of the high post to which he had been appointed; which made some of the simple burghers wonder why he undertook it, not knowing that it is a point of eitquette with a public orator never to enter upon a public office without declaring himself unworthy to cross the threshold. He then proceeded in a manner highly classic and erudite to speak of government generally, and of the government of ancient Greece in particular, together with the wars of Rome and Carthage, and the rise and fall of sundry outlandish empires which the worthy burghers had never read nor heard of. Having thus, after the manner of your learned orator, treated things in general, he came, by a natural, roundabout transition, to the matter in hand, namely, the daring aggressions of the Yankees.

As my readers are well aware of the advantage a potentate has in handling his enemies as he pleases in his speeches and bulletins, where he has the talk all on his own side, they may rest assured that William the Testy did not let such an opportunity escape of giving the Yankees what is called "a taste of his quality." In speaking of their inroads into the territories of their High Mightinesses, he compared them to the Gauls who desolated Rome, the Goths and Vandals who overran the fairest plains of Europe; but when he came to speak of the unparalleled audacity with which they of Weathersfield had advanced their patches up to the very walls of Ford Goed Hoop, and threatened to smother the garrison in onions, tears of rage started into his eyes, as though he nosed the very offence in question.

Having thus wrought up his tale to a climax, he assumed a most belligerent look, and assured the council that he had devised an instrument, potent in its effects, and which he trusted would soon drive the Yankees from the land. So saying, he thrust his hand into one of the deep pockets of his broad-skirted coat and drew forth, not an infernal machine, but an instrument in writing, which he laid with great emphasis upon the table.

The burghers gazed at it for a time in silent awe, as a wary housewife does at a gun, fearful it may go off half-cocked. The document in question had a sinister look, it is true; it was crabbed in text, and from a broad red ribbon dangled the great seal of the province, about the size of a buckwheat pancake. Still, after all, it was but an instrument in writing. Herein, however, existed the wonder of the invention. The document in question was a *Proclamation* ordering the Yankees to depart instantly from the territories of their High Mightinesses, under pain of suffering all the forfeitures and punishments in such a case made and provided. It was on the moral effect of this formidable instrument that Wilhelmus Kieft calculated, pledging his valor as a governor that, once fulminated against the Yankees, it would, in less than two months, drive every mother's son of them across the borders.

The council broke up in perfect wonder; and nothing was talked of for some time among the old men and women of New Amsterdam but the vast genius of the governor, and his new and cheap mode of fighting by proclamation.

As to Wilhelmus Kieft, having despatched his proclamation to the frontiers, he put on his cocked hat and corduroy small-clothes, and mounting a tall raw-boned charger, trotted out to his rural retreat of Dog's Misery. Here, like the good Numa, he reposed from the toils of state, taking lessons in government, not from the nymph Egeria, but from the honored wife of his bosom; who was one of that class of females sent upon the earth a little after the flood, as a punishment for the sins of mankind, and commonly known by the appellation of *knowing women*. In fact, my duty as an historian obliges me to make known a circumstance which was a great secret at the time, and consequently was not a subject of scandal at more than half the tea-tables in New Amsterdam, but which, like many other great secrets, has leaked out in the lapse of years,—and this was, that Wilhelmus the Testy, though one of the most potent little men that ever breathed, yet submitted at home to a species of government, neither laid down in Aristotle nor Plato; in short, it partook of the nature of a pure, unmixed tyranny, and is familiarly denominated *petticoat government*—an absolute sway, which, although exceedingly common in these modern days, was very rare among the ancients, if we may judge from the rout made about the domestic economy of honest Socrates; which is the only ancient case on record.

The great Kieft, however, warded off all the sneers and sarcasms of his particular friends, who are ever ready to joke with a man on sore points of the kind by alleging that it was a government of his own election, to which he submitted through choice, adding at the same time a profound maxim which he had found in an ancient author, that "he who would aspire to *govern*, should first learn to *obey*."

3. In which are recorded the sage projects of a ruler of universal genius—The art of fighting by proclamation—And how that the valiant Jacobus Van Curlet came to be fully dishonored at Fort Goed Hoop.

Never was a more comprehensive, a more expeditious, or, what is still better, a more economical measure devised, than this of defeating the Yankees by proclamation,—an expedient, likewise, so gentle and humane, there were ten chances to one in favor of its succeeding; but then there was one chance to ten that it would not succeed,—as the ill-natured fates would have it, that single chance carried the day! The proclamation was perfect in all its parts, well constructed, well written, well sealed, and well published; all that was wanting to insure its effect was, that the Yankees should stand in awe of it; but, provoking to relate, they treated it with the most absolute contempt, applied it to an unseemly purpose; and thus did the first warlike proclamation come to a shameful end,—a fate which I am credibly informed has befallen but too many of its successors.

So far from abandoning the country, those varlets continued their encroachments, squatting along the green banks of the Varsche River, and founding Hartford, Stamford, New Haven, and other border-towns. I have already shown how the onion patches of Pyquag were an eye-sore to Jacobus Van Curlet and his garrison; but now these moss-troopers increased in their atrocities, kidnapping hogs, impounding horses, and sometimes grievously rib-roasting their owners. Our worthy forefathers could scarcely stir abroad without danger of being outjockeyed in horse-flesh, or taken in in bargaining; while, in their absence, some daring Yankee peddler would penetrate to their household, and nearly ruin the good housewives with tin ware and wooden bowls.*

* The following cases in point appear in Hazard's *Collection of State Papers.*

"In the meantime, they of Hartford have not onely usurped and taken in the lands of Connecticott, although unrighteously and against the lawes of nations but have hindered our nation in sowing theire own purchased broken up lands, but have also sowed them with corne in the night, which the Nederlanders had broken up an intended to sowe: and have beaten the servants of the high and mighty,

I am well aware of the perils which environ me in this part of my history. While raking with curious hand but pious heart, among the mouldering remains of former days, anxious to draw therefrom the honey of wisdom, I may fare somewhat like that valiant worthy, Samson, who, in meddling with the carcass of a dead lion, drew a swarm of bees about his ears. Thus, while narrating the many misdeeds of the Ya-nokie or Yankee race, it is ten chances to one but I offend the morbid sensibilities of certain of their unreasonable descendants, who may fly out and raise such a buzzing about this unlucky head of mine, that I shall need the tough hide of an Achilles, or an Orlando Furioso, to protect me from their stings.

Should such be the case, I should deeply and sincerely lament,—not my misfortune in giving offence, but the wrong-headed perverseness of an ill-natured generation, in taking offence at anything I say. That their ancestors did use my ancestors ill is true,

---

the honored companie, which were laboring upon theire master's lands, from theire lands, with sticks and plow staves in hostile manner laming, and among the rest, struck Ever Duckings (Evert Duychink) a hole in his head, with a stick, so that the bloode ran downe very strongly downe upon his body."

"Those of Hartford sold a hogg, that belonged to the honored companie, under pretence that he had eaten of their grounde grass, when they had not any foot of inheritance. They groffered the hogg for 5s. if the commissioners would have given 5s. for damage; which the commissioners denied, because noe man's own hogg (as men used to say) can trespass upon his owne master's grounde."

and I am very sorry for it. I would, with all my heart, the fact were otherwise; but as I am recording the sacred events of history, I'd not bate one nail's breadth of the honest truth, though I were sure the whole edition of my work would be bought up and burnt by the common hangman of Connecticut. And in sooth, now that these testy gentlemen have drawn me out, I will make bold to go further, and observe that this is one of the grand purposes for which we impartial historians are sent into the world, to redress wrongs and render justice on the heads of the guilty. So that, though a powerful nation may wrong its neighbors with temporary impunity, yet sooner or later an historian springs up, who wreaks ample chastisement on it in return.

Thus these moss-troopers of the east little thought, I'll warrant it, while they were harassing the inoffensive province of Nieuw Nederlandts, and driving its unhappy governor to his wit's end, that an historian would ever arise and give them their own, with interest. Since, then, I am but performing my bounden duty as an historian, in avenging the wrongs of our revered ancestors, I shall make no further apology; and, indeed, when it is considered that I have all these ancient borderers of the east in my power, and at the mercy of my pen, I trust that it will be admitted I conduct myself with great humanity and moderation.

It was long before William the Testy could be persuaded that his much-vaunted war-measure was ineffectual; on the contrary, he flew in a passion whenever it was doubted, swearing that, though slow in operation, yet when it once began to work, it would soon purge the land of these invaders. When convinced, at length, of the truth, like a shrewd physician he attributed the failure to the quantity, not the quality of the medicine, and resolved to double the dose. He fulminated, therefore, a second proclamation, more vehement than the first, forbidding all intercourse with these Yankee intruders, ordering the Dutch burghers on the frontiers to buy none of their pacing horses, measly pork, apple-sweetmeats, Weathersfield onions, or wooden bowls, and to furnish them with no supplies of gin, gingerbread, or sourkrout.

Another interval elapsed, during which the last proclamation was as little regarded as the first; and the non-intercourse was especially set at naught by the young folks of both sexes, if we may judge by the active bundling which took place along the borders.

At length, one day the inhabitants of New Amsterdam were aroused by a furious barking of dogs, great and small, and beheld, to their surprise, the whole garrison of Fort Goed Hoop straggling into town all tattered and wayworn, with Jacobus Van Curlet at their head, bringing the melancholy intelligence of the capture of Fort Goed Hoop by the Yankees.

The fate of this important fortress is an impressive warning to all military commanders. It was neither carried by storm nor famine; nor was it undermined; nor bombarded; nor set on fire by red-hot shot; but was taken by a stratagem no less singular than effectual, and which can never fail of success, whenever an opportunity occurs of putting it in practice.

It seems that the Yankees had received intelligence that the garrison of Jacobus Van Curlet had been reduced nearly one eighth by the death of two of his most corpulent soldiers, who had overeaten themselves on fat salmon caught in the Varsche River. A secret expedition was immediately set on foot to surprise the fortress. The crafy enemy, knowing the habits of the garrison to sleep soundly after they had eaten their dinners and smoked their pipes, stole upon them at the noontide of a sultry summer's day, and surprised them in the midst of their slumbers.

In an instant the flag of their High Mightinesses was lowered, and the Yankee standard elevated in its stead, being a dried codfish, by way of a spread eagle. A strong garrison was appointed, of long-sided, hard-fisted Yankees, with Weathersfield onions for cockades and feathers. As to Jacobus Van Curlet and his men, they were seized by the nape of the neck, conducted to the gate, and one by one dismissed by a kick in the crupper, as Charles XII dismissed the heavy-bottomed Russians at the battle of Narva; Jacobus Van Curlet receiving two kicks in consideration of his official dignity.

4.   Containing the fearful wrath of William the
     Testy, and the alarm of New Amsterdam—
     How the Governor did strongly fortify the
     city—Of the rise of Anthony the Trumpeter,
     and the windy addition to the armorial bear-
     ings of New Amsterdam.

Language cannot express the awful ire of William the
Testy on hearing of the catastrophe at Fort Goed
Hoop. For three good hours his rage was too great
for words, or rather the words were too great for
him (being a very small man), and he was nearly
choked by the misshapen, nine-cornered Dutch oaths
and epithets which crowded at once into his gullet.
At length his words found vent, and for three days he
kept up a constant discharge, anathematizing the
Yankees, man, woman, and child, for a set of
dieven, schobbejacken, deugenieten, twistzoekeren,
blaes-kaken, loosen-schalken, kakken-bedden, and
a thousand other names, of which, unfortunately for
posterity, history does not mention. Finally, he
swore that he would have nothing more to do with
such a squatting, bundling, guessing, questioning,
swapping, pumpkin-eating, molasses-daubing, shin-
gle-splitting, cider-watering, horse-jockeying, notion-

peddling crew; that they might stay at Ford Goed Hoop and rot, before he would dirty his hands by attempting to drive them away: in proof of which he ordered the new-raised troops to be marched forthwith into winter-quarters, although it was not as yet quite mid-summer. Great despondency now fell upon the city of New Amsterdam. It was feared that the conquerors of Fort Goed Hoop, flushed with victory and apple-brandy, might march on to the capital, take it by storm, and annex the whole province to Connecticut. The name of Yankee became as terrible among the Nieuw Nederlanders as was that of Gaul among the ancient Romans; insomuch that the good wives of the Manhattoes used it as a bugbear wherewith to frighten their unruly children.

Everybody clamored around the governor, imploring him to put the city in a complete posture of deference; and he listened to their clamors. Nobody could accuse William the Testy of being idle in time of danger, or at any other time. He was never idle, but then he was often busy to very little purpose. When a youngling, he had been impressed with the words of Solomon, "Go to the ant, thou sluggard, observe her ways and be wise"; in conformity to which he had ever been of a restless, ant-like turn, hurrying hither and thither, nobody knew why or wherefore, busying himself about small matters with an air of great importance and anxiety, and toiling at a grain of mustard-seed in the full conviction that he was moving a mountain. In the present instance, he called in all his inventive powers to his aid, and was continually pondering over plans, making diagrams, and worrying about with a troop of workmen and projectors at his heels. At length, after a world of consultation and contrivance, his plans of defence ended in rearing a great flag-staff in the centre of the fort, and perching a wind-mill on each bastion.

These warlike preparations in some measure allayed the public alarm, especially after an additional means of securing the safety of the city had been suggested by the governor's lady. It has already been hinted in this most authentic history, that in the domestic establishment of William the Testy "the gray mare was the better horse"; in other words, that his wife "ruled the roost," and in governing the governor, governed the province, which might thus be said to be under petticoat government.

Now it came to pass, that about this time there lived in Manhattoes a jolly, robustious trumpeter, named Antony Van Corlear, famous for his long wind; and who, as the story goes, could twang so potently upon his instrument, that the effect upon all within hearing was like that ascribed to the Scotch bagpipe when it sings right lustily i' the nose.

This sounder of brass was moreover a lusty bachelor, with a pleasant, burly visage, a long nose, and huge whiskers. He had his little *bowerie,* or retreat, in the country, where he led a roistering life, giving dances to the wives and daughters of the burghers of the Manhattoes, insomuch that he became a prodigious favorite with all the women, young and old. He is said to have been the first to collect that famous toll levied on the fair sex at Kissing Bridge, on the highway of Hellgate.*

To this sturdy bachelor the eyes of all the women were turned in this time of darkness and peril, as the very man to second and carry out the plans of defence of the governor. A kind of petticoat council was forthwith held at the government house, at which the governor's lady presided; and this lady, as has been hinted, being all potent with the governor, the result of these councils was the elevation of Antony the Trumpeter to the post of commandant of wind-mills and champion of New Amsterdam.

The city being thus fortified and garrisoned, it would have done one's heart good to see the governor snapping his fingers and fidgeting with delight, as the trumpeter strutted up and down the ramparts, twanging defiance to the whole Yankee race, as does a modern editor to all the principalities and powers on the other side of the Atlantic. In the hands of Antony Van Corlear this windy instrument appeared to him as potent as the horn of the paladin Astolpho, or even the more classic horn of Alecto; nay, he had almost the temerity to compare it with the rams' horns celebrated in Holy Writ, at the very sound of which the walls of Jericho fell down.

Be all this as it may, the apprehensions of hostilities from the east gradually died away. The Yankees

---

* The bridge here mentioned by Mr. Knickerbocker still exists; but it is said that the toll is seldom collected nowadays, excepting on sleighing parties, by the descendants of the patriarchs, who still preserve the traditions of the city.

made no further invasion; nay, they declared that they had only taken possession of Fort Goed Hoop as being erected with their territories. So far from manifesting hostility, they continued to throng to New Amsterdam with the most innocent countenances imaginable, filling the market with their notions, being as ready to trade with the Nederlands as ever, and not a whit more prone to get to the windward of them in a bargain.

The old wives of the Manhattoes, who took tea with the governor's lady, attributed all this affected moderation to the awe inspired by the military preparations of the governor, and the windy prowess of Antony the Trumpeter.

There were not wanting illiberal minds, however, who sneered at the governor for thinking to defend his city as he governed it, by mere wind; but William Kieft was not to be jeered out of his wind-mills: he had seen them perched upon the ramparts of his native city of Saardam, and was persuaded they were connected with the great science of defence; nay, so much piqued was he by having them made a matter of ridicule, that he introduced them into the arms of the city, where they remain to this day, quartered with the ancient beaver of the Manhattoes, an emblem and memento of his policy.

I must not omit to mention that certain wise old burghers of the Manhattoes, skillful in expounding signs and mysteries, after events have come to pass, consider this early intrusion of the wind-mill into the escutcheon of our city, which before had been wholly occupied by the beaver, as portentous of its after fortune, when the quiet Dutchman would be elbowed aside by the enterprising Yankee, and patient industry overtopped by windy speculation.

5. On the jurisprudence of William the Testy, and his admirable expedients for the suppression of poverty.

Among the wrecks and fragments of exalted wisdom, which have floated down the stream of time from venerable antiquity, and been picked up by those humble but industrious wights who ply along the shores of literature, we find a shrewd ordinance of Charondas the Locrian legislator. Anxious to preserve the judicial code of the State from the additions and amendments of country members and seekers of popularity, be ordained that, whoever proposed a new law, should do it with a halter about his neck; whereby, in case his proposition were rejected, they just hung him up—and there the matter ended.

The effect was, that for more than two hundred

years there was but one trifling alteration in the
judicial code; and legal matters were so clear and
simple that the whole race of lawyers starved to
death for want of employment. The Locrians, too,
being freed from all incitement to litigation, lived
very lovingly together, and were so happy a people
that they make scarce any figure in history; it being
only your litigious, quarrelsome, rantipole nations
who make much noise in the world.

I have been reminded of these historical facts in
coming to treat of the internal policy of William the
Testy. Well would it have been for him had he in the
course of his universal acquirements stumbled upon
the precaution of the good Charondas, or had he
looked nearer home at the protectorate of Oloffe the
Dreamer, when the community was governed without
laws. Such legislation, however, was not suited to
the busy, meddling mind of William the Testy. On the
contrary, he conceived that the true wisdom of legislation consisted in the multiplicity of laws. He accordingly had great punishments for great crimes, and
little punishments for little offences. By degrees the
whole surface of society was cut up by ditches and
fences, and quickset hedges of the law, and even the
sequestered paths of private life so beset by petty
rules and ordinances, too numerous to be remembered, that one could scarce walk at large without
the risk of letting off a spring-gun or falling into a
man-trap.

In a little while the blessings of innumerable laws
became apparent; a class of men arose to expound

and confound them. Petty courts were instituted to take cognizance of petty offences, pettifoggers began to abound; and the community was soon set together by the ears.

Let me not be thought as intending anything derogatory to the profession of the law, or to the distinguished members of that illustrious order. Well am I aware that we have in this ancient city innumerable worthy gentlemen, the knights-errant of modern days, who go about redressing wrongs and defending the defenceless, not for the love of filthy lucre, nor the selfish cravings of renown, but merely for the pleasure of doing good. Sooner would I throw this trusty pen into the flames, and cork up my ink-bottle forever, than infringe even for a nail's breadth upon the dignity of these truly benevolent champions of the distressed. On the contrary, I allude merely to those caitiff scouts who, in these latter days of evil, infest the skirts of the profession, as did the recreant Cornish knights of yore the honorable order of chivalry—who, under its auspices, commit flagrant wrongs—who thrive by quibbles, by quirks and chicanery, and like vermin increase the corruption in which they are engendered.

Nothing so soon awakes the malevolent passions as the facility of gratification. The courts of law would never be so crowded with petty, vexatious, and disgraceful suits, were it not for the herds of pettifoggers. These tamper with the passions of the poorer and more ignorant classes, who, as if poverty were not a sufficient misery in itself, are ever ready to imbitter it by litigation. These, like quacks in medicine, excite the malady to profit by the cure, and retard the cure to augment the fees. As the quack exhausts the constitution, the pettifogger exhausts the purse; and as he who has once been under the hands of a quack is forever after prone to dabble in drugs, and poison himself with infalliable prescriptions, so the client of the pettifogger is ever after prone to embroil himself with his neighbors, and impoverish himself with successful lawsuits. My readers will excuse this digression into which I have been unwarily betrayed; but I could not avoid giving a cool and unprejudiced account of an abomination too prevalent in this excellent city, and with the effects of which I am ruefully acquainted: having been nearly ruined by a lawsuit which was decided against me; and my ruin having been completed by another, which was decided in my favor.

To return to our theme. There was nothing in the whole range of moral offences against which the jurisprudence of William the Testy was more strenuously directed than the root of all evil, and determined to cut it up, root and branch, and extirpate it from the land. He had been struck, in the course of his travels in the old countries of Europe, with the wisdom of those notices posted up in country towns, that "any vagrant found begging there would be put in the stocks," and he had observed that no beggars were to be seen in these neighborhoods; having doubtless thrown off their rags and their poverty, and become rich under the terror of the law. He determined to improve upon this hint. In a little while a new machine, of his own invention, was erected hard by Dog's Misery. This was nothing more nor less than a gibbet, of a very strange, uncouth, and unmatchable construction, far more efficacious, as he boasted, than the stocks, for the punishment of poverty. It was for altitude not a whit inferior to that of Haman so renowned in Bible history; but the marvel of the contrivance was, that the culprit, instead of being suspended by the neck, according to venerable custom, was hoisted by the waistband, and kept dangling and sprawling between heaven and earth for an hour or two at a time—to the infinite entertainment and edification of the respectable citizens who usually attend exhibitions of the kind.

It is incredible how the little governor chuckled at beholding caitiff vagrants and sturdy beggars thus swinging by the crupper, and cutting antic gambols in the air. He had a thousand pleasantries and mirthful conceits to utter upon these occasions. He called them his dandelions—his wild-fowl—his high-fliers —his spread-eagles—his goshawks—his scarecrows —and finally, his *gallows-birds;* which ingenious appellation, though originally confined to worthies who had taken the air in this strange manner, has since grown to be a cant name given to all candidates for legal elevation. This punishment, moreover, if we may credit the assertions of certain grave etymologists, gave the first hint for a kind of harnessing, or strapping, by which our forefathers braced up their multifarious breeches, and which has of late years been revived, and continues to be worn at the present day.

Such was the punishment of all petty delinquents, vagrants, and beggars and others detected in being guilty of poverty in a small way; as to those who had offended on a great scale, who had been guilty of flagrant misfortunes and enormous backslidings of the purse, and who stood convicted of large debts, which they were unable to pay, William Kieft had them straightway inclosed within the stone walls of a prison, there to remain until they should reform and grow rich. This notable expedient, however, does not appear to have been more efficacious under William the Testy than in more modern days: it being found that the longer a poor devil was kept in prison the poorer he grew.

6.   Projects of William the Testy for increasing
     the currency—He is outwitted by the Yankees
     —The Great Oyster War.

Next to his projects for the suppression of poverty
may be classed those of William the Testy for increasing the wealth of New Amsterdam. Solomon, of
whose character for wisdom the little governor was
somewhat emulous, had made gold and silver as
plenty as the stones in the streets of Jerusalem.
William Kieft could not pretend to view with him as
to the precious metals, but he determined, as an
equivalent, to flood the streets of New Amsterdam
with Indian money. This was nothing more nor less
than strings of beads wrought of clams, periwinkles,
and other shell-fish, and called seawant or wampum.
These had formed a native currency among the simple
savages, who were content to take them of the Dutchmen in exchange for peltries. In an unlucky moment,
William the Testy, seeing this money of easy pro-
duction, conceived the project of making it the current coin of the province. It is true it had an intrinsic

value among the Indians, who used it to ornament their robes and moccasins, but among the honest burglers it had no more intrinsic value than those rags which form the paper currency of modern days. This consideration, however, had no weight with William Kieft. He began by paying all the servants of the company, and all the debts of government, in strings of wampum. He sent emissaries to sweep the shores of Long Island, which was the Ophir of this modern Solomon, and abounded in shell-fish. These were transported in loads to New Amsterdam, coined into Indian money, and launched into circulation.

And now, for a time, affairs went on swimmingly; money became as plentiful as in the modern days of paper currency, and, to use the popular phrase, "a wonderful impulse was given to public prosperity." Yankee traders poured into the province, buying everything they could lay their hands on, and paying the worthy Dutchmen their own price—in Indian money. If the latter, however, attempted to pay the Yankees in the same coin for their tin ware and wooden bowls, the case was altered; nothing would do but Dutch guilders and such like "metallic currency." What was worse, the Yankee introduced an inferior kind of wampum made of oyster-shells, with which they deluged the province, carrying off in exchange all the silver and gold, the Dutch herrings, and Dutch cheeses: thus early did the knowing men of **the east manifest their skill in** bargaining the New

Amsterdammers out of the oyster, and leaving them the shell.*

It was a long time before William the Testy was made sensible how completely his grand project of finance was turned against him by his eastern neighbors; nor would he probably have ever found it out, had not tidings been brought him that the Yankees had made a descent upon Long Island, and had established a kind of mint at Oyster Bay, where they were coining up all the oyster-banks.

Now this was making a vital attack upon the province in a double sense, financial and gastronomical. Ever since the council-dinner of Oloffe the Dreamer at the founding of New Amsterdam, at

* In a manuscript record of the province, dated, 1659, Library of the New York Historical Society, is the following mention of Indian money:

"*Seawant* alias wampum. Beads manufactured from the *Quahaug or wilk:* a shell-fish formerly abounding on our coasts, but lately of more rare occurrence, of two colors, black and white; the former twice the value of the latter: six beads of the white and three of the black for an English penny. The seawant depreciates from time to time. The New-England people make use of it as a means of barter, not only to carry away the best cargoes which we send thither, but to accumulate a large quantity of beavers and other furs; by which the company is defrauded of her revenues, and the merchants disappointed in making returns with that speed with which they might wish to meet their engagements; while their commissioners and the inhabitants remain overstocked with seawant,—a sort of currency of no value except with the New England savages, etc."

which banquet the oyster figured so conspicuously, this divine shell-fish has been held in a kind of superstitious reverence at the Manhattoes; as witness the temples erected to its cult in every street and lane and alley. In fact, it is the standard luxury of the place, as is the terrapin at Philadelphia, the soft crab of Baltimore, or the canvas-back at Washington.

The seizure of Oyster Bay, therefore, was an outrage not merely on the pockets, but the larders of the New Armsterdammers; the whole community was aroused, and an oyster crusade was immediately set on foot against the Yankees. Every stout trencherman hastened to the standard; nay, some of the most corpulent burgomasters and schepens joined the expedition as a *corps de reserve*, only to be called into action when the sacking commenced.

The conduct of the expedition was intrusted to a valiant Dutchman, who for size and weight might have matched with Colbrand the Danish champion, slain by Guy of Warwick. He was famous throughout the province for strength of arm and skill at quarter-staff, and hence was named Stoffel Brinkerhoff, or rather Brinkerhoofd, that is to say Stoffel, the head-breaker.

This sturdy commander, who was a man of few words but vigorous deeds, led his troops resolutely on through Nineveh, and Babylon, and Jericho, and Patch-hog, and other Long Island towns, without encountering any difficulty of note; though it is said that some of the burgomasters gave out at Hard-scramble Hill and Hungry Hollow, and that others lost heart and turned back at Pusspanick. With the rest he made good his march until he arrived in the neighborhood of Oyster Bay.

Here he was encountered by a host of Yankee warriors, headed by Preserved Fish, and Habakkuk Nutter, and Return Strong, and Zerubbabel Fisk, and Determined Cock! at the sound of whose names Stoffel Brinkerhoff verily believed the whole parliament of Praise-God Barebones had been let loose upon him. He soon found, however, that they were merely the "selectmen" of the settlement, armed with no weapon but the tongue, and disposed only to meet him on the field of argument. Stoffel had but one mode of arguing, that was, with the cudgel; but he used it with such effect that he routed his antagonists, broke up the settlement, and would have driven the inhabitants into the sea if they had not managed to escape across the Sound to the mainland by the Devil's stepping-stones, which remain to this day monuments of this great Dutch victory over the Yankees.

Stoffel Brinkerhoff made great spoil of oysters and clams, coined and uncoined, and then set out on his return to the Manhattoes. A grand triumph, after the manner of the ancients, was prepared for him by William the Testy. He entered New Amsterdam as a conqueror, mounted on a Narraganset pacer. Five dried codfish on poles, standards taken from the enemy, were borne before him, and an immense store of oysters and clams, Weathersfield onions, and Yankee "notions" formed the *spolia opima;* while several coiners of oyster-shells were led captive to grace the hero's triumph.

The procession was accompanied by a full band of boys and Negroes, performing on the popular instruments of rattlebones and clam-shells, while Antony Van Corlear sounded his trumpet from the ramparts.

A great banquet was served up in the stadthouse from the clams and oysters taken from the enemy; while the governor sent the shells privately to the mint, and had them coined into Indian money, with which he paid his troops.

It is moreover said that the governor, calling to mind the practice among the ancients to honor their victorious general with public statues, passed a magnanimous decree, by which every tavern-keeper was permitted to paint the head of Stoffel Brinkerhoff upon his sign!

7. Growing discontents of New Amsterdam
    under the government of William the Testy.

It has been remarked by the observant writer of the
Stuyvesant manuscript, that under the administration
of William Kieft the disposition of the inhabitants of
New Amsterdam experienced an essential change, so
that they became very meddlesome and factious. The
unfortunate propensity of the little governor to experiment and innovation, and the frequent exacerba-
tions of his tempter, kept his council in a continual
worry; and the council being to the people at large
what yeast or leaven is to a batch, they threw the
whole community in a ferment; and the people at
large being to the city what the mind is to the body,
the unhappy commotions they underwent operated
most disastrously upon New Amsterdam—insomuch
that, in certain of their paroxysms of consternation
and perplexity, they begat several of the most
crooked, distorted, and abominable streets, lanes,
and alleys with which this metropolis is disfigured.
    The fact was, that about this time the community,

like Balaam's ass, began to grow more enlightened
than its rider, and to show a disposition for what is
called "self-government." This restive propensity was
first evinced in certain popular meetings, in which the
burghers of New Amsterdam met to talk and smoke
over the complicated affairs of the province, gradually obfuscating themselves with politics and tobacco-
smoke. Hither resorted those idlers and squires of
low degree who hang loose on society and are blown
about by every wind of doctrine. Cobblers abandoned their stalls to give lessons on political economy; blacksmiths suffered their fires to go out while
they stirred up the fires of faction; and even tailors,
though said to be the ninth part of humanity, neglected their own measures to criticize the measures
of government.

Strange! that the science of government, which
seems to be so generally understood, should invariably be denied to the only one called upon to exer-
cise it. Not one of the politicians in question, but,
take his word for it, could have administered affairs
ten times better than William the Testy.

Under the instructions of these political oracles
the good people of New Amsterdam soon became
exceedingly enlightened, and, as a matter of course,
exceedingly discontented. They gradually found out
the fearful error in which they had indulged, of
thinking themselves the happiest people in creation,
and were convinced that, all circumstances to the
contrary notwithstanding, they were all very unhappy, deluded, and consequently ruined people!

We are naturally prone to discontent, and avaricious after imaginary causes of lamentation. Like lubberly monks we belabor our own shoulders, and take a vast satisfaction in the music of our own groans. Nor is this said by way of paradox; daily experience shows the truth of these observations. It is almost impossible to elevate the spirits of a man groaning under ideal calamities; but nothing is easier than to render him wretched, though on the pinnacle of felicity; as it would be an Herculean task to hoist a man to the top of a steeple, though the merest child could topple him off thence.

I must not omit to mention that these popular meetings were generally held at some noted tavern, these public edifices possessing what in modern times are thought the true fountains of political inspiration. The ancient Greeks deliberated upon a matter when drunk, and reconsidered it when sober. Mob-politicians in modern times dislike to have two minds upon a subject, so they both deliberate and act when drunk; by this means a world of delay is spared; and as it is universally allowed that a man when drunk sees double, it follows conclusively that he sees twice as well as his sober neighbors.

8. Of the edict of William the Testy against
    tobacco—Of the Pipe-plot, and the rise of
    feuds and parties.

Wilhelmus Kieft, as has already been observed, was a
great legislator on a small scale, and had a micro-
scopic eye in public affairs. He had been greatly annoyed by the factious meeting of the good people
of New Amsterdam, but, observing that on these occasions the pipe was ever in their mouth, he began to
think that the pipe was at the bottom of the affair, and
that there was some mysterious affinity between
politics and tobacco-smoke. Determined to strike at
the root of the evil, he began forthwith to rail at
tobacco, as a noxious, nauseous weed, filthy in all
its uses; and as to smoking, he denounced it as a
heavy tax upon the public pocket—a vast consumer
of time, a great encourager of idleness, and a deadly
bane to the prosperity and morals of the people.
Finally the issued an edict, prohibiting the smoking
of tobacco throughout the New Netherlands. Ill-
fated Kieft! Had he lived in the present age and at-

tempted to check the unbounded license of the press, he could not have struck more sorely upon the sensibilities of the million. The pipe, in fact, was the greatest organ of reflection and deliberation of the New Netherlander. It was his constant companion and solace: was he gay, he smoked; was he sad, he smoked; his pipe was never out of his mouth; it was part of his physiognomy; without it his best friends would not know him. Take away his pipe? You might as well take away his nose!

The immediate effect of the edict of William the Testy was a popular commotion. A vast multitude, armed with pipes and tobacco-boxes, and an immense supply of ammunition, sat themselves down before the governor's house, and fell to smoking with tremendous violence. The testy William issued forth like a wrathful spider, demanding the reason of this lawless fumigation. The sturdy rioters replied by lolling back in their seats, and puffing away with redoubled fury, raising such a murky cloud that the governor was fain to take refuge in the interior of his castle.

A long negotiation ensued through the medium of Antony the Trumpeter. The governor was at first wrathful and unyielding, but he was gradually smoked into terms. He concluded by permitting the smoking of tobacco, but he abolished the fair long pipes used in the days of Wouter Van Twiller, denoting ease, tranquility, and sobriety of deportment; these he condemned as incompatible with the despatch of business, in place whereof he substituted little captious short pipes, two inches in length, which, he observed, could be stuck in one corner of the mouth, or twisted in the hatband, and would never be in the way. Thus ended this alarming insurrection, which was long known by the name of The Pipe-Plot, and which, it has been somewhat quaintly observed, did end, like most plots and seditions, in mere smoke.

But mark, oh, reader! the deplorable evils which did afterwards result. The smoke of these villainous little pipes, continually ascending in a cloud and the nose, penetrated into and befogged the cerebellum, dried up all the kindly moisture of the brain, and rendered the people who used them as vaporous and testy as the governor himself. Nay, what is worse, from being goodly, burly, sleek-conditioned men, they became, like our Dutch yeomanry who smoke short pipes, a lantern-jawed, smoke-dried leathern-hided race.

Nor was this all. From this fatal schism in tobacco-pipes we may date the rise of parties in the Nieuw Nederlandts. The rich and self-important burghers who had made their fortunes, and could afford to be lazy, adhered to the ancient fashion, and formed a kind of artistocracy known as the *Long Pipes;* while the lower order, adopting the reform of William Kieft as more convenient in their handicraft employments, were branded with the plebeian name of *Short Pipes.*

A third party sprang up, headed by the descendants of Robert Chewit, the companion of the great Hudson. These discarded pipes altogether and took to chewing tobacco; hence they were called *Quids*— an appellation since given to those political mongrels which sometimes spring up between two great parties, as a mule is produced between a horse and an ass.

And here I would note the great benefit of party distinctions in saving the people at large the trouble of thinking. Hesiod divides mankind into three classes —those who think for themselves, those who think as others think, and those who do not think at all. The second class comprises the great mass of society; for most people require a set creed and a file-leader. Hence the origin of party: which means a large body of people, some few of whom think, and all the rest talk. The former take the lead and discipline the latter; prescribing what they must say, what they must approve, what they must hoot at, whom they must support, but, above all, whom they must hate; for no one can be a right good partisan, who is not a thorough-going hater.

The enlightened inhabitants of the Manhattoes, therefore, being divided into parties, were enabled to hate each other with great accuracy. And now the great business of politics went bravely on, the long pipes and short pipes assembling in separate beer-houses, and smoking at each other with implacable vehemence, to the great support of the State and profit of the tavernkeepers. Some, indeed, went so far as to bespatter their adversaries with those odoriferous little words which smell so strong in the Dutch language, believing, like true politicians, that they served their party, and glorified themselves in proportion as they bewrayed their neighbors. But, however they might differ among themselves, all parties agreed in abusing the governor, seeing that he was not a governor of their choice, but appointed by others to rule over them.

Unhappy William Kieft! exclaimed the sage writer of the Stuyvesant manuscript, doomed to contend with enemies too knowing to be entrapped, and to reign over a people too wise to be governed. All his foreign expeditions were baffled and set at naught by the all-pervading Yankees; all his home measures were canvassed and condemned by "numerous and respectable meetings" of pot-house politicians.

In the multitude of counsellors, we are told, there is safety; but the multitude of counsellors was a continual source of perplexity to William Kieft. With a temperament as hot as an old radish, and a mind subject to perpetual whirlwinds and tornadoes, he never failed to get into a passion with every one who undertook to advise him. I have observed, however, that your passionate little men, like small boats with large sails, are easily upset or blown out of their course; so was it with William the Testy, who was prone to be carried away by the last piece of advice blown into his ear. The consequence was, that, though a projector of the first class, yet by continually changing his projects he gave none a fair trial; and by endeavoring to do everything, he in sober truth did nothing.

In the meantime, the sovereign people got into the

saddle, showed themselves, as usual, unmerciful riders; spurring on the little governor with harangues and petitions, and reproaches, in much the same way as holiday apprentices manage an unlucky devil of a hack-horse—so that Wilhelmus Kieft was kept at a worry or a gallop throughout the whole of his administration.

9.   Of the folly of being happy in time of pros-
     perity—Of troubles to the south brought on
     by annexation—Of the secret expedition of
     Jan Jansen Alpendam, and his magnificent
     reward.

If we could but get a peep at the tally of dame Fortune, where like a vigilant landlady she chalks up the debtor and creditor accounts of thoughtless mortals, we should find that every good is checked off by an evil, and that, however we may apparently revel scot-free for a season, the time will come when we must ruefully pay off the reckoning. Fortune in fact is a pestilent shrew, and withal an inexorable creditor; and though for a time she may be all smiles and courtesies and indulge us in long credits, yet sooner or later she brings up her arrears with a vengeance, and washes out her scores with our tears. "Since," says good old Boëtius, "no man can retain her at his pleasure; what are her favors but sure prognostications of approaching trouble and calamity?"

This is the fundamental maxim of that sage school of philosophers, the croakers, who esteem it true wisdom to doubt and despond when other men rejoice, well knowing that happiness is at best but transient—that, the higher one is elevated on the seesaw balance of fortune, the lower must be his subsequent depression—that he who is on the uppermost round of a ladder has most to suffer from a fall, while he who is at the bottom runs very little risk of breaking his neck by tumbling to the top.

Philosophical readers of this stamp must have doubtless indulged in dismal forebodings all through the tranquil reign of Walter the Doubter, and considered it what Dutch seamen call a weather-breeder. They will not be surprised, therefore that the foul weather which gathered during his days should now be rattling from all quarters on the head of William the Testy.

The origin of some of these troubles may be traced quite back to the discoveries and annexations of Hans Reinier Oothout, the explorer, and Wynant Ten Breeches, the land-measurer, made in the twilight days of Oloffe the Dreamer; by which the territories of the Nieuw Nederlandts were carried far to the south to the Delaware river and parts beyond. The consequence was, many disputes and brawls with the Indians, which now and then reached the drowsy ears of Walter the Doubter and his council, like the muttering of distant thunder from behind the mountains, without, however, disturbing their repose. It was not till the time of William the Testy that the thunderbolt reached the Manhattoes. While the little governor was diligently protecting his eastern boundaries from the Yankees, word was brought him of the irruption of a vagrant colony of Swedes in the south, who had landed on the banks of the Delaware and displayed the banner of that redoubtable virago Queen Christina, and taken possession of the country in her name. These had been guided in their expedition by one Peter Minuits, or Minnewits, a renegade Dutchman, formerly in the service of their High Mightinesses, but who now declared himself governor of all the surrounding country, to which was given the name of the province of NEW SWEDEN

It is an old saying that "a little pot is soon hot," which was the case with William the Testy. Being a little man, he was soon in a passion, and once in a passion, he soon boiled over. Summoning his council on the receipt of this news, he belabored the Swedes in the longest speech that had been heard in the colony since the wordy warfare of Ten Breeches and Tough Breeches. Having thus taken off the fire-edge of his valor, he resorted to his favorite measure of proclamation, and despatched a document of the kind, ordering the renegade Minnewits and his gang of Swedish vagabonds to leave the country immediately, under pain of the vengeance of their High

Mightinesses the Lords States-General, and of the potentates of the Manhattoes.

This strong measure was not a whit more effectual
than its predecessors, which had been thundered
against the Yankees; and William Kieft was preparing to follow it up with something still more formidable, when he received intelligence of other invaders
on his southern frontier, who had taken possession
of the banks of the Schuylkill, and built a fort there.
They were represented as a gigantic, gunpowder race
of men, exceedingly expert at boxing, biting, gouging,
and other branches of the rough-and-tumble mode of
warfare, which they had learned from their proto-
types and cousins-german, the Virginians, to whom
they have ever borne considerable resemblance. Like
them, too, they were great roisterers, much given to
revel on hoe-cake and bacon, mint-julep and apple-
toddy; whence their newly formed colony had already acquired the name of Merryland, which, with a
slight modification, it retains to the present day.

In fact, the Merrylanders and their cousins, the
Virginians, were represented to William Kieft as off-
sets from the same original stock as his bitter enemies
the Yanokie, or Yankee tribes of the east, having both
come over to this country for the liberty of conscience, or, in other words, to live as they pleased:
the Yankees taking to praying and money-making,
and converting quakers; and the Southerners to horse-
racing and cock-fighting, and breeding Negroes.

Against these new invaders Wilhelmus Kieft immediately despatched a naval armament of two sloops
and thirty men, under Jan Jansen Alpendam, who

was armed to the very teeth with one of the little governor's most powerful speeches, written in vigorous Low Dutch.

Admiral Alpendam arrived without accident in the Schuylkill, and came upon the enemy just as they were engaged in a great "barbecue," a kind of festivity or carouse much practised in Merryland. Opening upon them with the speech of William the Testy, he denounced them as a pack of lazy, canting, julep-tippling, cock-fighting, horse-racing, slave-trading, tavern-hunting, Sabbath-breaking, mulatto-breeding upstarts, and concluded by ordering them to evacuate the country immediately: to which they laconically replied in plain English, "they'd see him d——d first!"

Now, this was a reply on which neither Jan Jansen Alpendam nor Wilhelmus Kieft had made any calculation. Finding himself, therefore, totally unprepared to answer so terrible a rebuff with suitable hostility, the admiral concluded his wisest course would be to return home and report progress. He accordingly steered his course back to New Amsterdam, where he arrived safe, having accomplished this hazardous enterprise at small expense of treasure and no loss of life. His saving policy gained him the universal appellation of the Saviour of his Country; and his services were suitably rewarded by a shingle monument, erected by subscription on the top of Flattenbarrack Hill, where it immortalized his name for three whole years, when it fell to pieces and was burnt for firewood.

10.   Troublous times on the Hudson—How Kil-
      lian Van Rensellaer erected a feudal castle,
      and how he introduced club-law into the
      province.

About this time the testy little governor of the New
Netherlands appears to have had his hands full, and
with one annoyance and the other to have been kept
continually on the bounce. He was on the very point
of following up the expedition of Jan Jansen Alpendam by some belligerent measures against the
marauders of Merryland, when his attention was suddenly called away by belligerent troubles springing
up in another quarter, the seeds of which had been
sown in the tranquil days of Walter the Doubter.

The reader will recollect the deep doubt into which
that most pacific of governors was thrown on Killian
Van Rensellaer's taking possession of Bearn Island by
wapen recht. While the governor doubted and did
nothing, the lordly Killian went on to complete his
sturdy little castellum of Rensellaerstein, and to garrison it with a number of his tenants from the Helderberg, a mountain region famous for the hardest

heads and hardest fists in the province. Nicholas Koorn, a faithful squire of the patroon, accustomed to strut at his heels, wear his cast-off clothes, and imitate his lofty bearing, was established in this post as wachtmeester. His duty it was to keep an eye on the river, and oblige every vessel that passed, unless on the service of their High Mightinesses, to strike its flag, lower its peak, and pay toll to the lord of Rensellaerstein.

This assumption of sovereign authority within the territories of the Lords States-General, however it might have been tolerated by Walter the Doubter, had been sharply contested by William the Testy on coming into office; and many written remonstrances had been addressed by him to Killian Van Rensellaer, to which the latter never deigned a reply. Thus, by degrees, a sore place, or, in Hibernian parlance, a *raw,* had been established in the irritable soul of the little governor, insomuch that he winced at the very name of Rensellaerstein.

Now it came to pass, that, on a fine sunny day, the Company's yacht, the *Half-Moon,* having been on one of its stated visits to Fort Aurania, was quietly tiding it down the Hudson. The commander, Govert Lockerman, a veteran Dutch skipper of a few words but great bottom, was seated on the high poop, quietly smoking his pipe under the shadow of the proud flag of Orange, when on arriving abreast of Bearn Island, he was saluted by a stentorian voice from the shore, "Lower thy flag, and be d—d to thee!"

Govert Lockerman, without taking his pipe out of his mouth, turned up his eye from under his broad-brimmed hat to see who hailed him thus discourteously. There, on the ramparts of the fort, stood Nicholas Koorn, armed to the teeth, flourishing a brass-hilted sword, while a steeple-crowned hat and cock's tailfeather, formerly worn by Killian Van Rensellaer himself, gave an inexpressible loftiness to his demeanor.

Govert Lockerman eyed the warrior from top to toe, but was not to be dismayed. Taking the pipe slowly out of his mouth, "To whom should I lower my flag?" demanded he. "To the high and mighty Killian Van Rensellaer, the lord of Rensellaerstein!" was the reply.

"I lower it to none but the Prince of Orange and my masters the Lords States-General." So saying, he resumed his pipe and smoked with an air of dogged determination.

Bang! went a gun from the fortress; the ball cut both sail and rigging. Govert Lockerman said nothing, but smoked the more doggedly.

Bang! went another gun; the shot whistled close astern.

"Fire, and be d——d," cried Govert Lockerman, cramming a new charge of tobacco into his pipe, and smoking with still increasing vehemence.

Bang! went a third gun. The shot passed over his head, tearing a hole in the "princely flag of Orange."

This was the hardest trial of all for the pride and patience of Govert Lockerman. He maintained a stubborn, though swelling silence; but his smothered rage might be perceived by the short vehement puffs of smoke emitted from his pipe, by which he might be tracked for miles, as he slowly floated out of shot and out of sight of Bearn Island. In fact he never gave vent to his passion until he got fairly among the highlands of the Hudson; when he let fly whole volleys of Dutch oaths, which are said to linger to this very day among the echoes of the Dunderberg, and to give particular effect to the thunder-storms in that neighborhood.

It was the sudden apparition of Govert Lockerman at Dog's Misery, bearing in his hand the tattered flag of Orange, that arrested the attention of William the Testy, just as he was devising a new expedition against the marauders of Merryland. I will not pretend to describe the passion of the little man when he heard of the outrage of Rensellaerstein. Suffiice it to say, in the first transports of his fury, he turned Dog's Misery topsy-turvy; kicked every cur out of doors, and threw the cats out of the window; after which, his spleen being in some measure relieved, he went into a council of war with Govert Lockerman, the skipper, assisted by Antony Van Corlear, the Trumpeter.

11. On the Diplomatic mission of Antony the
     Trumpeter to the Fortress of Rensellaer-
     stein—And how he was puzzled by a caba-
     listic reply.

The eyes of all New Amsterdam were now turned to
see what would be the end of this direful feud between William the Testy and the patroon of Rensel-
laerwick; and some, observing the consulation of the
governor with the skipper and the trumpeter, predicted
warlike measures by sea and land. The wrath of William Kieft, however, though quick to rise, was quick
to evaporate. He was a perfect brushheap in a blaze,
snapping and crackling for a time, and then ending
in smoke. Like many other valiant potentates, his
first thoughts were all for war, his sober second
thoughts for diplomacy.

Accordingly, Govert Lockerman was once more
despatched up the river in the Company's yacht, the
Goed Hoop bearing Antony the Trumpeter as am-
bassador, to treat with the belligerent powers of Rensellaerstein. In the fulness of time the yacht arrived
before Bearn Island, and Antony the Trumpeter,

mounting the poop, sounded a parley to the fortress. In a little while the steeple-crowned hat of Nicholas Koorn, the wacht-meester, rose above the battlements, followed by his iron visage, and ultimately his whole person, armed, as before, to the very teeth; which, one by one, a whole row of Helderbergers reared their round burly heads above the wall, and beside each pumpkin-head peered the end of a rusty musket. Nothing daunted by this formidable array, Antony Van Corlear drew forth and read with audible voice a missive from William the Testy, protesting against the usurpation of Bearn Island, and ordering the garrison to quit the premises, bag and baggage, on pain of the vengeance of the potentate of the Manhattoes.

In reply, the wacht-meester applied the thumb of his right hand to the end of his nose, and the thumb of his left hand to the little finger of the right, and spreading each hand like a fan, made an aërial flourish with his fingers. Antony Van Corlear was sorely perplexed to understand this sign, which seemed to him something mysterious and masonic. Not liking to betray his ignorance, he again read with a loud voice the missive of William the Testy, and again Nicholas Korn applied the thumb of his right hand to the end of his nose, and the thumb of his left hand to the little finger of the right, and repeated this kind of nasal weather-cock. Antony Van Corlear now persuaded himself that this was some shorthand sign or symbol, current in diplomacy, which, though unintelligible to a new diplomat, like himself, would speak

volumes to the experienced intellect of William the
Testy; considering his embassy therefore at an end, he
sounded his trumpet with great complacency, and set
sail on his return down the river, every now and
then practising this mysterious sign of the wacht-
meester, to keep it accurately in mind.

Arrived at New Amsterdam he made a faithful
report of his embassy, to the governor, accompanied by a manual exhibition of the response of
Nicholas Koorn. The governor was equally perplexed
with his embassy. He was deelpy versed in the mysteries of free-masonry; but they threw no light on the
matter. He knew every variety of wind-mill and
weather-cock, but was not a whit the wiser as to the
aërial sign in question. He had even dabbled in Egyp-
tian hieroglyphics and the mystic symbols of obe-
lisks, but none furnished a key to the reply of Nicholas Koorn. He called a meeting of his council. Antony Van Corlear stood forth in the midst, and putting the thumb of his right hand to his nose, and the
thumb of his left hand to the finger of the right,
he gave a faithful facsimile of the portentous sign.
Having a nose of unusual dimensions, it was as if
the reply had been put in capitals; but all in vain:
the worthy burgomasters were equally perplexed with
the governor. Each one put his thumb to the end of
his nose, spread his fingers like a fan, imitated the
motion of Antony Van Corelear, and then smoked
in dubious silence. Several times was Antony obliged
to stand forth like a fugleman and repeat the sign,

and each time a circle of nasal weather-cocks might be seen in the council-chamber.

Perplexed in the extreme, William the Testy sent for all the soothsayers, and fortune-tellers and wise men of the Manhattoes, but none could interpret the mysterious reply of Nicholas Koorn. The council broke up in sore perplexity. The matter got abroad, and Antony Van Corlear was stopped at every corner to repeat the signal to a knot of anxious newsmongers, each of whom desparted with his thumb to his nose and his fingers in the air, to carry the story home to his family. For several days all business was neglected in New Amsterdam; nothing was talked of but the diplomatic mission of Antony the Trumpeter—nothing was to be seen but knots of politicians with their thumbs to their noses. In the meantime the fierce feud between William the Testy and Killian Van Rensellaer, which at first had menaced deadly warfare, gradually cooled off, like many other war-questions, in the prolonged delays of diplomacy.

Still to this early affair of Rensellaerstein may be traced the remote origin of those windy wars in modern days which rage in the bowels of the Helderberg, and have wellnigh shaken the great patroonship of the Van Rensellaers to its foundation; for we are told that the bully boys of the Helderberg, who served under Nicholas Koorn the wacht-meester, carried back to their mountains the hieroglyphic sign which had so sorely puzzled Antony Van Corlear and the sages of the Manhattoes; so that to the present day

the thumb to the nose and the fingers in the air is apt
to be the reply of the Helderbergens whenever
called upon for any long arrears of rent.

12. Containing the rise of the great Amphictyonic council of the Pilgrims, with the decline
and final extinction of William the Testy.

It was asserted by the wise men of ancient times,
who had a nearer opportunity of ascertaining the
fact, that at the gate of Jupiter's palace lay two huge
tuns, one filled with blessings, the other with misfortunes; and it would verily seem as if the latter had
been completely overturned and left to deluge the unlucky province of Nieuw Nederlandts: for about this
time, while harassed and annoyed from the south
and the north, incessant forays were made by the bor-
der-chivalry of Connecticut upon the pigsties and
hen-roosts of the Nederlanders. Every day or two
some broad-bottomed express-rider, covered with
mud and mire, would come floundering into the gate
of New Amsterdam, freighted with some new tale of
aggression from the frontier; whereupon Antony Van

Corlear, seizing his trumpet, the only substitute for a newspaper in those primitive days, would sound the tidings from the ramparts with such doleful notes and disastrous cadence as to throw half the old women in the city into hysterics; all which tended greatly to increase his popularity; there being nothing for which the public are more grateful than being frequently treated to a panic—a secret well known to the modern editors.

But, oh ye powers! into what a paroxysm of passion did each new outrage of the Yankees throw the choleric little governor! Letter after letter, protest after protest, bad Latin, worse English, and hideous Low Dutch were incessantly fulminated upon them, and the four-and-twenty letters of the alphabet, which formed his standing army, were worn out by constant campaigning. All, however, was ineffectual; even the recent victory at Oyster Bay, which had shed such a gleam of sunshine between the clouds of his fair-weather reign, was soo followed by a more fearful gathering up of those clouds, and indignations of more portentous tempest; for the Yankee tribe on the banks of the Connecticut, finding on this memorable occasion their incompetency to cope, in fair fight, with the sturdy chivalry of the Manhattoes, had called to their aid all the ten tribes of their brethren who inhabit the east country, which from them has derived the name of Yankee-land. This call was promptly responded to. The consequence was a great confederacy of the tribes of Massachusetts, Connecticut, New Plymouth, and New Haven, under the title of the "United Colonies of New England"; the pretended object of which was mutual defence against the savages, but the real object the subjugation of the Nieuw Nederlandts.

For, to let the reader into one of the great secrets of history, the Nieuw Nederlandts had long been regarded by the whole Yankee race as the modern land of promise, and themselves as the chosen and peculiar people destined, one day or other, by hook or by crook, to get possession of it. In truth, they are a wonderful and all-prevalent people, of that class who only require an inch to gain an ell, or a halter to gain a horse. From the time they first gained a foothold on Plymouth Rock, they began to migrate, progressing and progressing from place to place, and from land to land, making a little here and a little there, and controverting the old proverb, that a rolling stone gathers no moss. Hence they have facetiously received the nickname of THE PILGRIMS: that is to say, a people who are always seeking a better country than their own.

The tidings of this great Yankee league struck William Kieft with dismay, and for once in his life he forgot to bounce on receiving a disagreeable piece of intelligence. In fact, on turning over in his mind all that he had read at the Hague about leagues and combinations, he found that this was a counterpart of the Amphictyonic league, by which the states of Greece attained such power and supremacy; and the very idea made his heart quake for the safety of his empire at the Manhattoes.

The affairs of the confederacy were managed by an annual council of delegates held at Boston, which Kieft denominated the Delphos of this truly classic league. The very first meeting gave evidence of hostility to the Nieuw Nederlanders, who were charged, in their dealings with the Indians, with carrying on a traffic in "guns, powther, and shott,—a trade damnable and injurious to the colonists." It is true the Connecticut traders were fain to dabble a little in this damnable traffic; but then they always dealt in what were termed Yankee guns, ingeniously calculated to burst in the pagan hands which used them.

The rise of this potent confederacy was a deathblow to the glory of William the Testy, for from that day forward he never held up his head, but appeared quite crestfallen. It is true, as the grand council augmented in power, and the league, rolling onward, gathered about the red hills of New Haven, threatening to overwhelm the Nieuw Nederlandts, he continued occasionally to fulminate proclamations and protests, as a shrewd sea-captain fires his guns into a water-spout; but alas! they had no more effect than so many blank cartridges.

Thus end the authenticated chronicles of the reign of William the Testy; for henceforth, in the troubles, perplexities, and confusion of the times, he seems to have been totally overlooked, and to have slipped forever through the fingers of scrupuolus history. It is a matter of deep concern that such obscurity should hang over his latter days; for he was in truth a mighty and great-little man, and worthy of be-

ing utterly renowned, seeing that he was the first
potentate that introduced into this land the art of
fighting by proclamation, and defending a country by trumpeters and wind-mills.

It is true, that certain of the early provincial poets,
of whom there were great numbers in the Nieuw
Nederlandts, taking advantage of his mysterious
exit, have fabled, that, like Romulus, he was trans-
lated to the skies, and forms a very fiery little star,
somewhere on the left claw of the Crab; while others,
equally fanciful, declare that he had experienced a
fate similar to that of the good king Arthur, who, we
are assured by ancient bards, was carried away to the
delicious abodes of fairyland, where he still exists
in pristine worth and vigor, and will one day or another return to restore the gallantry, the honor, and
the immaculate probity, which prevailed in the glorious days of the Round Table.*

All these, however are but pleasing fantasies, the
cobweb visions of those dreaming varlets, the poets,

---

* The old Welsh bards believed that King Arthur was not
dead, but carried awaie by the fairies into some pleasant
place, where he shoulde remain for a time, and then re-
urn againe and reigne in as great authority as ever.—
HOLLINSHED.

The Britons suppose that he shall come yet and conquer
all Britaigne, for certes, this is the prophicye of Merlyn—
He say'd that his deth shall be douteous; and said soth for
men thereof yet have doubte and shuillen for ever more—
or men wyt not whether that he lyveth or is dede.—
DR. LEEW, CHRON.

to which I would not have my judicious readers attach any credibility. Neither am I disposed to credit an ancient and rather apocryphal historian, who asserts that the ingenious Wilhelmus was annihilated by the blowing down of one of his wind-mills; nor a writer of later times, who affirms that he fell a victim to an experiment in natural history, having the misfortune to break his neck from a garret window of the stadt-house in attempting to catch swallows by sprinkling salt upon their tails. Still less do I put my faith in the tradition that he perished at sea in conveying home to Holland a treasure of golden ore, discovered somewhere among the haunted region of the Catskill mountains.*

* Diedrich Knickerbocker, in his scrupulous search after truth, is sometimes too fastidious in regard to facts which border a little on the marvellous. The story of the golden ore rests on something better than mere tradition. The venerable Adrian Van der Donck, Doctor of Laws, in his description of the New Netherlands, asserts it from his own observation as an eye-witness. He was present, he says, in 1645, at a treaty between Governor Kieft and the Mohawk Indians, in which one of the latter, in painting himself for the ceremony, used a pigment, the weight and shining appearance of which excited the curiosity of the governor and Mynheer Van der Donck. They obtained a lump, and gave it to be proved by a skillful doctor of medicine, Johannes de la Montague, one of the councillors of the New Netherlands. It was put into a crucible, and yielded two pieces of gold, worth about three guilders. All this, continues Adrian Van der Donck, was kept secret. As soon as peace was made with the Mohawks, an officer and a

The most probable account declares, that, what with the constant troubles on his frontiers, the incessant schemings and projects going on in his own pericranium, the memorials, petitions, remonstrances, and sage pieces of advice of respectable meetings of the sovereign people, and the refractroy disposition of his councillors, who were sure to differ from him on every point, and uniformly to be in the

---

few men were sent to the mountain (in the region of the Kaatskill), under the guidance of an Indian, to search for the precious mineral. They brought back a bucket full of ore; which, being submitted to the crucible, proved as productive as the first. William Kieft now thought the discovery certain. He sent a confidential person, Arent Corsen, with a bag full of the mineral, to New Haven, to take passage in an English ship for England, thence to proceed to Holland. The vessel sailed at Christmas, but never reached her port. All on board perished.

In the year 1647, Wilhelmus Kieft himself, embarked on board the *Princess* taking with him specimens of the supposed mineral. The ship was never heard of more!

Some have supposed that the mineral in question was not gold, but we have the assertion of Adrian Van der Donck, an eye-witness, and the experiment of Johannes de la Montagne, a learned doctor of medicine, on the golden side of the question. Cornelius Van Tienhoven, also, at that time secretary of the New Netherlands, declared in Holland that he had several specimens of the mineral, which proved satisfactory.**

** See Van der Donck's "Description of the New Netherlands." *Collect. New York Hist. Society,* Vol. I., p. 161.

wrong, his mind was kept in a furnace-heat, until he became as completely burnt out as a Dutch family-pipe which has passed through three generations of hard smokers. In this manner did he undergo a kind of animal combustion, consuming away like a farthing rush-light: so that when grim death finally snuffed him out, there was scarce left enough of him to bury!

It would appear, however, that these golden treasures of the Kaatskill always brought ill-luck: as is evidenced in the fate of Arent Corsen and Wilhelmus Kieft, and the wreck of the ships in which they attempted to convey the treasure across the ocean. The golden mines have never been explored, but remain among the mysteries of the Kaatskill mountains, and under the protection of the goblins which haunt them.

THE LEGEND OF
DON MUNIO SANCHO DE HINOJOSA

In the cloisters of the ancient Benedictine convent of San Domingo, at Silos, in Castile, are the mouldering yet magnificent monuments of the once powerful and chivalrous family of Hinojosa. Among these reclines the marble figure of a knight, in complete armor, with the hands pressed together, as if in prayer, On one side of his tomb is sculptured, in relief, a band of Christian cavaliers capturing a cavalcade of male and female Moors; on the other side, the same cavaliers are represented kneeling before an altar. The tomb, like most of the neighboring monuments, is almost in ruins, and the sculpture is nearly unintelligible, excepting to the keen eye of the antiquary. The story connected with the sepulchre, however, is still preserved in the old Spanish chronicles, and is to the following purport:

In old times, several hundred years ago, there was a noble Castilian cavalier, named Don Munio Sancho

de Hinojosa, lord of a border castle, which had
stood the brunt of many a Moorish foray. He had
seventy horsemen as his household troops, all of the
ancient Castilian proof, stark warriors, hard riders,
and men of iron; with these he scoured the Moorish lands, and made his name terrible throughout the
borders. His castle hall was covered with banners and
scimitars and Moslem helms, the trophies of his prowess. Don Munio was, moreover, a keen huntsman;
and rejoiced in hounds of all kinds, steeds for the
chase, and hawks for the towering sport of falconry.
When not engaged in warfare, his delight was to beat
up the neighboring forests; and scarcely ever did he
ride forth without hound and horn, a boar-spear in
his hand, or a hawk upon his fist, and an attendant
train of huntsmen.

His wife, Doña Maria Palacin, was of a gentle
and timid nature, little fitted to be the spouse of so
hardy and adventurous a knight; and many a tear did
the poor lady shed when he sallied forth upon his
daring enterprises, and many a prayer did she offer
up for his safety.

As his doughty cavalier was one day hunting, he
stationed himself in a thicket, on the borders of a
green glade of the forest, and dispersed his followers
to rouse the game and drive it towards his stand. He
had not been here long when a cavalcade of Moors,
of both sexes, came pranking over the forest lawn.
They were unarmed, and magnificently dressed in
robes of tissue and embroidery, rich shawls of India,

bracelets and anklets of gold and jewels that sparkled in the sun.

At the head of this gay cavalcade rode a youthful cavalier, superior to the rest in dignity and loftiness of demeanor, and in splendor of attire; beside him was a damsel, whose veil, blown aside by the breeze, displayed a face of surpassing beauty, and eyes cast down in maiden modesty, yet beaming with tenderness and joy.

Don Munio thanked his stars for sending him such a prize, and exulted at the thought of bearing home to his wife the glittering spoils of these infidels. Putting his hunting-horn to his lips, he gave a blast that rung through the forest. His huntsmen came running from all quarters, and the astonished Moors were surrounded and made captives.

The beautiful Moor wrung her hands in despair, and her female attendants uttered the most piercing cries. The young Moorish cavalier alone retained self-possession. He inquired the name of the Christian knight who commanded this troop of horsemen. When told that it was Don Munio Sancho de Hinojosa, his countenance lighted up. Approaching that cavalier, and kissing his hand, "Don Munio Sancho," said he, "I have heard of your fame as a true and valiant knight, terrible in arms, but schooled in the noble virtues of chivalry. Such do I trust to find you. In me you behold Abadil, son of a Moorish alcaid. I am on the way to celebrate my nuptials with his lady; chance has thrown us in your power, but I confide in your magnanimity. Take all our treasure

and jewels; demand what ransom you think proper
for our persons, but suffer us not to be insulted or
dishonored."

When the good knight heard this appeal and beheld the beauty of the youthful pair, his heart was
touched with tenderness and courtesy. "God forbid,"
said he, "that I should disturb such happy nuptials.
My prisoners in troth shall ye be, for fifteen days,
and immured within my castle, where I claim, as
conqueror, the right of celebrating your espousals."

So saying, he despatched one of his fleetest horsemen in advance, to notify Doña Maria Palacin of the
coming of this bridal party; while he and his hunts
men escorted the cavalcade, not as captors, but as a
guard of honor. As they drew near to the castle, the
banners were hung out, and the trumpets sounded
from the battlements, and on their nearer approach,
the drawbridge was lowered, and Doña Maria came
forth to meet them, attended by her ladies and
knights, her pages and her minstrels. She took the
young bride, Allifra, in her arms, kissed her with
the tenderness of a sister, and conducted her into the
castle. In the meantime, Don Munio sent forth missives in every direction, and had viands and dainties
of all kinds collected from the country round; and
the wedding of the Moorish lovers was celebrated
with all possible state and festivity. For fifteen days
the castle was given up to joy and revelry. There
were tiltings and jousts at the ring, and bull-fights,
and banquets, and dances to the sound of minstrelsy.
When the fifteen days were at an end, he made the

bride and bridegroom magnificent presents, and conducted them and their attendants safely beyond the borders. Such, in old times, were the courtesy and generosity of a Spanish cavalier.

Several years after this event, the king of Castile summoned his nobles to assist him in a campaign against the Moors. Don Munio Sancho was among the first to answer the call, with seventy horsemen, all stanch and well-tried warriors. His wife, Doña Maria, hung about his neck. "Alas, my lord!" exclaimed she, "how often wilt thou tempt thy fate, and when wilt thy thirst for glory be appeased?"

"One battle more," replied Don Munio, "one battle more, for the honor of Castile, and I here make a vow that when this is over, I will lay by my sword, and repair with my cavaliers in pilgrimage to the Sepulchre of our Lord at Jerusalem." The cavaliers all joined with him in the vow, and Doña Maria felt in some degree soothed in spirit; still, she saw with a heavy heart the departure of her husband, and watched his banner with wistful eyes until it disappeared among the trees of the forest.

The king of Castile led his army to the plains of Salmanara, where they encountered the Moorish host, near to Ucles. The battle was long and bloody. The Christians repeatedly wavered, and were as often rallied by the energy of their commanders. Don Munio was covered with wounds, but refused to leave the field. The Christians at length gave way, and the king was hardly pressed, and in danger of being captured.

Don Munio called upon his cavaliers to follow

him to the rescue. "Now is the time," cried he, "to prove your loyalty. Fall to, like brave men! We fight for the true faith, and if we lose our lives here, we gain a better life hereafter."

Rushing with his men between the king and his pursuers, they checked the latter in their career, and gave time for their monarch to escape; but they fell victims to their loyalty. They all fought to the last gasp. Don Munio was singled out by a powerful Moorish knight, but having been wounded in the right arm, he fought to disadvantage, and was slain. The battle being over, the Moor paused to possess himself of the spoils of this redoubtable Christian warrior. When he unlaced the helmet, however, and beheld the countenance of Don Munio, he gave a great cry; and smote his breast. "Woe is me!" cried he, "I have slain my benefactor! the flower of knightly virtue! the most magnanimous of cavaliers!"

While the battle had been raging on the plain of Salmanara, Doña Maria Palacin remained in her castle, a prey to the keenest anxiety. Her eyes were ever fixed on the road that led from the country of the Moors, and often she asked the watchman of the tower, "What seest thou?"

One evening, at the shadowy hour of twilight, the warden sounded his horn. "I see," cried he, "a numerous train winding up the valley. There are mingled Moors and Christians. The banner of my lord is in the advance. Joyful tidings!" exclaimed the old seneschal; "my lord returns in triumph, and brings cap-

tives!" Then the castle courts rang with shouts of
joy; and the standard was displayed, and the trumpets were sounded, and the drawbridge was lowered,
and Doña Maria went forth with her ladies, and her
knights, and her pages, and her minstrels, to welcome
her lord from the wars. But as the train drew nigh,
she beheld a sumptuous bier, covered with black velvet, and on it lay a warrior, as if taking his repose; he
lay in his armor, with his helmet on his head, and his
sword in his hand, as one who had never been conquered, and around the bier were the escutcheons
of the house of Hinojosa.

A number of Moorish cavaliers attended the
bier, with emblems of mourning and with dejected
countenances; and their leader cast himself at the feet
of Doña Maria, and hid his face in his hands. She
beheld in him the gallant Abadil, whom she had
once welcomed with his bride to her castle, but who
now came with the body of her lord, whom he had
unknowingly slain in battle!

The sepulchre erected in the cloisters of the Convent of San Domingo was achieved at the expense of
the Moor Abadil, as a feeble testimony of his grief
for the death of the good knight Don Munio, and
his reverence for his memory. The tender and faithful Doña Maria soon followed her lord to the tomb.
On one of the stones of a small arch, beside his
sepulchre, is the following simple inscription: *"Hic
jacet Maria Palacin, uxor Munonis Sancij de Hinojosa";* Here lies Maria Palacin, wife of Munio Sancho de Hinojosa.

The legend of Don Munio Sancho does not conclude with his death. On the same day on which the battle took place on the plain of Salmanara, a chaplain of the Holy Temple at Jerusalem, while standing at the outer gate, beheld a train of Christian cavaliers advancing, as if in pilgrimage. The chaplain was a native of Spain, and as the pilgrims approached, he knew the foremost to be Don Munio Sancho de Hinojosa, with whom he had been well acquainted in former times. Hastening to the patriarch, he told him of the honorable rank of the pilgrims at the gate. The patriarch, therefore, went forth with a grand procession of priests and monks, and received the pilgrims with all due honor. There were seventy cavaliers, beside their leader, all stark and lofty warriors. They carried their helmets in their hands, and their faces were deadly pale. They greeted no one, nor looked either to the right or to the left, but entered the chapel, and kneeling before the Sepulchre of our Saviour, performed their orisons in silence. When they had concluded, they rose as if to depart, and the patriarch and his attendants advanced to speak to them, but they were no more to be seen. Every one marvelled what could be the meaning of this prodigy. The patriarch carefully noted down the day, and sent to Castile to learn tidings of Don Munio Sancho de Honojosa. He received for reply, that on the very day specified that worthy knight, with seventy of his followers, had been slain in battle. These, therefore, must have been the blessed spirits of those Christian warriors, come to fulfil their vow of a pilgrimage to the Holy Sepulchre at Jerusalem. Such was Castilian faith in the olden time, which kept its word even beyond the grave.

If any one should doubt of the miraculous apparition of these phantom knights, let him consult the *History of the Kings of Castile and Leon* by the learned and pious Fray Prudencio de Sandoval, Bishop of Pamplona, where he will find it recorded in the *History of the King Don Alonzo VI.,* on the hundred and second page. It is too precious a legend to be lightly abandoned to the doubter.

About the author of

THE LEGEND OF SLEEPY HOLLOW

Washington Irving was born April 3, 1783, in New York City, the youngest of a rich merchant's eleven children. He was a frail, bright and impressionable child. Though he was to practice law on Wall Street, work in his family's cutlery business and even serve (later in life) as U.S. minister to Spain, his first love was literature and by the time he was 35 he had renounced most of his earlier activities to live by his pen.

Irving was much influenced by his travels, undertaken as a youth for health reasons. Excursions up the Hudson River were followed, when he was 21, by a two-year stay in southern Europe, where he filled notebooks primarily with his impressions of people. His early work included satires based on those impressions and his popular *Knickerbocker's History of New York* (1809). His most famous stories and legends, however, were written from 1818 on, in such picturesque volumes as *The Sketch Book* (1819-1820), *Tales of a Traveller* (1824) and *The Alhambra* (1832).

Irving also wrote biographies of Oliver Goldsmith, Mahomet and George Washington. After a full and vigorous life, he died in Irvington, New York, on November 28, 1859.

If your dealer does not have any of the MAGNUM EASY EYE CLASSICS, send price of book plus 10 cents to cover postage to MAGNUM CLASSICS, 18 East 41st Street, Room 1501, New York, N.Y. 10017.